3RD & OAK

3RD & OAK

STORIES

NOVELITICS WRITERS COLLECTIVE

EDITED BY

KIM TAYLOR BLAKEMORE & KERRY CATHERS

SYCAMORE CREEK press

First Edition 2024

ISBN (ebook): 979-8-9912591-1-8

ISBN (paperback): 979-8-9912591-0-1

Cover design by Jackie Zureich

Copyright © 2024 by Sycamore Creek Press

CONTENTS

FOREWORD
TONYA MITCHELL

Life is story. Story is life.

Humans have been telling stories before recorded time. Before the written word existed to put them down. We are as inextricably linked to stories as we are our DNA. Story is *in* our DNA.

The best stories are a blazing light in the darkness—they do more than distract us from an ordinary day. They confirm something within us that makes us feel seen, they enlighten us when we come upon a character, idea, or turn of phrase that pulls us into a new perspective, they take us prisoner. Stories remind us of who we are.

As the creators of the varied worlds stories inhabit, writers must ask themselves: what is it I want my reader to take away? What's the point of the story? Oftentimes, writers don't know the answer to these questions until the words are flung down. Many writers, including Flannery O'Connor, Joan Didion, and Stephen King have expressed in some form or another that they don't know what they think until they read what they're saying. Translation: stories are as much an act of discovery for the writer as they are for the reader.

At its core, story is about conflict. This discord becomes the heart of the story. Without conflict—however minor it might be—there is no story. This friction is irresistible to readers because we love to try and work out what happens next. We become emotionally invested. When you think about it, it's a sort of alchemy. We decipher symbols inked on wood pulp that have the power to make us feel elation, melancholy, empathy, disgust. These emotions—altered states of mind if you will—are as limitless as the stories themselves.

Which brings me to the dozen stories collected here. They have one thing in common: the building at the intersection of 3rd & Oak. Be prepared to enter twelve very different worlds. The real and the magical, the mundane and the macabre, the past and the present.

Stories of rescue and revenge, of heroism, unrequited love and more await.

THE PLUMBER
MICAH THORP

It seemed like such a simple thing, the kitchen sink. Hardly the underpinning of rebellion.

Pete initially ignored the loose handle and the gurgling sounds the pipes made, but when water that should have come from the spout spurted from a crack in the compression coupling beneath the drain, he decided the problem needed to be addressed. For two hours he tried to fix it, removing the strainer flange, friction gasket, and spout assembly before realizing his ability to disassemble the artifice of tubes and pipes exceeded his ability to reassemble them. Finally, he put down the wrench he borrowed from his roommate and sat in a meditative pose for several minutes, as recommended by an online therapy app. When he opened his eyes, he decided the best next course of action was to seek professional help for the sink and potentially his psyche.

With his newfound clarity he rose, marched down the hall to the elevator, and punched the button to the basement.

Jerry never looked good. Pete was used to that. But when Pete entered Jerry's office, he looked particularly moribund.

"I need someone to fix my sink," Pete said matter-of-factly.

Jerry took a swig of coffee from the Styrofoam cup in his left hand, followed by a Marlboro chaser from the cigarette in his right. A bit of ash fell onto his mustard tie, flowing like a four-inch waterfall over a cream shirt, struggling to hold back his protruding abdomen. "Get in line. The plumbing's falling apart. It's a freaking disaster."

"A disaster?" Pete replied as he studied Jerry, wondering if this particular disaster would be the one that closed what remained of Jerry's coronary arteries.

"The goddamned Condo Association won't allow goddamned union plumbers into the goddamned building."

Pete briefly wondered how God had managed to damn the building, the Condo Association, and union plumbers all at the same time. He thought about saying something to Jerry, but held back, remembering Jerry's coronaries.

"Well, maybe you can get a plumber that's not in a union."

Jerry took a long puff from his Marlboro before setting it in an ashtray on his desk next to a large file folder labeled *Building Super*. "Son, do you have any idea how hard it is to find a non-union plumber?"

Pete shook his head.

"They're like unicorns. Creatures with magical powers that bring happiness and joy. People think they're real. People go looking for them. But they're never found. Why? Because they exist only in the imagination."

"Then maybe the Condo Association should change its policy?"

Jerry coughed. He picked his cigarette up from the ashtray and pulled a draught of smoke into his lungs which, much to Pete's surprise, seemed to lessen his cough. After a moment, Jerry leaned across his desk. "The Association is a den of iniquity filled with mendacity and deceit. Hell has fewer demons than the COA. Only a fool would ask the Condo Association to change a policy."

Pete sighed. "So, what do I do about my sink?"

Jerry shrugged. "Don't know. Don't care. Use the bathtub."

Pete turned to leave. "Great, either enter a den of iniquity or find a unicorn. Thanks for your help."

~

Pete did everything he could to avoid Mrs. Burton-Hedges. An oversized blustery woman fond of wearing large hats, silk scarves, and real fur, she frequently made her way from the tenth floor to the building lobby via the freight elevator, which had been carpeted and paneled with wood at her direction. It was assumed she avoided the main elevators to minimize interaction with other occupants who resided on the "common floors" of the building at 3rd and Oak.

Despite condescension for her neighbors, Mrs. Burton-Hedges managed to maintain the chairmanship of the building's Condominium Association for as long as anyone could remember. How she garnered enough of the necessary votes to retain her position was a source of constant gossip. Some suggested her support came from bribes to an unknown number of condo owners, while others speculated her husband, the building's original developer, had written something in the Association bylaws that afforded her lifelong rights to hold the chair, choose the directors, and treat residents like peasants in her ten-story feudal state.

And if her authoritarian rule over the building wasn't enough to pacify the residents, circumstances surrounding the mysterious disappearance of her husband only codified the intimidation and terror her presence could induce. Shortly after Mr. Burton's will had been signed, he stepped across the threshold of his tenth-floor penthouse and was never seen again. Local law enforcement had reportedly found traces of strychnine in a cocktail glass, but a body was never found. From the outset of the investigation Mrs. Burton-Hedges surrounded herself with a phalanx of attorneys and, with no other evidence, his disappearance remained cloaked in mystery.

It was with this context that Pete avoided Mrs. Burton-Hedges. But by Thursday morning he decided he had little choice but to seek an exception to the Association rule. For two hours, he waited in the building lobby near the freight elevator. At five minutes after ten the bell on the elevator rang and a loud grating voice echoed across the tiled lobby floor. "Jerold, I heard a knocking sound coming from the radiator.

Do we have *vermin* in the pipes again?" Mrs. Burton-Hedges emerged from the elevator like an unpenned bull charging into a rodeo corral. Her large blue hat shaded most of her face, hiding all but her bulbous nose and substantial jowls. Her neck was covered by a fur draped over a long cashmere coat. An expensive purse hung from her left arm. Her heels clicked loudly as she marched toward the building lobby.

Jerry waddled behind her, clipboard in hand, sweat beaded on his forehead.

"No Mrs. B, that sound was probably just some air kicking around. I'll look into it."

Pete took a deep breath and casually approached Mrs. Burton-Hedges.

"Jerold, there is a *vagrant* in the lobby!" Mrs. Burton-Hedges exclaimed.

Jerry looked at Pete. "He lives on the third floor."

"Did we open a *shelter* on the third floor? Jerold, why was I not informed?"

Jerry shook his head. "No, he lives in a condominium. He's a resident."

Mrs. Burton-Hedges pulled a silk handkerchief from her purse and held it over her nose and mouth. "Jerold, give him what he wants and make him go away."

Pete held up his hands. "Ma'am, I just want to get my sink fixed. I live in 3C with my cousin. Our sink hasn't worked for a month, and I need to hire a plumber. Jerry says there is a policy about not hiring unionized plumbers, and I can't find a non-union plumber, so I need an exception to the policy."

Mrs. Burton-Hedges put the handkerchief back in her purse and took a step toward Pete. She cleared her throat and straightened her back. "Young man, there will never, ever, under any circumstances be a union plumber allowed in the building."

Jerry stood behind Mrs. Burton-Hedges shaking his head, motioning for Pete to stop. Instead, Pete pursed his lips. "Why? Why no union plumbers?"

A sneer grew on Mrs. Burton-Hedges face. "They are a virus. First, we allow unionized plumbers. Then it's unionized janitorial staff. Then the garbage collectors. And the doormen. Everyone thinks *they* should be allowed to work, or not work, under *their* rules. It would be anarchy. And I do not tolerate anarchy." She pointed her index finger at Pete's chest. "Do you understand? No one examines the pipes in this building unless I say they do."

"Whoa man. Don't smash the herbs," Bogs said when Pete set down his satchel on the table in the middle of the room. Pete picked up the satchel, brushed off the bottom, and threw it onto a chair.

Bogs didn't appear to have moved since Pete had left for work. Bogs didn't get off the couch when Pete wasn't at work, so it came as no surprise that he didn't get off the couch when Pete *was* working.

"You look wiped out. Getting beaten down by the man?" Bogs intoned in a manner suggesting that he was both mildly concerned and deeply disinterested in Pete's well-being.

"Just trying to get the sink fixed."

Bogs brushed something off his dirty tie-dyed t-shirt. "It's broken?"

"Dude? Seriously? It hasn't worked for a month."

Bogs scratched his beard. "Didn't notice."

"Water doesn't come out of the tap." Pete sighed. "And when you pour something down the drain it leaks."

Bogs stopped scratching his beard and, as a quizzical look crossed his face, he pulled a toothpick from the tangled brown nest just below his chin. He brushed it off and set it on the coffee table. "So, is the super going to send someone?"

"No."

"Why not?"

"He won't hire a union plumber."

Bogs stretched his back across the dark brown faux leather couch. Apart from a pair of reclining chairs, a very used kitchen table, and an oversized television, the couch was the only furniture in the condominium's main room. "Why don't you just hire a non-union plumber?"

"Apparently all plumbers belong to the union."

Bogs yawned. "Not all of them. I know one who doesn't."

Pete's right eyebrow rose. "Really. Can you give him a call?"

"I'm not sure she has a phone number." Bogs closed his eyes. "Or for that matter a phone."

Pete reached into his satchel and pulled out a pencil and yellow note pad. "Well then give me an address."

"Can't really say she has an address either."

Pete shook his head. "She?"

"Alexandra."

Pete's eyebrows rose. "I imagined a hairy, overweight guy with jeans that don't cover his butt when he bends over."

Bogs shifted his weight on the couch. "Dude, you are so regressive. You need to get out more."

Pete considered reminding Bogs that "getting out" required leaving the couch, but decided maintaining focus on the issue at hand would be more productive. "What's the name of her business?"

"World-Famous Sports Bar," Bogs replied.

Pete rolled his eyes. "Her plumbing company is named after a bar?"

"No man, she hangs out at the World-Famous Sports Bar. Or maybe she works there." Bogs scratched his beard again and stopped when another toothpick fell out. "It's on Sixth and Alder. Tell them you want to order a liquid plumber."

"Why can't I just tell them I want to talk to Alexandra?"

"The bar might get the wrong idea." Bogs pointed at his head.

Pete closed his eyes and rubbed his temples. "What kind of place is this? A bar fronting as a plumbing business where you can't ask for a plumber?"

"Yup." Bogs replied as he rolled over on the couch and closed his eyes.

~

When Pete entered the World-Famous Sports Bar, he assumed he was in the wrong place. The bar was empty save for a few tables, a pinball machine, two large television screens, and a long polished bar with well-worn barstools. It didn't appear worldly or famous, or associated with sports. A woman with black hair pulled up in a ponytail stood behind the bar holding a phone next to her ear speaking a language Pete didn't recognize. She appeared annoyed.

Pete sat on a barstool and watched as the woman behind the bar continued her conversation, ignoring him. She was dressed in black, wore black fingernail polish, and had deep-set eyes. Across her left arm was a tattoo of an eagle with a monkey wrench in its talons. After a long minute the conversation ended, and she turned her attention to Pete.

"What can I get you?" Her accent was as unknown to Pete as the language she had been speaking.

"I need a *liquid plumber*," Pete replied.

The woman reached for a bottle of gin and a martini glass. She pulled a shaker from beneath the bar.

Pete shook his head. "No, I need a liquid plumber."

The woman stopped. "Yes. Gin, orange juice, lime, and melon liqueur. Is this not how it's made?"

Pete shook his head again. "No, I mean I need a…" He paused. "I need to talk to Alexandra."

"She isn't here. Maybe you should leave a message."

Pete sighed. "Okay. Can I leave an address? I need to hire her to fix my sink."

The woman shrugged and pulled out a Post-It note and pen. She handed them to Pete, who wrote down his phone number and address. "Any idea how soon I can expect to hear from her?"

"No." The woman behind the bar said emphatically. "She will contact you when she chooses."

Pete's shoulders slumped. "Okay." He handed the note to the woman behind the bar. "Maybe I will have a drink."

"We're closed," the woman replied.

It was ten thirty at night when Pete heard a knock at the door. At first, he didn't feel the need to respond and simply turned up the television volume. Bogs had gone to bed, having endured a long day of eating and napping. But as the pounding on the door continued, he pulled himself off the couch, pulled a bathrobe over his t-shirt, and stumbled to the door.

It took a moment before Pete recognized the woman from the World-Famous Sports Bar standing in the hallway. She wore a black leather jacket, black baseball cap, and black jeans. As Pete opened the door, he noticed a red toolbox sitting on the floor next to her.

"Hello?" Pete asked.

"You asked for a plumber," the woman stated flatly.

"Yeah. You were there."

"And now I am here," she said as she picked up the toolbox.

"It's ten thirty."

The woman pushed past Pete. "Closer to eleven I think."

"How did you get in the building? I didn't buzz you in. The doors are locked."

The woman didn't answer.

Pete closed the door and followed her into the kitchen. She put the toolbox on the floor and opened it. She picked up the top tray, piled high with wrenches and a pipe cutter. As she set the tray down, Pete noticed a silver handgun in the bottom of the box.

"Alexandra, can I call you Alexandra? Is that a gun?" Pete paused and took a deep breath. "In your toolbox. Is that a gun?"

"Call me Alex. These are plumbing tools. In my toolbox. You want a plumber to fix your sink. The plumber needs tools to fix the problem."

"And a handgun is helpful?"

Alex picked up a monkey wrench and twisted one of the pipes. "Sometimes."

Alex tapped the pipes below the sink. After a moment she stood. "The sink is not the problem."

Pete shook his head. "What do you mean? It leaks. There's water coming out of the drain. Nothing comes from the faucet."

Alex put her tools back in the toolbox. "There are things that need to be fixed if your sink is going to work properly."

"What things?"

"Plumbing things."

"And how are you going to fix them?"

Alex turned toward Pete. "They will be fixed. Alex will fix them. The problem is not the sink. The problem is…existential."

Pete scratched his head. "How is a sink an existential problem? You turn the handle and water comes out. You pour water in, and it goes down the drain. It's a sink."

"Flow like water and you will find your way through the rock," Alex replied.

Pete sighed. "But apparently not the nozzle on my sink. What existential problem do I need to fix?"

Alex picked up her toolbox and marched back to the front door. "You do nothing. You hired a plumber; the plumber will fix."

Pete sighed. "And when will I know it's done?"

Alex smirked ever so slightly. "When your sink works. Obviously."

THE NEXT MORNING, AS PETE WALKED THROUGH THE LOBBY JERRY approached him with a panicked look on his face.

"What did you do?" Jerry asked.

"What do you mean?"

"Mrs. Jenkins in 4C called and thanked me for fixing her shower drain."

Pete shrugged. "Great."

"No, it's not great. Mrs. Jenkins has been complaining about it for over a year. And now it's fixed." Jerry wiped some sweat off his forehead and leaned toward Pete. "And I didn't get anyone to fix it."

Pete nodded. "You can thank me later."

Jerry took a step back. His eyes widened. He reached in his back pocket, pulled out a small flask, unscrewed the lid, and took a swig.

"You didn't do what I think you did...Did you?" He took a longer drink from the flask.

"That depends. What do you think I did?"

Jerry put his flask back in his pocket and leaned forward breathing heavily. "Peter, did you hire a union plumber?"

Pete thought for a moment before responding. "I actually don't know."

"What do you mean you don't know?"

Pete shrugged. "Well, I'm pretty sure she's not in a union. But I'm not sure if she's actually a plumber. Either way, she probably isn't in a union, so why does it matter?"

Jerry closed his eyes and cleared his throat. "So, you brought someone in to fix the plumbing who isn't a plumber?"

"Maybe."

Jerry opened his eyes and pulled out a wrinkled piece of paper from his pocket. "Someone dropped this in the freight elevator yesterday morning."

Pete smoothed out the yellow paper with his hand. *Revolution Plumbing* was printed in large block letters across the flyer above the catchphrase *"Ready to Lead You to Plumbing Independence"* and a bald eagle holding a monkey wrench.

Pete handed the flyer back to Jerry. "What does this have to do with me? And how do you know they're a union outfit? Did you call them?"

Jerry carefully folded the flyer and placed it in his shirt pocket. "I tried to look them up. No phone number, no address. It's like they don't exist." He coughed before continuing in a low voice. "The union plumber thing, it isn't about unions, it's about plumbing."

Pete thought about mentioning the World-Famous Sports Bar, but couldn't imagine how it would help. "So, it doesn't matter who I hired, it matters that I tried to fix my sink?"

Jerry's brow glistened with sweat. "No. She doesn't want anyone touching the plumbing. Anyone." He pulled a handkerchief from his pocket and wiped his forehead. "Mrs. B was livid when she found this, especially after several residents thanked her for fixing their showers and toilets. She wants to hold an inquest to find out who hired the plumber."

Pete shrugged. "Not my inquest, not my problem."

"Actually, it is. When you asked her to change the condo policy you got her attention. She's quite certain you are behind the improved plumbing in the building and intends to kick you out. The inquest is just a formality."

Pete raised an eyebrow. "She can't actually do that, can she?"

Jerry grimaced. "What do you think?"

Pete felt a sense of panic come over him. "I can't get kicked out. It's my condo!"

Jerry shrugged. "Well, I hope at the very least your sink works."

Pete thought for a moment before realizing he hadn't checked to see if it did.

WHEN PETE RETURNED TO THE BUILDING THAT AFTERNOON, HE STARTED TO open the glass door to the lobby when he heard a loud "Psst." An elderly man in khakis and a blue jacket waved his hand and motioned for Pete to come closer. Pete walked up next to the man, who looked around nervously and said cryptically, "Follow me."

The elderly man led Pete across the street to the pay lot where a black sedan and light blue van were parked next to one another. The man approached the side door of the van and knocked three times. The door slid open. Four people sat on bench seats. Pete didn't recognize any of them.

The elderly man cleared his throat. "We understand you're leading the revolution." He paused, waiting for Pete to respond. When he didn't, the old man continued. "We want to join you."

A woman with large and circular tinted glasses and cat hair on her blouse nodded. "Yes, we're all here to help in the fight against the Condo Association."

A young man wearing a black leather jacket leaned forward. "We've already started sticking it to them." His brow furrowed. "Yesterday I hired a carpet cleaner."

The woman with a bedazzled pink hoodie and blue hair smiled. "I ordered ten pizzas and had them delivered to the building staff." Her eyes got big. "And you should have seen Burton-Hedge's face when one of the groundskeepers thanked her!"

Pete put his hands in his pockets. "Sounds very…revolutionary, but I'm not trying to start anything." Noticing blank stares, Pete added, "I just needed to fix my sink."

The elderly man nodded. "Start something? You did. And when you stood up to the witch on the tenth floor the rest of the building took notice. The people are rising up. They've started hiring outside handymen, getting their walls painted." He paused for effect. "And even requesting to attend Condo Association meetings."

A very serious look crossed the face of the woman with cat hair on her blouse. "We are sending around a petition to remove the current board chair."

Pete closed his eyes. "Seriously, I'm not trying to start anything. I just hired a…well, I think I hired a plumber."

The bedazzled woman patted the knee of the young man sitting next to her, "Such a reluctant leader. Like George Washington."

The young man nodded. "Or Che Guevara."

The elderly man in the khakis put his hand on Pete's shoulder. "We just need someone to organize the building. Someone to show the way. We just need to know, what do we do next?"

Pete sighed. "I have no idea. Finish fixing the plumbing, maybe?"

There was a moment of silence as the rebels looked at one another. Finally, the bedazzled woman spoke. "Brilliant. We defy the COA's most sacred command. We fix the plumbing!"

THE NOTICE WAS REMARKABLY INAUSPICIOUS. *YOUR PRESENCE IS REQUIRED AT the 3rd and Oak Condominium Association Meeting. Seven O'clock. Tenth floor. Tardiness may result in punishment.*

At five minutes to seven, Pete found himself standing outside an ornate door on the tenth floor. A small golden placard read *3rd and Oak Condominium Association—In Session*. Not seeing a doorbell, he considered for a moment whether or not he should knock. As he raised his fist, the large door silently opened.

Pete stepped into a darkened hallway. A door at the end opened and a bright light caused him to squint. He made his way through the door into a large windowless room with a parquet floor and ornamental rug. On one side was a large portrait of Mrs. Burton-Hedges holding a small dog, on the other side a much smaller portrait of a middle-aged man, presumably Mr. Burton, with a chagrined look on his face.

Mrs. Burton-Hedges sat on a small dais behind an ornate wooden table. She wore a purple dress, pearl necklace, and black scarf which failed to hide the skin folds in her neck. Jerry sat at a smaller desk on one side. He wore a short-sleeved white shirt exposing three skin-colored NicoDerm patches on the back of his arm.

As Pete entered the room, Mrs. Burton-Hedges motioned toward a chair in the middle of the room facing the desk. A large light had been positioned directly above the chair to highlight whoever was being questioned.

Mrs. Burton-Hedges scowled as she stared at Pete. "Young man, your insidious efforts to infiltrate the pipes of this building have come to the attention of this body."

Pete nodded. "Okay."

Jerry cleared his throat. "I think the Chairwoman is asking whether or not you hired someone to work on the building's plumbing without notifying the Association and without ensuring the Association's rules were being followed."

"I was told not to hire a union plumber, and I didn't." Pete replied.

Mrs. Burton-Hedges leaned forward. "Was this plumber licensed and bonded? Mister..." She turned to Jerry, "What's his name?"

"Peter Simpson."

"Mr. Simpson, did you hire someone to do work on the building at 3rd and Oak without the expressed permission of this Condo Association?"

Pete thought for a moment before answering. "Maybe."

Jerry cleared his throat. "What do you mean, maybe?"

"I got someone to fix my sink. I didn't hire her to do anything to the rest of the building." Pete raised an eyebrow. "And what is this Condo Association? So far, I only see you?"

Mrs. Burton-Hedges ignored the question. "By 'maybe' you mean 'yes.'" She straightened her back and cleared her throat. "Clearly, Mr. Simpson, you have decided you are above the law. You have decided your needs come first. Let me assure you, they do not." She turned to Jerry. "Jerold, take a note." She turned back to Pete. "This very morning someone decided they could steam clean the carpet in the seventh-floor hallway. Someone else made the unfortunate decision to change the lobby light fixtures from bright white to soft white. Next, they'll want planters with flowers on the sidewalk." She pounded her fist on the table. "It's an insurrection, I tell you, and I won't stand for it! The residents of this building place their faith in this Association and its chair. That faith has been put in jeopardy." She leaned forward and her face darkened. "I find *your* lack of faith disturbing."

Pete could feel the heat from the light above his head. "I'd like to discuss this with the rest of the Condo Association, if you don't mind."

Mrs. Burton-Hedges stood. "I do mind. For your purposes I *am* the 3rd and Oak Condominium Association. Let me be clear. If it turns out you hired someone who was not licensed and bonded you will be removed from this building. You will have to sell your condominium." With that, she nodded at Jerry, lumbered off the dais, and left the room.

As if on cue, Jerry began to cough. His face turned a scarlet red. Pete briefly considered stepping behind him and using the Heimlich maneuver, but wasn't sure what Jerry might have accidentally swallowed.

After several moments of coughing, Jerry stopped, took a deep breath, and nodded at Pete. "I would suggest you have a conversation with the person you hired."

～

THE NEXT DAY, WHEN PETE ENTERED THE WORLD-FAMOUS SPORTS BAR, Alex was seated at one of the tables watching a hockey match on television.

"Alex, I'm getting kicked out of my condo."

Alex continued to stare at the hockey match as she replied, "No, you are not."

Pete frowned. "Yes. The condo board is kicking me out. The chairwoman knows I hired you to fix my sink. Unless you're licensed and bonded and not in a union, she is going to kick me out of my condo."

"You mean the fat woman who killed her husband."

Pete slumped in his chair. "Yes, Mrs. Burton-Hedges."

Alex pounded her fist on the table as one of the hockey teams scored a goal. "Maqsat!" she shouted.

Alex turned to Pete. "Did you see *Star Wars*?"

Pete cocked his head to one side. "The movie?"

Alex nodded.

"Of course. But I'm not sure what that has to do with anything."

"How did Luke Skywalker overthrow the Empire?" Alex paused, leaned forward, and whispered, "Plumbing."

Pete closed his eyes. "What are you talking about? He blew up the Death Star."

"How did he blow it up? He used a pipe. Fired the torpedo right down the drain. Like sending a snake down the toilet." Alex leaned across the table. "You want the fat lady to sing, you send a torpedo down her drainpipe." She clapped her hands. "Boom."

"You aren't going to kill Mrs. Burton-Hedges, are you? I didn't tell you to murder anyone. I just needed to fix my sink."

Alex winked at Pete. "No killing. No, we fix the plumbing in your building another way. Like the *Star Wars* torpedo. We find a weakness and cause a chain reaction." She made a whistling sound followed by another "Boom."

Pete sighed. "And how do I shoot a torpedo down the drainpipe in my building? Which, by the way, I don't want to blow up."

Alex turned back to the television. "No worry. Alex already flew her X-wing fighter into the trench and fired the shot."

Pete rolled his eyes. "I think I need a beer."

Alex continued to stare at the television. "We're closed."

THAT AFTERNOON, WHEN PETE ENTERED THE BUILDING, HE WAS SURPRISED TO find the lobby was filled with police officers.

Jerry stood in the corner, a sandwich in one hand and coffee in the other.

"What's happening?" Pete asked.

"Apparently an informant told the police they found Mr. Burton's wedding ring in the building's drainage pipes." Jerry took a bite of his sandwich before continuing. "Was enough evidence to get a search warrant for the penthouse."

"How did his wedding ring make its way into the building's plumbing?"

A large glob of mayonnaise dropped onto Jerry's shirt. He wiped it off with the back of his hand. "Garbage disposal. Looks like that's how she got rid of him."

"She put him down the garbage disposal? Is that even possible?"

Jerry shrugged. "Must have carved him up pretty good. Explains why the plumbing's been so messed up."

Pete felt a wave of nausea wash over him. "You mean the plumbing in the building has been full of…Mr. Burton?"

Jerry nodded. He took a swig of coffee. "Look at it this way, at least it was only the drainage pipes. It's not like you were showering in him. We were all just helping wash him out."

Pete took a deep breath. "I'm not sure that makes it better."

As Pete spoke, the elevator door behind him opened. A handcuffed Mrs. Burton-Hedges entered the lobby, escorted by two police officers. Wearing a dark gray jacket and loafers, she struggled as the officers prodded her toward the front door. "Unhand me. I'll have your jobs!"

As Mrs. Burton-Hedges was pulled toward the building doors she noticed Jerry. "Jerold, call my attorney!"

Jerry held up his sandwich. "Yes, Mrs. B. Right away." He turned and whispered to Pete. "As soon as I get an exercise bike." He waved as the police pushed the oversized woman through the front door. "Real soon Mrs. B, real soon."

Pete put his hands in his pockets. "What happens now?"

Jerry shrugged. "The Condo Association holds a new election." He coughed. "And you should run. You might get elected."

BOGS WAS IN THE KITCHEN WHEN PETE GOT HOME. HE STOOD OVER THE sink, turning the facet off and on. He looked at Pete. "Looks like Alexandra fixed it."

Pete nodded. "Fixed the sink and the Association." He set his bag down on the kitchen table. "I'm thinking about running."

"You should." Bogs turned the faucet off a final time. "Maybe you can get the lights in the hallway fixed."

"They aren't working?" Pete asked, wondering how Bogs would know about the lights in the hallway as he never entered it.

Bogs sauntered back to the couch. "Yeah. They're pretty bad. You'll probably need to hire an electrician."

IN A FARAWAY PLACE

KERRY CATHERS

The clink of a metal spoon against fine china brought Liza Cunningham's attention from the window and the collection of people streaming past it to the woman seated across the linen-draped table from her.

"Fix your posture." Miss Fitzgerald delivered the scold with a bright smile. Arguments drew attention, and of all the things they did not need, attention was one of the last of them. "If you would remove the pained look from your face, I would be ever so grateful." Miss Fitzgerald sipped from her steaming cup.

"It isn't an expression of pain; it's one of boredom." Liza took a mouthful of tepid tea and winced. "How much longer before we concede defeat?"

"We don't. Patrick's information has yet to be false. Mr. Reeleder will pass this way."

"And Mr. Reeleder is a bad man."

"Beyond his habit of transporting items covertly, I've no notion as to his character. Its goodness or badness."

"He's a smuggler." Another sip and Liza pushed the cup away, not certain which displeased her more, the tea or the man's occupation. Hypocritical for the most part, given that she was a mostly-reformed thief.

"A judgmental term which reflects negatively upon those who employ such men and women."

Liza's grin was mischievous. "You've employed smugglers. Does the detective know?"

"I have. Yes, he does. And, no. You cannot tease him about that."

Liza looked to the people crowding London's streets. Across from the tea shop, Detective Philip Armitage leaned against a lamppost pretending to read a broadsheet, his tailored suit exchanged for workingman's garb. Tall, brown-blond, imposing, and with a boxer's physique, he stood with a deceptive air of disinterest. Miss Fitzgerald had brought him into their makeshift coven to provide protection, and to run interference should any of their activities catch too much police attention.

"And what are we to do once we have Mr. Reeleder?" Liza asked, fighting the urge to set her chin in her palm.

"We're going to have a chat."

Liza gave a tiny unladylike snort. "You think he'll talk?"

"They always talk."

Her gaze snapped to Miss Fitzgerald. Magic or intimidation or violence to coerce him into conversation, Liza didn't want to know which would be chosen. Perhaps all of them. The sorceress seated across from her was poised, her expression serene despite the tension that hovered around them. Raven hair arranged to perfection, eyes ice blue, her dark gown complementing her pale complexion as it pulled her into the background.

The two women were recently acquainted, as Miss Fitzgerald described it. Liza had become part of the group less than a month ago after an ill-conceived robbery had gone horribly wrong. Her theft of an innocuous-looking object of potent magic had thrust her into the middle of a war between covens, a war which had cost Liza dearly. After the chaos had settled, Liza had remained, finding the world of magic as intriguing as it was intimidating.

"These objects he's smuggling, any of them particularly dangerous?" Only part of her wanted to know what he traded in.

"Anything touched by magic is particularly dangerous."

"But will anything turn us into toads if we drop it?"

"Nothing can do that." She gave Liza a don't-be-ridiculous glare then turned her attention to the outside crowd. "We proceed with caution. Mr. Reeleder might be in possession of items that could shorten our lives, but he also might be surrounded by men who can do that just as easily."

"But we're protected from the worst of the magic stuff?" Liza spun the bracelet Miss Fitzgerald had given her that morning. Silver with lapis-lazuli flowers over it, the reverse cluttered with etched glyphs.

"Mostly,"

"*Mostly*? How mostly?"

"He's here." Miss Fitzgerald stood, fishing a handful of coins from her pocket. She laid the strap of her satchel across her body and strode from the tea shop like an empress leaving court.

Liza scrambled not to be left behind.

Outside was a typical London day, the streets congested with people going here and there on business or pleasure or both. It made following anyone difficult. Only vaguely aware of Mr. Reeleder's features, Liza followed Miss Fitzgerald's hat as it wove through the mass. Boredom gave way to disquiet and her hand went to her waist by instinct. Beneath the floral print a long thin blade lay secreted. Another stood in her corset. Thugs, criminals, corrupt police, she knew how to contend with those. The people and things touched by magic remained uncertain territory, and such uncertainty tended to get people killed.

She caught her first sight of their quarry when he darted across the street, drawing ire as he slipped between hansom cabs. Liza followed, reaching the other side as Mr. Reeleder turned into a smaller street. He moved at a jaunty pace, seeming to be without a single care and eased into an alley halfway along the street. Liza shivered. Few good things happened in alleys when day was approaching night.

The pace, press of bodies, and the warmth of the summer sun brought beads of sweat to her hairline, and the tight fit of the dress's collar and corset made her feel claustrophobic. She'd be panting like a well-run dog by the time they caught up with him. If they ever did. Which they might not, given his pace.

Until he stopped. Abruptly at the corner of the alley where it met up with a lane packed with merchant stalls and customers.

Miss Fitzgerald eased to one side, positioning herself so a walnut vendor stood between her and their quarry. Liza drew close, lungs pumping against the confines of her dress as she struggled for air.

Their wait was short. From among the crowd emerged a petite woman with a dress of pale yellow, a parasol dangling from her arm, and an oversized hat obscuring her face. She greeted him in the French way, with a small peck to each cheek, then held out her hand. By his expression, Mr. Reeleder refused and seemed to bargain with her. Their words lost in the distance and the din of voices from the lane.

The woman pulled a stack of folded bank notes from her pocket and set them on display. The brazenness of the act in a place such as this made Lizas's innards curdle. People ended up dead in alleys for less than that. When Mr. Reeleder reached for the notes, she snatched them back. After more words, he produced a folded page and a statuette that fit easily into his palm. A quick inspection of both and the notes were surrendered and stashed away in Mr. Reeleder's inner pocket. An easy place for pilfering; Liza's fingers itched.

The woman tucked her treasures into her pocket, and, by chance, lifted her gaze and met the eyes of Miss Fitzgerald. Anger quickly became mischief as she curtsied, smiled, and blew a kiss. She was off into the lane in a blur of yellow.

Miss Fitzgerald raised her hand, snapped her fingers, and a moment later Armitage was beside them. She spoke, leading them forward at a rush. "I know her from Marseille."

"Mr. Reeleder?" Armitage asked moving Liza in front of him.

"Loath as I am to allow his escape, she poses a greater danger. We contend with her, then revisit our smuggling problem when she's no longer a threat."

They pushed through bodies, ignoring the insults and curses that followed. The woman's hat wove an intricate pattern ahead and marked their path from the market into a street less congested, then another lined on one side by tenements and on the other by a high brick wall.

The woman halted in front of a door, turned like a dancer, waved, and smiled before slipping through it. Armitage ran forward, catching it before it closed. Liza followed Miss Fitzgerald through. Two steps over the threshold and the world lurched, pitching her forward, off balance, into a bright, well-furnished parlor. The wrongness of it raised Liza's hackles. Wherever they were, they needed to get out. She spun on her heels and made it one step closer to the door. The woman from Marseille blew a kiss and slammed the door shut.

A wave went through, like a bullock of a man, lifting Liza from her feet and tossing her deeper into the parlor before dropping her on a carpet, her head landing with a thud. When she climbed to her feet, shaking off the dizziness, Miss Fitzgerald was at the door, studying marks in the wood.

"Take this." Armitage unwrapped a gold-colored lozenge and held it toward her.

"What is it?" Liza held it between finger and thumb.

"To help with the bump to the head."

"You're not taking one?"

"I have more." He pulled another from an inner jacket pocket. "Under the tongue so it dissolves faster."

"Explains much about your personality."

He offered an inquisitive look as he slid the lozenge into his mouth.

"A few too many hits to the head." She put the disc beneath her tongue and doubled over from the taste. Nausea rose like a tide, but the lozenge was gone before she could spit it out. "Why does nothing in magic have a good side?"

"I never have to worry about my tea going cold." Miss Fitzgerald stepped back from the door, hands on hips, and whispered something in French that might have been profanity. "Portal magic. I loathe portal magic."

Liza gave their surroundings a closer inspection; something scratched at the back of her mind, warning her something was very wrong. A sizeable room, bathed in bright sunlight entering through four windows framed by thick curtains, two to each wall. To the other side stood rooms whose purpose she didn't feel inclined to explore. The furniture was plentiful and elegant and set out for entertaining. Painted landscapes pressed close together on the walls. The trappings of wealth.

All left to rot.

Liza went to a writing table and took the top letter from a pile resting on a salver tarnished so much it was almost black. When she read the address, the world lurched. That's what was amiss with the room. The sun was in the wrong place.

"We're not where we think we are." The pit of Liza's stomach went cold.

"How so?" Miss Fitzgerald studied a glyph.

"We're in a residence on the corner of 3rd and Oak."

"I don't think London has a 3rd Street," Miss Fitzgerald responded, attention elsewhere.

"Doesn't. But we're not in London." She held the letter toward them as proof. "We're in America. That place situated on the other side of the Atlantic from where we were moments ago."

"That far?" Miss Fitzgerald took the letter from Liza as Armitage went to a window. "How curious."

"I can think of a more appropriate word," Liza grumbled.

"I did not think enough magic could be conjured to stretch a portal that distance. But it does answer a few questions." Miss Fitzgerald seemed to think the accomplishment a challenge to her talent.

"Is one of them: How do we get home?" Liza asked.

"There are marks along each of the windows. Same as on the doorframe." Armitage joined them.

"The letter is over twenty years old, yet the room is undisturbed. Two decades of keeping people out requires considerable power and talent."

"Or someone returning to renew the spell." He pointed to the chair.

Miss Fitzgerald went to the window to inspect the glyphs there. Liza followed to have her first sight of a country she'd heard so much about. Below them stood empty stables, their walls and roof standing in disrepair. To the far side, a row of brick shops, expertly designed to cater to the affluent members of society, left to decay.

"Try it." Miss Fitzgerald stepped away from the window. "They're containment, not protection."

He swung the chair and it splintered against the glass.

"Why don't we go back the way we came?" Liza shivered.

"Not how it works." Miss Fitzgerald looked more intrigued than fearful.

"Of course, it doesn't," Liza sighed.

"One door in, another out," Miss Fitzgerald explained without condescension.

"And if there's no other door?" Liza didn't want to know the answer.

"There's always another door," said Miss Fitzgerald, certain in the declaration.

"Not in here." Liza pointed to the frames that lacked doors.

"Our only option is to find the door leading to London. Miss Cunningham, we have need of your skills. And do not dawdle with questions about safety. The longer we are here, the less likely we are to leave."

Liza pulled her kit from her skirt pocket and knelt in front of the lock. "I open the door, we go into the city, find transport to the coast and a ship home."

"Eventually."

"Eventually?"

"I want to look around," Miss Fitzgerald declared.

Liza sighed. A question came out of her she wasn't certain she wanted answered. It would be nothing good. "Do I want to know why?"

"Great evil was done here. Somewhere in this building. And I'm not leaving until I find out what that evil is."

"ARE WE GOING TO FIND BODIES BEHIND ANY OF THESE DOORS?" LIZA ASKED Armitage, half her attention on the lock in front of her, working it by instinct. She crouched in front of a door in a hallway. They'd gone first to the top floor, trying every lock, inspecting every residence, before proceeding to the next one down.

"Possibly,"

"*Possibly*? You're supposed to say: Absolutely not."

"Absolutely not." He leaned against the doorframe. After so many doors opened, his vigilance had given way to something more relaxed. His hovering less annoying.

"You're not funny." Liza set the final pin into place, stood, and declared the door open.

Armitage moved off the frame and turned to Miss Fitzgerald, who stood at the door one down from theirs. She nodded and joined them.

"There are no marks on the next one. It can be opened safely."

Liza nodded and stood away from the door, aware that her definition of safe did not quite match Miss Fitzgerald's. She looked down the hall in the direction they were moving. Three floors had been searched with nothing of significance found or seen. Each apartment was bedecked with expensive furniture and art, wardrobes filled with clothes suited to the prosperous, if not the overly affluent. A few insignificant charmed items were left where they were found. Not one apartment possessed anything that could be the portal home.

An eerie, unnatural silence occupied the rooms, the halls, the stairwells. Every creak of the floor echoed like a promise of something awful to come. The building seemed more like the interior of a mausoleum than a former home. Not a soul had been seen or heard, but she could not shake the feeling of being watched.

"Nothing." Miss Fitzgerald strode from the apartment and down the hall. Liza followed at a slower pace, playing with the tools from her kit. Another lock opened, another home searched.

Liza moved aside for the others, allowing them to open yet another door and inspect the space behind it. She glanced down the hall to measure their progress and caught sight of a shadow that didn't seem to fit the emptiness. She moved a few steps toward it when Miss Fitzgerald's call halted her. A glance away and back, and the shadow was gone.

She shook her head to drive out the paranoia, and was in front of another lock.

"Listen," Miss Fitzgerald's tone was like honed steel. Silence hovered long enough to believe there was nothing to hear. Then a thump came like a drum and a ping.

"Out. Out." Miss Fitzgerald ran down the hall, Armitage in tow. He grabbed Liza's arm and pulled her along behind him.

She opened her mouth to ask the urgency when the air heated to that inside of an oven, stifling her breath and cooking her throat. A roar pushed itself along the hall. At the intersection of two halls, they fell sideways into the adjoining one, Armitage giving Liza a slight toss. She fell, rolled, and looked up to see an inferno race past, its heat forcing aside Liza's gaze. It flared out as quickly as it had come.

On her feet first, Miss Fitzgerald stepped into the hall they'd abandoned. "Either there are traps we've sprung, or we are not alone."

Liza, standing on knees slightly wobbly, was not certain which she preferred.

"There are glyphs," Armitage announced, pointing to the closest door.

"Excellent." Miss Fitzgerald ran her fingers over them. Liza was less than convinced.

"Portal magic?" Armitage asked as Liza peeked into the hall to find nothing burned. Nothing changed.

"We might have found our way home," Miss Fitzgerald purred. "If I can find which of them ignites the spell."

"We'll be home soon?" Liza joined them, hopeful, ready to be away from the oddness of the place.

"Soon. There is more exploring to be done," Miss Fitzgerald responded, stepping back from the door to test the handle. Locked. "Miss Cunningham, would you be so kind."

Liza knelt, her knees starting to hurt from so long perched on them. The lock, mundane in its appearance, proved trickier. The pattern of the pins was less obvious and moved with reluctance, as though rusted. Closing her eyes, she ignored the discussion behind her, set aside her unease, and listened to what the lock was telling her.

A thump like a drum and a ping.

"Miss Cunningham."

"I know."

"Time is short."

"I know." The pins weren't moving as they should. Weren't obeying her motions.

"Sooner, preferable to later."

Another. Another. Another. A few left.

Another thump like a drum and a ping, and a slow rumble from far away.

"Miss Cunningham."

A shiver ran down her spine as she moved the final pins and pulled the tools free. A sigh of relief more than victory as she turned the handle.

The door opened with a jerk, suction pulling it inward toward the abyss.

And taking Liza with it.

SHE STRUCK GROUND WITH ENOUGH FORCE TO KNOCK THE BREATH FROM HER and send up a puff of sediment that stung her eyes. Lungs tight, her gasps ragged, Liza pulled herself to her hands and knees, eyes squeezed shut and watering. She spat out the layer of grime from her mouth, brought herself to her feet, and opened her eyes to darkness so thick it felt eternal.

"Where are we?" Her whisper sounded like a shout.

"Lux." Miss Fitzgerald sounded annoyed. A pop and the world was bathed in a dim gray light.

An unfinished ceiling hung low above them, but the walls were wide apart and lacking windows. The floor was unexpectedly made from wooden beams. Shelves in various stages of dereliction lined the edges, and a waist-high heavy table dominated one side of the chamber. Jars, books, tools of the trade lay scattered as much as stood sentry on the shelves. To Liza's left, a single cupboard reached almost the height of the ceiling with drawers beneath a door that hung from one hinge. The air reeked of sulphur and decay.

"I think I prefer the darkness," Liza mumbled, half to herself.

"We know what happened to the residents," Armitage spoke from a short distance away, crouching and staring into the space behind the room's only staircase, the top of which was marked by a tall narrow door.

Liza stared through gaps where risers should have been, eyes following the line of darker shadows of things she did not want to see. "Where *are* we?"

"I believe we are in the conjuring room of a coven located in 3rd and Oak's cellar." Miss Fitzgerald brushed at her skirts like she was hitting someone she didn't like. "I suspect this is a residential house where coven members lived."

"I thought that practice had ended." Armitage made a slow circle of the vicinity, eyes on the floor. He picked up various items, tested their weight, and abandoned them.

"It would seem they kept the practice this side of the Atlantic. In Russia, as well. They seem to like them there."

"They murdered their members?" Liza wiped the filth from her face with a dusty sleeve.

"This was done by people using taboo magic. *This* is the result of an infestation like we're seeing in London."

"The old magic is returning." Armitage sounded defeated.

"As is its evil." Miss Fitzgerald went to the shelves, inspecting. "This damage is not from age. Someone was looking for something."

"A relic?" Armitage paused, his body tensing like a predator about to strike.

"Possibly." Miss Fitzgerald mused.

"Perhaps I am alone in my inclination, but I suggest we get ourselves out of here before something worse happens." Liza lifted her skirts above what was prim and went toward the staircase.

Miss Fitzgerald's iron grip on her elbow halted her. "Use your intelligence." The cut of her voice was like a porcelain knife. "Nothing bars the stairwell, yet there's a pile of bodies beneath it. Neither chains nor cages nor any form of restraint to be found."

Armitage moved in line with the staircase at a distance and signaled for them to stand to the side. He tossed a lump of something onto the third step. A thump and light exploded with a severity that sent Liza to her knees, arms raised to protect her face. The air crackled and sizzled like bacon in too much fat. As it subsided, she risked a look. Crooked spider webs of light danced the length and width of the stairwell.

"Superb." Liza stood, stomach souring as its contents threatened to rise. "There wouldn't happen to be another door somewhere?"

"I'd force a tunnel through the wall," Miss Fitzgerald said, "but I've not the ingredients. Anything I find on the shelf is likely as old as the letter. Too stale for something that complex. And the magic here is rotten. It's the stairs or we stay here and rot."

"We're trapped."

"Trapped is for people who lack the ingenuity to manufacture an escape." Her voice was half distracted as she surveyed the line of steps. To Armitage she said, "I need to see the glyphs. If I know how the spell was built, I can break it."

"The tenants never succeeded in breaking it." Liza took in the grimness of the chamber. What a horrid place to die.

"Expounding the failures of others does nothing to increase our chances of success. Detective, we'll need something heavy enough to break the bottom step. And cloth to wind around your hands. And something to shield your face."

"Is that wise?" Liza eased closer to the staircase.

"Daring, not wisdom, is called for in such situations." Miss Fitzgerald stated.

"Daring got us into this."

"And without it we'd be charred lumps of flesh and bone in an upper hallway." A sigh and Miss Fitzgerald's tone softened minutely. "It is a precarious situation we find ourselves in, but not an impossible one. What we must do is gather the tools we shall need for our escape. I am certain, given the extent of the detritus, that we will find exactly what we require or something close enough to it to serve our needs."

Liza scanned the gaping chamber behind her, gray, chilled, and unfriendly. "You want me to rummage around this nightmare?"

"Do you have another suggestion?"

∼

THERE WAS LESS TO LOOK THROUGH THAN LIZA HAD THOUGHT, BUT THE grime was thicker than she'd feared. Jars broken, their contents scattered, tins, tools of the trade, remnants of lives ended in this miserable place. There were expensive items of jewelry she might have pocketed a few weeks ago, before her life became entangled in magic. A few nails, a hammer without its handle, wires, and a shovel. All and sundry seemed to have made its way to the conjuring room.

Miss Fitzgerald seemed to be meeting with more success on the occasions when Liza glimpsed her. Difficult to know exactly, except that her expression had eased from homicidal to something more tolerant. Armitage looked content, finding sizeable items and carting them back to the staircase. If tossing a single item on the step caused a lightning storm, Liza wasn't certain she wanted to witness what breaking one would do.

She kicked some rubble aside and stepped onto what she thought was secure. It shifted, she staggered, arms flailing, and regained her footing. Not trusting what she'd stepped on, she went in the opposite direction and caught her toe under a wire and tumbled into the debris. The racket drew the attention of her comrades.

Armitage eased toward her. "Are you—"

"I'm fine," she barked harsher than was deserved. She kicked at the mess surrounding her, frustrated as much as fearful. And stopped.

Liza dragged her boot heel toward her with careful slowness. Felt it. Shoved her boot heel away from her. Felt it again. Faint. Hardly noticeable. But there.

On her knees, Liza brushed the floor clean, not caring how filthy it made her. And found it. A line along the boards. Too regular to be anything but purposeful. Not part of the floor's regular layout. Left and right. Following the thin gap. Laying bare a rectangle too small for an adult to pass through, and barely discernible. Unless you knew where to look and that there was something to find.

"I found something you both should see."

"The floor?" Armitage stated when he drew close.

"You're not funny." She pointed to what she thought was obvious. "Look."

"At what?" Miss Fitzgerald asked, coming up on her left side.

"It's the top of a ken." Neither offered indication they understood. "Every peeler *knows* what a ken is."

"A hidden location where ne'er-do-wells hide their ill-gotten goods."

"Precisely." A shrug and a hopeful look at Miss Fitzgerald. "Maybe your relic is hidden here."

Miss Fitzgerald cleared a wider space. "Unlikely. There are neither glyphs of protection nor concealment. Nor those to open it."

Triumphantly smug, Liza announced. "Doesn't need them. There'll be a concealed lock. Not everything is about magic." Back on her knees, her fingers danced over the edge of the hatchway until they caught on roughness where the knot in the wood sat. With a bit of pressure, Liza pulled the small panel away, revealing a lock. Taking out her kit, she went to work. What looked simple proved to be complicated, but nothing she had not conquered before. The mechanism gave way before Miss Fitzgerald could complain about lost time. With a pop, a handle came up from the wood. Armitage pulled it.

Beneath was a white marble casing in which sat an ivory urn, wider than it was tall. Miss Fitzgerald touched it, and, when nothing happened, reached in and brought it out.

"This was worth the inconvenience." The awe in her voice marked its importance more than its appearance did. "Mesopotamian." She turned it in her hands, examining everything. "Primitive glyphs. Perhaps the earliest manifestations of them and of magic."

"Worth killing for." Liza eased closer while Armitage remained at a distance.

"Worth slaughtering for. With this, and with enough magic at your disposal, you can create new spells."

"In the wrong hands, it could be catastrophic." Armitage closed the lid to the ken. "I don't need to suppose that it is coming with us."

"Most definitely," She twisted the top, removed it. "Whatever was inside is mercifully gone."

"Our stay is extended, I presume?" Armitage seemed nonplussed.

"Considerably. Having the relic is not enough. We must know why they have it and what they were doing with it."

A faint click and screeching hinges brought their attention to the stairwell.

"Hide it." Miss Fitzgerald shoved the urn at Liza and hurried to the stairs followed closely by Armitage.

Liza placed it on the floor with care, not entirely convinced it wouldn't turn her into something unpleasant. After concealing it beneath fraying cloth, she abandoned it, scurrying to the base of the stairs, arriving as their guest did.

"Isn't this a delight. I had long since ceased to expect company." He was tall, his height exaggerated by his elevated position on the first step. His hair was thinning and his face long. The limbs were spindly and the fine clothes fitted to his slight frame.

"Your friend, Mademoiselle LaFleur, was kind enough to invite us."

"She is a bit of a minx, is she not?" His gaze went over all of them, to the dim mess beyond. "You'll find nothing of use in there. We searched it thoroughly."

"It would be negligent of us not to try." Miss Fitzgerald offered a frigid smile.

"You are aware I cannot allow you to leave."

"It would be negligent of us not to try." The smile faded.

"Foolish, is a more apt word."

"Perhaps. But that is for us to decide."

"The others tried and failed." He leered more than smiled. "I will have your secrets before I am done with you. Soon. I have a few more tools to gather." He turned to go up the stairs.

Armitage was in motion, rushing forward as he pulled the revolver from beneath his jacket. The man was faster, drawing his own weapon and firing twice. The sound was like an explosion in Liza's head, hurting her ears and making them buzz. When the chamber fell silent, Armitage was on the ground, clutching his abdomen. Miss Fitzgerald rushed to him and pressed her hands to the wounds. The man on the steps grinned like a penny dreadful villain.

"Please." Liza rushed to him, up on the step and clutching before he could react. "Don't leave me. I'll tell you their secrets. But don't let me die here. Don't." She was hysterical. Hands on his lapels. His sleeves.

Reaching inside his jacket. Each time he pushed a hand off, she had it fixed to another part of his clothing. Begging. Pleading. Coming close to tears.

"Off me." He bellowed, the noise almost as loud as the gunshots. He took her by the arms and threw her aside.

She landed hard and rolled. By the time she was on her feet, the gun was pointed at her. His hand was steady and his expression fanatical. Liza crouched, showed herself to be no threat. A moment, when her life might have ended, he turned and went up the steps. "I'll return with my best tools. Best you speak before I use them."

Miss Fitzgerald shouted her own threat in French as Liza hurried to where she was crouched. The look she gave put ice on Liza's bones.

"I'll explain when there's time." Liza's voice held despite the racing of her heart. "Is he bad?"

"Put pressure here." No answer was the worst answer of all. When Miss Fitzgerald brought her hands away from Armitage's abdomen, they were red.

She put all her weight on the wounds, felt the warmth of blood and the ooze of it through her fingers. "How bad?"

"It isn't the wounds that are the threat. The magic in the chamber is fetid and it will fester in his blood, killing him before anything I do can fix him."

She worked as she spoke, drawing a length of cloth from the satchel and handing it to Liza, who stuffed it under her hands. Next came a wide squat jar with a cork lid. She scooped out a sizeable portion of foul-smelling cream that looked like oatmeal left to rot. Liza moved her hands, allowed Miss Fitzgerald to smear the wounds before returning the pressure. She chanced a look at Armitage. His face was paler than it should be. Miss Fitzgerald drew two symbols on his abdomen in his own blood as she spoke words of magic.

"There is no time to decipher and counter the spells on the steps," Miss Fitzgerald barked.

But there was no other way out.

Miss Fitzgerald looked behind, studied the cupboard before seeming to come to a decision. "We make a portal."

"Where? There's no other door." Liza followed Miss Fitzgerald's gaze. *"It's a cupboard."*

"It's a door."

"But will it work?"

"Theoretically."

"You've not done this before?"

"And where would I have had the need to try?" She was on her feet, testing the door. "Portals are made over thresholds, but…" She ran her hand over the bottom shelf of the cupboard. "It should suffice."

"To England."

"No. Not to England." Miss Fitzgerald turned, words harsh. "We'll get nowhere unless I can fix the door to the cupboard."

"I found nails." Liza was up and away as soon as Miss Fitzgerald placed her hands on Armitage. Scrambling through rubble, frantic, angry that she had not paid more attention. Where? Where? Where?

"Bring the relic," Miss Fitzgerald shouted.

Finding the nails under a messy pile on the floor, she almost wept. The hammer's head not far away. At a run, she went to the cupboard, setting the relic close to Armitage's head. She lifted the door and struggled to hold the nails and the broken hinge in place until Miss Fitzgerald joined her. Liza stared at her, shocked, unable to look at Armitage.

"It will make no difference." Miss Fitzgerald's voice was eerie in its softness.

Liza nodded and went to work, hammering as best she could. Missing the nail more than once, hitting her fingers often, until the hinge was secured.

"Take the gunpowder from the detective's bullets and put it in the relic. No questions. I've smeared the bullets with an oil so they'll come apart easily."

Liza hesitated then obeyed. She worked the bullets as Miss Fitzgerald painted symbols on the narrow space between the door and the edge of the cupboard. With the knife from her waist, Liza cut a short strip of her slip, twisted it, and set one end in the relic, touching the powder, and draped the other over the edge before setting the lid, but not sealing it.

"I thought we were to take it with us?"

"Its magic is too powerful, too old. If I take it through the portal it will explode."

Liza opened her mouth to speak, then snapped it shut at the sound of the door opening. "Our friend has returned." She was up, grabbing the first thing her hand touched and tossing it onto the step. Light crackled and spat and the door swung shut. When it eased, she tossed something else.

"Much longer?" Liza called, hiding her face behind her upraised arms.

"Soon."

"Soon is a horrible word."

"It's better than never."

A can tossed and sparks danced about the stairwell. A candlestick. A pipe.

"Done."

Liza tossed items one after another and rushed to where Miss Fitzgerald was helping Armitage to his feet. She slid herself beneath his free arm and took half his weight on her shoulders. He sucked in a breath and held it as he walked, his motions slow, his effort extreme. He was dead weight draped over them.

At the cupboard, Miss Fitzgerald took a nail and scratched a final glyph into the wood. Light flared and died behind the door.

"I'll be impressed if this works." Miss Fitzgerald opened the cupboard to blackness.

Behind them the door's hinges creaked.

"The relic," Miss Fitzgerald hissed as they shoved Armitage upward, using the lower shelf as a step.

"Worry about Armitage." Liza gave a shove and abandoned them.

She moved the relic further from the stairwell, closer to the cupboard. From her pocket, Liza pulled a box of matches and struck one as the man reached the middle landing. She touched the flame to the twist of fabric and prayed it would be enough.

The man reached the bottom. Looked at her. Looked at the relic. Liza darted to the cupboard and clamored her way up and through it as an eruption filled the room behind her.

~

She landed on her side and rolled onto her back, this landing aching more than the others did. A terrifying rumble sounded behind her. She sat up, watching in horror as 3rd and Oak shuddered and collapsed in on itself, sending a plume of dust and foulness over them. Liza held her breath and closed her eyes until the heat faded.

Armitage sat beside her looking far healthier than moments ago.

"You'll live," Miss Fitzgerald affirmed. "Now that you're away from the magic." She gave her attention to the pile of rubble. "Shame. I would have given my left pinky to find out what they were doing with the relic."

Liza went to where Miss Fitzgerald stewed, reached into her pocket. "There might be something of worth in this." She held out a notebook.

Miss Fitzgerald quirked a smile. "Your hysterics. Well done, Miss Cunningham."

"Do you think he's dead? Whoever he is."

"I do hope so. If not, he'll find us and kill us."

"You're not much for offering comfort, are you?"

"I saved the detective's life. That's enough comforting for one day." She flipped through the book.

"What now?" Liza looked around at the derelict buildings. She didn't want to think how the three of them looked. Filthy, bloodied, battered. "We'll never find a place to take us in."

"I've money enough to overcome any aversion to renting us two rooms."

"We let the local coven know about what happened before we go home?" Liza asked.

"We cannot be certain they'll be friendly to our presence or what we did." Miss Fitzgerald picked foreign bits from her dress.

"Shouldn't we—"

She snapped the book shut and faced Liza squarely. "We tell no one of this. If word spreads about what we found and destroyed, what we walked away with..." She held up the notebook. "There won't be a spell or a person who can protect us."

Liza nodded, understanding.

"Chop chop, Detective." Miss Fitzgerald clapped her hands, turned toward the officer. "We must find the swiftest route to London. We've a smuggler to capture and question."

Armitage got to his feet with a grunt.

"Prepare yourself for the journey, Miss Cunningham. It will be a less-than-pleasant trip to the coast." Miss Fitzgerald brushed at her skirt with filthy hands. "I've heard the Americans have yet to learn how to make a proper cup of tea."

MISSED IMPRESSIONS

SALLY K LEHMAN

My shoulders shrugged up and forward in an effort to cover more of my neck with the scarf and jacket I'd thrown on before leaving. The gloves that completed this particular winter ensemble were lying on top of the pellet stove at home—forgotten, warm, and cozy—in the rush to leave. *Charlie's always in a rush*, I thought, and wondered how long it takes for frostbite to seep in and destroy hands through wool coat pockets.

I looked up at just the right moment to catch a snowflake on my eyelashes, smudging the street signs that marked 3rd Avenue and Oak Street. Why had I agreed to leave my car a block away? Why had I agreed to come with Charlie to this part of town in the middle of the night?

Because she was freaking out and practically crying and needed someone to drive her in the snow. I snuggled my face further into my scarf and blinked away the snowflake. *And because Mom and Dad would never have agreed to bring her here.*

I looked right, left, right, saw no traffic. *Not surprising since it's god-awful late at night and snowing,* I thought and crossed 3rd to loiter in front of the closed shops there. The sidewalk was littered with trash at the edges from people quickly vacating their tent homes in favor of shelter beds. I peeked in a shop window. What looked like it could have been a cute little store had become a vacant linoleum floor and a For Lease sign on the window. Next door, a shoe store sat behind a window with a person-sized crack and spider-webbed crackles in a pattern that was somewhere between avant-garde and ready-to-collapse chic. The next window had Black Lives Matter spray-painted on it.

Three empty businesses all in a row, like some off-putting nursery rhyme for the twenty-first century screaming look how dismal the city had become since politics and Covid and legalized drugs and the houseless crisis and crazy-high inflation and protests and and and…

I counted them off on the fingers still embedded in my coat pockets.

My sigh sent a rush of foggy air out my nose—*like the bull in Bugs Bunny cartoons*, I thought, just as I always have since childhood, my parents restricting us to old cartoons 'because modern cartoons are too violent.'

"Like Bugs isn't violent," I whispered just to hear my voice, a voice, any voice. It was too quiet for downtown without the students and unhoused people and cops on the street.

I wished there was one of those nice bank signs around, where they had the temperature and time. I arched my neck around the corner to zero avails. No banks, no simple helpful number sequences lighting up the night. Anyway, I was pretty sure the temperature was somewhere in the negative Fahrenheits and that the clocks had all basically stopped—given up in deference to the weather.

For a place known for wet weather, my city didn't deal well with snow. The flakes started falling and everyone forgot the basics of driving in favor of if-there's-a-space-there-I'm-going-to-drive-there pandemonium. All of the people in their 1990-something Honda Civics with bare tires deciding it is absolutely mandatory for them to charge up some ice-covered hill, only to leave their cars smashed on the side of the road when they failed. Finally, everybody giving up, every business closing its doors, and every person plopping down indoors to wait it out.

That night, Snowmageddon had closed the entire metro area as people hunkered down and waited for the next-day's sun to raise the thermometers back to the standard just-above-forty to change it all back to rain. Except for me. I, in capitulation to my parents always telling me to take care of my little sister, was standing around outside some concrete-gray, midcentury, gone-to-hell building waiting for said sister to remember she had left me behind so I could drive us both back to our suburban home.

The snow became thicker. Heavier. Big, fat snowflakes that seemed to stop in the air and wait to be seen, that looked beautiful but made the world too still. Made the world hold its breath.

I'd stood still long enough to get sleepy-cold. Leaving the depressing storefronts behind, I walked to the corner of Oak Street again, looked right, left, right for the zero cars that drove around in the frozen wee smalls, and crossed twice to stand in the parking lot that faced the apartment building Charlie was in. Hopefully. Maybe? *She seemed to go in there, right?*

Charlie had pissed me off beyond anything ever before. I had barely pulled my car into the parking space when she undid her seatbelt and jumped out saying "Wait here in the car," like I was some chauffeur instead of her big sister doing her a favor. Like I was actually going to let her go running off into the night alone in the not-really-that-big-but-still-scary city.

After getting my car into park, after checking the doors were locked like fourteen times, after crunching across the pavement, sliding along the first bit of sidewalk, and cussing myself out for wearing my not-skid-resistant boots in the rush to leave, I was just able to see her disappear into the creepy-sad building I stood across from. And I was contemplating the best ways to murder my sister. Didn't even care by then if I got away with it.

The icy parking lot asphalt had cracked from the previous summer's crazy hot weather and the rain had seeped in. Winter-dead weeds pushed through the puzzle pieces left behind like mini stalagmites of icicle trying to attack my freezing toes.

Good lord, I was tired and morose and really annoyed with my sister for leaving me out in the cold while she—in my mind's eye—was sitting in some over-hot, little dark room completing some clandestine deal that the stupid building across the street just screamed out was happening there. I walked the edge of the lot, accidentally kicked an old needle left behind when the cops gathered up people and took them inside for the night.

Dang it, Charlie, I thought, *what have you gotten yourself into this time?*

As I stomped my feet against the icy pavement in an attempt to warm them up, a loud bang came from the direction of the apartment building. "Shit," I whispered.

I ran across the street, back to the apartments, thinking, *Was that a gun? It was a gun! Why am I running toward the gun?* But I kept running.

There were no doors on the outside of the stupid building, just windows—many with cardboard covering up broken glass, others covering up who knew what. I could feel my heart beat against my ribs, and in my temple, and in my stomach. As fast as possible, I walked along the sidewalk hoping to find some opening that would get me to where my sister was, repeatedly telling myself that I should know where Charlie went, that Mom and Dad were going to kill me if something happened to their sweet baby Charlene. The sense of having legs left me, and I was skimming above the ground as a mass of nervous energy that just-so-happened could float. My hands came out of my pockets, leaving them exposed and in pain from the cold air and wind. I should have watched her closer. Should have kept up with her. Should never have let her leave the car alone.

"Mom is going to kill me," I whispered to myself, as another gunshot echoed through the air.

That was it. My heart beat in my throat, my hands cupped my mouth, and I gave in to the panic. "Charlie!" I hollered at the building. "Charlie!" I was losing it. "Charlie!"

A non-cardboarded window opened, and a woman looked out. With a voice that sounded more confused than angry, she asked, "What are you yelling about?"

I bolted toward the window, slid on the icy cement, almost landed on my butt, and barely righted myself as I got close enough to talk without shouting. My body swayed and my words rushed out so fast, I'm sure I sounded completely deranged. "My baby sister's in there somewhere and there was just something—it sounded like a gun—it was probably a gun—you know, one shooting? And then another gun was shooting—or maybe it was the same gun—I mean, I don't know the difference between guns, but that just happened, and I don't know where Charlie —my sister's name is Charlie—I don't know where she is."

The woman blinked while I caught my breath. She had that confused look of someone who was parsing out the words spattered at her and trying to find meaning. "Why don't you come into the courtyard to talk," she said after a couple second's parse.

It all caught up to me, and I very nearly wailed, "I don't know how!"

"Sweetie, just go around to the other side, back where Oak meets 4th, and I'll come meet you."

I sort of lope-ran toward 4th Avenue. As I reached the corner and tried to keep up my speed through the turn, my not-great-for-snow boots slid out from under me. In what felt like slow motion, my body arched up out of alignment with the world, my feet came off the ground, my eyes saw the line of buildings slide up-up-up until I looked straight at the snowy clouds that filled the night sky, and I landed flat on my back.

I lay where I landed. Snowflakes gently falling into my face as my brain reoriented the city. It was oddly peaceful. The cold ground a safe place to be.

The woman from the window's face popped into the space above me, interrupting the falling snow. Her voice had that rush voices get when worried. "Are you okay?"

I think I answered.

Two sets of hands lifted me from the pavement by my armpits, setting my feet back on the ground, and guiding me through a black-scrolled iron door that I could have sworn was not in the side of the building before. The hands continued me along through a sweet little courtyard where two trees sat as skeletons waiting for the cold to go away so they could turn green again. A plastic Big Wheel sat beneath one, its seat and handlebars barely encased in snow, as if someone had ridden it recently. A bench sat beneath the other.

The hands belonged to two boys who led me through an opened doorway off the courtyard, through a small entryway, and into a living room with warm burgundy walls and a pale gray sofa alongside a beautiful wooden dining table which my mother, the antique-lover, would've drooled over.

The boys set me softly down in a paisley-encased armchair and slowly backed away, hands out like they could still steady me if I decided to fall from the chair. They then sat on the sofa facing me. I tilted my head as I looked at them, fuzzy thoughts attempting to make sense out of things, but the head tilt made my neck scream loud important obscenities at me, so my head got straightened again.

The woman from the window came up beside me and brushed the snow off my jacket and hair. "Now, what were you doing standing outside at this time of night?"

"Outside?"

Her voice stayed calm. "Do you know today's date?"

I had to think about that one. I'd left home around midnight. Did that mean that it was still the day before or was she looking for the after-midnight date?

Before I could answer, she asked, "Are you experiencing any dizziness or pain?"

The whole night seemed to have made me dizzy, and Charlie was certainly a pain, but where to start with all of that?

I must have paused too long, because the woman said, "Oh no, she might have gone and got herself a head injury. Scottie, you call an ambulance. Benji, you go pour her some of that tea I was making. She's too cold for her own good."

The two boys stood, ready to obey orders, but I reached my hands out to stop them. "No, no, thank you, but I can't be hurt right now," I said. "I've got to find my sister."

The woman paused for no more than a second. "Benji, get her the tea at least. She's got to warm up some," she said to the younger of the two. "Now, what is your name?" she asked me.

"Lucy," I said. "Lucy Parsons."

"Hello, Lucy-Lucy," she said with a smile. "My name is Maureen-Maureen Ford. These are my grandsons, Scottie and Benji." She gestured to the older kid sitting on the sofa then the younger kid who was handing me a cup of hot tea.

Benji looked about twelve. Still in that waiting-for-puberty phase that screams Middle School. Scottie looked sixteen or seventeen, tall but not done growing, still getting comfortable with that sudden addition of height and muscle boys get in high school. Both good-looking kids with kind eyes.

"Now," Maureen said, "have you tried calling your sister?"

I semi-pointed toward a wall. "Outside," I said, "I was…" My words dwindled away.

She almost laughed. Dipped her voice a little as she asked, "On the phone?"

I shook my head slightly, worried about aggravating the pain that had arrived when I'd head tipped before. Thought, *Where did I leave my phone*? Then said all Eureka-y, "I left my phone on the charger at home."

"Okay," Maureen said. "Would your sister answer her phone if she didn't recognize the number?"

"No," I said, dragging the word out to emphasize how much of a 'no' it really was.

"So, you are picking your sister up and can't find her?"

"I actually brought her here," I said, feeling all confessional, "and lost her."

"Okay," she said. "Then what do you know about where your sister was going? Maybe we can help find her?"

The steam of warm jasmine tea slipped into my head, making me realize two things at once. One, I had no idea if Charlie had even gone into this building. Two, my entire defrosting body hurt.

As I tried to structure everything in my mind into words, I sipped the tea and felt the warmth travel down my chest and into my stomach. "That's the problem," I said. "I don't know where my sister was going." And I was embarrassed to add, "Or who she might be with."

Maureen Ford looked at me with an expression that seemed to say I was a fairly stupid girl to come along on an errand that I knew nothing about. I'd shared that sentiment back when I was standing at the corner of 3rd and Oak.

I raised my one hand and patted the air between us, as if I could calm her worries with a little air pat. "This is just Charlie. She does stuff like this, where she has to be running out late at night and can't tell anyone anything about the whys or wherefores. But she always comes out of it safely."

Maureen raised her eyebrows and tipped her head to the side. Implying that she could guess there were lots of times my sister wasn't all that fine.

I thought a little harder about Charlie and how she behaved. About the ways I'd complain about her to my friends at work.

"Well..." I drew the word out a bit more than was strictly called for. "She mostly comes out of it safely. I mean, this one time she had a cut on her hand and she wouldn't tell anyone how it happened, and this other time she..." My words straggled off as Maureen's eyes looked less and less like a stranger's and more and more like those of a worried mother —who was actually worried about me. "Anyway, she's mostly fine. But tonight, there were gunshots, and I freaked out and started shouting—"

"At three o'clock in the morning," Maureen said, more calmly than could really be expected.

I nodded and hesitantly agreed. "At three in the morning—"

"On a Monday," Maureen added.

"On a Monday," I agreed. I looked away from Maureen, to a wall where a copy of that Michelle Obama portrait that had caused such a fuss in 2018 hung. An a-ha moment hit that got me sitting up fast. "Oh my gosh, did I wake you all up? I'm so sorry."

Maureen's grandsons both put on the same expression—lowered eyebrows, half-sneers, and something in their eyes that said: Are you kidding? Of course you woke us up.

"Of course I woke you up," I said. "It's the middle of the night. A school night. I'm so sorry." My brain tried to jolt my body out of the chair, to get myself out of their way and back to the street to wait for Charlie to emerge from some unknown doorway at some unknowable time, but the rest of my body wasn't having it, so I fell back with a sorry-sounding squeak that my throat had never made before. "Ow," I added, not meaning to say it, but sometimes your brain conspires with your vocal cords.

Maureen kneeled beside the chair, her hand warm and motherly on my forearm. "Drink your tea. And don't worry, Lucy. I'm a nurse up at Good Sam. I just got home myself. The boys..." She hesitated, then finished with, "sometimes get up so they can talk to me since I'm asleep when they head to school."

"No, we don't," the older boy, Scottie, said, and Benji jabbed his narrow elbow into his brother's side.

"Snow day tomorrow," Benji said, with a smile that could have meant that I shouldn't worry, but probably meant that he was trying to appease the crazy woman who'd landed at and screamed into his window.

Outside, another gun shot went off.

"That!" I said. "Doesn't that sound like...I mean, isn't that a gun?"

Maureen stood and shook her head. "No, that's the train tracks. The wheels make that noise when they hit a certain juncture point." She shrugged. "I suppose it sounds like gunshot if you're expecting guns."

My head dropped fast. My eyes looked for some relief from embarrassment in the teacup I was holding too tightly.

"I'm sorry for—" I couldn't think of the right words. I was sorry for assuming that because this was a dingy apartment building across from empty stores and a crappy parking lot, that because the hour was late and they were all awake—*Because I woke them*, I told myself—that because—and I sighed inwardly—I thought there were gunshots because none of this was good enough to avoid being gun-adjacent in my brain.

I looked up and met Maureen's warm brown eyes. I wondered what she saw when she looked at me. All I could do was take a breath, straighten my shoulders, and say, "Can we start over?"

She smiled. A remarkable, full smile that made me feel less like a complete jerk and more like someone who had just been really scared in a place where I'd never been before. "Yes," she said. "Yes, we can." She reached out her right hand and said, "Hi, I'm Maureen."

I took her hand in mine. "Hi, I'm Lucy, and I'm very worried about my sister, Charlie. It's making me a little cray-cray right now."

Maureen smiled wider and nodded. "I understand." She made

scooting hand gestures to her grandsons. "Boys, get back to bed. Thank you for helping Lucy in."

"Yes," I added, reaching my hands out like I was handing them my appreciation as a gift and twinging my sore neck and head as I did it, making me grimace. "Thank you so much."

They looked at both of us like we were insane, like friendships didn't start at three in the morning, like they were decidedly going to talk about us once they reached a bedroom. Scottie mumbled something in his deeper voice and Benji giggled.

Maureen grabbed herself a cup of tea and sat across from me. "Now, tell me more about this sister of yours and maybe I'll have an idea of where to look."

I thought for a second, then started in. "Tonight, or I guess last night, Charlie came home around midnight. I was doing homework."

Maureen nodded. "You in college?"

I nodded. "Getting my MBA online."

She nodded, like me getting an advanced degree explained something for her. In a found-the-solution kind of voice, she said, "And so you're living with your sister."

"Well…" I hesitated because some people got weird ideas about how I wasn't doing things like they were supposed to be done. "Charlie and I both live with our folks."

Maureen's eyebrow flinched slightly up. She controlled it well, but it was still a flinch. "How old are you?"she said, emphasizing the 'are' a little too much.

My face got warm. "I'm twenty-seven."

Her eyebrows actually-really-truly shot up then, but she held her tongue. I'd give her a six point five on the 'Being Cool And Not A Boomer Scale' for it.

I took a breath and started the standard list of pseudo accomplishments I used to help me justify my current existence. "My parents let me stay at home because I pay rent, am in school, and am saving to buy a house one day."

Maureen nodded, like it made sense to her. "And your sister?"

I stared at the little flecks of tea leaf floating near the bottom of my cup. "Charlie is twenty-one."

That was really all I could say. My sister drove a car our parents gave her 'because she has to drive to school,' lived rent free 'because she has to focus on school,' and was handed money regularly 'because she has no time for a job what with school.'

"She in school, too? Could she be with her college friends?"

I shook my head. "Dropped out." Then rushed to add, "You see, Charlie is special. She never really fit the mold of your average school kid—even from the start."

Maureen nodded slightly, encouragingly, egging-me-on-ly.

"Charlie didn't get stuff like reading and history. I mean, I spent hours with her trying to help her learn it, but it just never clicked for her." I looked Maureen full in the eyes. "She was always really good at math, though."

Maureen stood. "Let's keep warming you up while we think." She took my cup and walked to the kitchen. As she refilled both of our cups, she asked, "So, couldn't Charlie go to school for accounting or something like that?"

"She tried. But the classes, well, they didn't…suit her?"

Maureen's whole face went into a question mark. "Is that an answer or a question?"

My mouth was all fish-out-of-water gaping, looking for the right words, when Benji stepped into the living room, passed by me going to the kitchen, and said, "She's always saying that."

"Benjamin Aaron Ford, why aren't you in bed?" Maureen asked while she carried our cups back to the sofa and chair. Handed me mine.

He slapped on a cheeky grin that told me Maureen always middle-named him but he generally got around her. "I'm thirsty," he said with a shrug then filled a cup from the sink. "But you do always say that."

"That's because youths these days keep talking like fools with their sentences going up at the end as if everything is a question."

I half-raised my hand. "Mine was a question," I said. "I honestly don't know how classes didn't suit her, other than being in the morning and she wanted to sleep until the afternoon. Our mom and dad kept saying that they didn't suit as if it would explain why she didn't have a job and didn't go to school." I gave up on using any kind of filter for what I wanted to say, finished with, "She almost never pays rent."

"That sounds like crap," Benji said, a bit loud.

"Benjamin!" Maureen said.

"I didn't swear," he answered.

"It was darned close," she said.

"It does sound like cra—garbage though." He sat next to his grandmother on the sofa. "How come there are different rules for people living in the same house?"

"I know," I said. "It's probably because Charlie was the baby. She's a lot younger than me." I shrugged. "That's why I'm out here worrying about where she's off to, I suppose. She's the baby, so I'm responsible for her."

Benji nodded, like he understood exactly what I was talking about. "Like Scott getting a later bedtime and being allowed to hang with his friends when Grandma's at work," he said. "But I gotta stay inside where it's safe and boring."

Feeling the camaraderie, I gave him a smile and offered an up-nod to say *yep, we get each other.*

"So how exactly does Charlie pay rent when she manages to do it? Maybe that will tell us what she's doing this time of night," Maureen asked.

My mouth opened to answer, but again I was without words to fill it. I honestly never knew how she had any money our parents didn't hand to her.

"She's gotta be selling something," Benji said with a knowing nod.

Maureen swatted his arm softly. "You don't know that."

"Nah, he's right, Grandma," said a voice from the hallway, and Scottie stepped into the living room.

In that voice mothers reserve for getting the truth out of children, Maureen asked, "What do you mean, Scott?"

He looked at the rug all hang-dog-like. "I seen her."

"You *saw* her," Maureen corrected. "And where, may I ask, did you see this woman?"

Scottie looked embarrassed and his voice sounded as reluctant as a child tattling on his best friend. "Earlier tonight, before you got home. She was going into Hunt's apartment."

Like we were playing Jinx, Maureen and I both said, "How do you know it was her?"

His face said he thought it was one of the stupidest questions ever asked in the history of questions. Scottie pointed at me and said to Maureen, "She looks just like her."

I understood what he meant. Despite our age difference, people saw the same brown hair and same blue eyes, and my Dad's self-same smile on us, and assumed we were twins, which really annoyed Charlie since she was younger and thought I should have the decency to look older than her.

Maureen jumped up, tea spilling over the side of her cup, and she walked into the kitchen saying, "Oh, no, this is so wrong, Lucy. If Charlie is going into Hunt Payton's apartment, then she is up to zero amount of good."

I stood. Adrenaline had filled in for good sense, and my back and head felt the bounce of pain throughout. My brain was going millions-a-minute with questions. "Who's this Hunt guy? What's wrong with him? Why are we freaking out?"

Benji blurted out, "Hunt's a straight up pimp, dude."

Scottie nudged his brother. "No, man, you got the wrong word. Hunt's not a pimp."

But the image of my sister—my baby sister who I helped teach the alphabet to, who I'd bandaged knees for—putting out to some overly hairy, smelly, unwashed, old man screamed all over my brain. I almost yelled. "Are you saying that my Charlie is a prostitute?"

Scottie shoulders and hands went up into an I-don't-know gesture.

Benji said, "I think they call themselves sex workers now."

To which I had no response that could be safely said in front of a child.

"Okay," Maureen said, sounding like she was taking control of the situation. "Okay." Her hands pressed down the air in the middle of the circle we'd formed, her voice sounding less in control. "Okay." She paused as her face said she was trying to find a solution. "I'm sure it's not what we're thinking."

"Where does Hunt live?" I asked.

Maureen didn't answer. She just said, "Boys, stay here!" then turned to her front door and headed out with total angry-grandma energy.

I followed her.

The boys followed me.

We went up a set of outside stairs that led from the oasis of snow-covered trees to the walkway for the apartments above. On the second level, we marched along the black wrought iron half-wall railing, turned a corner, and lined up single file—Maureen, me, Benji, and Scottie—at a door marked two-fifteen.

Maureen launched a pound-on-the-door-because-I-mean-business knock that I would have been afraid to answer.

The door slowly opened, and half my sister's face peeked out.

At least she has common sense to seem scared, I thought as I moved to the front of our line and said in a terse half-whisper, "Charlie! What have you been doing? Are you prostituting yourself? Mom and Dad are going to kill me if you're—"

"Lucy?" Charlie half-whispered back. "What are you doing here? And who are these people? You can't just go following me around like that. I am a grown-ass adult."

I could hear the little stomp of her foot in her voice as she spoke, which made me angrier. We whisper-argued over each other some more.

"I told you to wait in the car. Why didn't you just listen to me for once? You are not my mother."

"What kind of grown-ass adult goes running around in the middle of the night, I'd like to know. And you need to answer the prostitution question still."

Maureen stepped up beside me. She left the whispering behind. "Young lady, your sister has been worried sick, standing alone out in the cold. Which, I might add, you are leaving us out in right now. So open that door and we'll figure out what's going on." She turned her head to the left and said, "And Mr. Callahan, you should be ashamed of yourself for eavesdropping."

The door next to us suddenly closed.

Charlie looked startled, but she opened the door and we all re-lined up and went in.

The entryway of this apartment was basically the same size as Maureen and the boys' place, yet where theirs was welcoming and warm, this was cluttered with several pairs of sneakers and bits of trash that had been forgotten about long enough for cobwebs to accumulate around them. Maureen led the way with more angry-grandma body language that included fists.

On the sofa, surrounded by gaming controllers, fast food wrappers, and empty soda cans was a young man. He was a good-looking guy with black hair, dark brown eyes, and a big bruise swelling up his left eye, a scab stretching against his bottom lip, and a left jawline stretched out and swollen to the point it looked like he had a huge jawbreaker shoved in his cheek. His skin was ashen-looking, and he cradled his right arm against his chest.

"What the hell, Charlie!" he said, holding himself stiff, his arm close and protected.

"Hunt, this is my sister, Lucy; Lucy, this is my friend, Hunt." Charlie pointed to me then him then me. "I don't know who these other people are, she just, like, brought them with her."

Maureen nodded to him, said, "Hunt..." in that dip down, then up way, like an up-nod in sound.

"Sorry, man," Scottie said, "I saw the girl coming in here, then her sister was like freaking out so I had to say something."

Maureen gave Scottie one of those looks that said she'd be having a talk with him later about what happens when she is away from home.

"Charlie, what the hell is going on?" I asked. "How do you even know this guy?"

Her arms circled up tight around her chest. I hadn't seen her look so vulnerable since her cat, Mr. Potty Bottoms, was hit by a car and had to have surgery. "Hunt and I went to high school together," she said. "I sometimes give him rides when he gets stranded places after a...well, a job."

"And what kind of jobs does he do?"

"He…well, he—"

"I do whatever the trick wants done." Hunt's voice was raw and scratchy. He looked right at me and pursed his lips. "You wanna taste, mamacita?"

"C'mon, Hunt, knock it off," Charlie said.

"So, you, Charlie, are not prostituting yourself?" I asked.

"No," she said, "and it's called sex work and there's nothing wrong with it if you make the choice yourself. I mean, Hunt's a good guy. He just had a really bad night tonight."

Maureen went to Hunt and put the back of her hand on his forehead. "What happened, Hunt?"

"Guy was unhappy with services rendered and had a little anger management issue."

Benji's eyes had gotten bigger and bigger as the conversation went on. I slipped my hand into his, gave it what I hoped was a reassuring, this-crap-doesn't-happen-to-all-boys squeeze.

Maureen gently pressed on Hunt's arm. He winced and pulled it closer to him like a kitten with a sticker in its paw. She almost touched his swollen jaw, tipping her head to the side to look at the facial injuries.

"You know your arm's probably broken, right? And your jaw might be, too."

Charlie scooted around the cluttered coffee table to the other side of Hunt. "I know! I've been trying to convince him to let me take him to the hospital, but he won't go."

"I don't have money for hospitals."

"You can't work with your arm all dented in," Charlie said.

"I'll figure it out." Hunt's teeth clenched together.

"You will not figure it out," Maureen said. She had seamlessly decided that someone needed to be the parent in the room and had nominated herself, accepted the position, and was past the point of thanking the crowd for their support. "You are going to the hospital. You can be driven there by one of us, or I can call 911. Choose."

Hunt glanced over at Scottie, who shrugged. "Man, that's just my Grams. You gotta choose, 'cause otherwise she's gonna call the po-po."

Hunt looked across all of our faces, landing on Charlie who gave him a hopeful smile. "Fine," he said. "I'll let one of you drive me to the fucking hospital."

Maureen sent Benji to grab Hunt's shoes from the entryway and Scottie to get his jacket off the kitchen counter. She made the boys help get the shoes on and drape the jacket over Hunt's shoulders. We agreed that Charlie and I should take Hunt to the university hospital up on the hill since my car had snow tires and he would be seen there without insurance. I hoofed it back to the car, got it over to 4th, and we got Hunt settled in the back seat and Charlie in the front.

Maureen gave me her phone number in case we ran into some other emergency, then made me promise to call to let her know when we were safe.

With my sister and her friend settled in the car, I came over to Maureen to say thank you. She opened her arms wide, knew exactly what I needed, and pulled me into a grandma-hug. My eyes misted up as my arms hugged her back.

She whispered, "You got this."

Three words I didn't realize I needed so badly at that moment.

Back in the driver's seat, I looked at my sister and realized that I had a lot to figure out about my relationship with her. And she wasn't going to make that easy.

"Let me GPS it," Charlie said, and put her nose into her phone.

"I know how to get to the hospital." I turned to look at her as we waited for no other cars at a red light. "Charlie, what were you thinking?"

"About what?"

"About running all over the place to pick up some…friend of yours who is selling his body?"

"You do know I can hear you, right?" Hunt said from the back seat.

"You do know that I don't care, right?" I said as the light turned green and we moved on.

Charlie kept looking at her phone.

The silence between the three of us was nearly complete between the noiseless Prius and the utter lack of anything else resembling standard noise-making humanity.

I broke the silence first. "Charlie, you need to answer me."

She sighed in that little girl way she used to get Mom and Dad—and me—to give in to her. As her breath gushed out, I was feeling manipulated for the three-hundred-and-seventy-second time that night.

I knew it would be easier to let her harrumph her way out of it all. That she was never going to change her behavior and would just continue to pretend everything that night was normal.

But I wasn't willing to give in anymore. "Answer me, Charlie!"

She jumped. Unused to having loud angry voices directed at her in any kind of persistent way.

And I turned the car onto Broadway.

"It's not her fault," Hunt said. "I can't afford a car, and she's been there to help. You should be proud of her."

I raised my index finger and met his eyes in the rearview mirror. Admonishment read and recorded as Hunt sneered then looked out his window at the empty city passing by.

When she finally spoke, Charlie's voice was barely a whisper. "Everyone else gives up on people. I can't do that."

She paused, then said a little louder, "You never give up on me. I figure Hunt deserves the same."

I looked at her then—really and truly looked at her. She wasn't the kid I was teaching things to anymore. Wasn't the obnoxious teen that spent her weekends ensconced in earbuds and alt-rock all day. She was my sister, but not my friend and that sucked. I'd never gotten to know her as the actual adult she was.

As the car looped around the curves going up the hill, none of us said another word.

SHANNON

KATIE NELSON STONE

St. Louis, Missouri
May 11, 1893

A knock against my door made me flinch.

"Shannon?" A familiar voice.

My name. I shuddered at the utterance. If I never heard my name again, I'd die a happy man.

Another soft knock came, followed by a train's whistle.

When my father owned the depot, I knew everyone within a two-block radius of the tracks. The morning stationmaster. The ticket takers. The waitress at Nell's Restaurant. The multiple freight agents. And—all the long-term residents and workers at 3rd and Oak Boarding.

I'd been somebody back then. But now—I was nobody. And my life depended on that.

The knock at the door came again. "Open up, darling." It was Clara, an old family friend.

Of course, she knew my affiliation with 3rd and Oak Boarding. With the amount of business our fathers did together, she spent nearly as much time here as I did. Ten years my senior, Clara had taught me how to count, how to tie my shoelaces, and how to play chess, although I never won. She was the closest thing I had to a sibling and Clara would rather subject herself to a hard day's work than put me in any sort of danger.

I trusted her. And yet, I ignored her.

"Shannon?" A second voice said. Her husband, Henry. "Open up, son."

Despite them being barely a decade older than my three and twenty years, ever since my father's death, they'd acted as if I were their child.

Their large, stupid child who'd made one of the most detrimental business blunders of the century. I squeezed my eyes shut and cringed at the thought of it.

"Nobody's mad at you, Shannon," Clara tried again.

"Well, *we're* not mad at you, son."

I rolled my eyes. *Son.*

"No one's mad at you," Clara repeated. I could feel her eyes blaring into Henry's.

"Quite right. Not a soul."

A moment of silence passed, interrupted by another of the depot's train whistles.

"Shannon Alabaster," Clara said. I could envision her with her fists on her hips. "I know you're in there. 'There's no place better to hide out than 3rd and Oak.' Sound familiar?"

I cursed—silently, of course—at the age-old adage we'd regularly bestow on some of the seedier boarders we'd observed during our boredom-induced eavesdropping sessions.

As the freight depot's owner and operator, it often made sense for my father to stay close to the station. With Mother departed from the world too soon, he and I often avoided staying in our primary residence. We'd been the boarding house's longest tenants—seven years. For most of my childhood, my world extended only a little beyond the freight depot and the hallways and dormitories of the boarding house.

When I was fifteen, Father was advised by a business colleague to send me away to school. Bad advice, as far as I was concerned. I'd protested, for certain. But in the end, Father won and I was shipped off to St. Louis's Smith Academy. Turned out that Father had known best, and I'd excelled in all areas, especially in business. I'd headed to Bryant and Stratton Business College in Chicago shortly thereafter.

I hated thinking of school.

Not because I'd floundered. I'd performed adequately. Well enough that my father wanted to keep me enrolled. No. I hated thinking of school because it's where I met Charles Hardwick. And Charles Hardwick is who introduced me to Zachery Pritchett.

Pritchett.

I gritted my teeth, balled my fist, and resisted the urge to punch a hole in the wall.

"Just open the door," Clara said. "All we want to do is talk to you."

It was because of Pritchett that I was back at the boarding house, two blocks from my dead father's train depot, hiding from the world.

"Shannon? It's me, Henry. Your friend."

I rolled my eyes. Henry had always been one for theatrics.

"Listen, son, there's a chance you won't have to go to debtors' prison. They hardly even do that anymore."

"We contacted Albert. He said there was some sort of relief program in place that you could claim," Clara said. "What was that called, Henry?"

"Bankruptcy."

"Bankruptcy! That's it. Oh, it doesn't sound too horrible now, does it?"

"Not at all," Henry's theatrical voice boomed through the door, punchy with fake positivity. "Open up and let us figure this out. Together."

They meant well, and their kindness made my throat tighten. I didn't deserve it. Certainly, not now. Because among the money I'd lost, I bore the guilt of Clara's most heavily.

"Fine. Stay in there. But I'm still going to talk." Clara cleared her throat. "Word has gotten out and I fear you'll be visited by those who do not have your best interests at heart."

"There's a rumor going around that Mr. Stetson has hired someone to come and—" Henry paused. "Retrieve what is owed to him."

"I think you should turn yourself in to the police."

"The police?" Henry said. "I thought debtors' prison was out of fashion."

"I'm sure they could do something. At least he'd be safe while this whole mess played out," Clara said in a hiss to Henry. "You'd be protected, Shannon! That's more than you'll be in this run-down old building." Clara stomped her foot, then kicked the door. "Shannon Alabaster, open this door right this minute. You're coming home with us."

"He's not here." I heard a third voice outside the door. Mary. The owner of 3rd and Oak Boarding.

Clara yelped, in surprise I supposed. "Was he kicked out?"

Mary sniffed. "We evacuated the building due to lice and bed bugs."

"Good heavens."

"You're telling me," Mary said. "Mr. Daughtry been busy all day throwing mattresses into the dumpster outside."

"Well, will you pass a message on to him?" Clara said, prim and proper.

Mary belched. "If I remember."

Clara cleared her throat. "Tell him he's welcome to come home whenever he likes. And tell him he'll be found by those that want to find him, and it's only a matter of time."

Mary grunted. "No one's coming into 3rd and Oak that I don't want in 3rd and Oak."

"Certainly. Regardless, please pass on our message."

As their footsteps moved further away and down the stairs, I thumped my forehead against the door once, twice, three times.

After a few moments, Mary declared, "They're gone."

I opened the door a crack and confirmed she was alone.

"Thank you, Mary, I owe you."

"You owe everyone." Mary shoved the door open and came into the room. "I wasn't fibbing, neither. Daughtry needs to take your bed out. The damn critters are running the place and if we're to survive another season, we best nip this in the bud."

"But—I paid through the week." And I had no extra funds for a room elsewhere.

She threw me something she'd carried in with her. "Here's a bedroll. Everyone else is gone, so don't come crying to me or Daughtry when you get ticks and lice."

Much like the rest of the recent world, the boarding house had fallen into hard times, with repairs neglected and regular cleanings foregone. Mary's gesture nearly crumpled me. Kindness can do that to you when you're down. "Thank you," I said and placed a hand on her shoulder.

She shrugged it off and pointed a finger at me. "You're staying because I liked your daddy." She jabbed that finger into my chest. "And I mean what I told that woman: no visitors. Wanted or not."

Mary shuffled me out of the bedroom as Daughtry came in, sweat causing his white shirt to cling to his barrel chest.

I wouldn't be a problem for Mary. I wouldn't be a problem for anyone.

I grabbed my hat and coat and made my way down the hallway toward the staircase that led to the front door and prayed Clara and Henry weren't waiting for me outside.

As I peeked out the door, guilt flooded me, hot and unabashed. Clara and Henry had never shown me anything but love, interest in my life, and investment in my career. I'd lost their money, and I couldn't forget that. Perhaps that's why I couldn't answer the door at their request. I treated them as if they were undertakers instead of the saviors I knew they were.

But I couldn't face them. Not yet.

I placed my hat on my head and turned my chin into my coat. Because if there was one thing Clara was right about, it was that Stetson's man was coming.

IF I WANTED TO GO ANYWHERE, I HAD TO WALK PAST THE TRAIN DEPOT, which meant I walked past the picket lines.

My father was a bootstrap puller, always believed if you set your mind to something, you could achieve it. His father was poor, and his father's father poorer. By the family's standards, my father's meager success and modest wealth were remarkable. Whenever I expressed jealousy at a classmate's success, or a desire for something outside our means, my father would take it in stride, stretch his arms toward the train depot and say, "You've got something none of them have—a free ride anywhere."

Of course, he'd been a teaser.

It was rainy for May in St. Louis. I weaved through the crowded streets, bumping into men who were shouting, "Fair wages, fair hours" in unison while waving picket signs that read: "Stand together, fight for our rights" and "United we stand, divided we fall."

Father always envisioned I'd take over the depot once he retired. He talked about how he'd settle down in the house he owned but never stayed at and I'd come over for supper on Fridays and luncheons on Sundays. Sometimes his daydreams involved my fictitious wife and made-up grandchildren. I'd always roll my eyes or act disgusted, and he'd laugh.

The truth of it was, I was a brat, and I didn't deserve him or the depot.

The day I told Father I didn't want his business looked different than I'd imagined. He could have screamed, or worse, laughed in my face. He could have chosen to see my dreams as an insult or a personal slight. But not my father. After I broke the news that I wouldn't run his life's work, that I wanted to get into stock trading and investments, he smiled, took me by my shoulders and said, "Of course, you can do it because you can do anything."

But that was then.

Despite its current dire and impoverished circumstances, St. Louis was a hub of innovation. It was something my father always loved about the city. And the train depot was at the center of it all. When it was announced that Chicago would host the 1883 World's Fair, my father buzzed with excitement. St. Louis, he claimed, would be resourced for everything ranging from beer and corn to lumber and iron. He believed the city, its residents, and the train depot would be swamped with work and revenue. My father had been right. St Louis busied itself producing and shipping textiles, machinery, even new inventions to be displayed at the fair.

In a cruel twist of fate, my father had died six months before the fair's kick off, amidst the busiest prep season for the event. Afterward, I'd organized the sale of the train depot from my office downtown.

It was difficult to say whether the new owner of the depot was unfair or if the train yard workers just felt the brunt of the season. Probably a bit of both. The increase in work from the World's Fair left the train yard workers feeling overworked, and the instability of the railway's future due to the recent stock market crash caused workers to panic.

My father had seen his depot on strike a time or two, but never beyond what could be remedied. I wondered if these men knew that it wasn't just their lives that were burning; the whole world was on fire.

While the Midwest prepared for the World's Fair—an event to show-case the utmost peculiarities, triumphs, and wonders—the stock market plummeted. Not much was known just yet, but they were calling it a panic. The beast had acted as a tempest that had swept through my once-thriving kingdom, leaving devastation in its wake. First to implode had been the investments, then there was the run on the banks. The market had tumbled and my investments had vanished along with those of my clients. With those had gone our livelihoods, our houses, cars, servants, and, of course, our status. When news of the crash had broken, our clients had come flocking to our establishment. Very quickly, I'd realized what had happened with Pritchett, and I'd snuck out the back door.

They called it a panic, as if it were some fleeting moment of irrational fear. No. It was a nightmare that refused to relent.

Outside the throng on the street corner, a woman sat atop a stoop with a toddler perched on each knee—one crying and the other burrowing his head into his mother's neck with his thumb in his mouth. In front of her stood a newsboy, probably no older than nine, selling papers in the rain.

"The newest news on everything—strike, bank run, grocery store credit—you name it, this paper's got it," he yelled.

"One, please," I said, then quickly secured the pages under my arm.

I tucked my chin further into my coat and made my way to the café to do what I did every day—scour the newspaper for any mention of my failings.

THE BELL ABOVE THE DOOR TINKLED AS I ENTERED THE CAFÉ, AND I CURSED.

Hard to be incognito when the door announces your arrival.

I scrunched my neck further down, clutching the newspaper to my side.

A hand raised in the corner.

Gregory Allen. Pritchett had introduced us shortly after I'd started working at the firm.

"Put your hand down," I hissed at my old business partner.

"Good morning," he said.

"Nothing good about it." I took the seat opposite him.

Gregory flinched, rubbed his neck, then picked up his coffee cup. The dark circles under his eyes felt friendly, familiar. "How are things?"

I snorted. "I could ask you the same question."

There was a slight shake to Gregory's hand as he set down his coffee cup. The dread I'd walked through all day crept from my feet to my stomach. No matter how scared and paranoid I felt, I knew Gregory felt worse—Gregory had a family. "Are Anna and the girls well?"

"They're safe. Staying nearby. Not at the house, of course."

"Of course," I repeated, and the dread that pillowed in my stomach released back down into my boots.

I'd spent many dinners at Gregory's house. Business celebrations. Holidays. Late conversations over cognac. It would be all too easy to assume his wife was a snob. With a lifetime of money and a business tycoon for a husband, Anna spoke like old money and looked as if she'd never worried a day in her life. She hosted the best parties and kept the best company, always knowing who to connect with whom at any given moment. She held just as much power as Gregory, just different. Anna could have behaved however she'd wanted to and gotten away with it.

But instead of waving smaller people away in disgust or dismissal,

Anna waved at them in welcome and embrace. I'd always liked her. We'd always been close.

I'd miss her.

"Are you here to put me out of my misery?" I asked.

"On the contrary," he straightened and pulled an envelope from his coat pocket, laying it in front of me. "I'm here to deliver you."

I eyed it before pulling it toward me. "What's this?"

"I said I'd make this right, and I have." He motioned toward the envelope. "Open it."

It crinkled as I peeked inside. A modest wad of cash peeked back.

I crunched the envelope shut and pushed it toward Gregory. "No."

"Anna and I are heading back to London."

"No," I repeated.

"Don't be obtuse. Take the money and go—"

"It's blood money," I said as my volume rose.

"Blood money?" Gregory laughed.

I thrust my thumb over my shoulder. At the union men picketing. At the child forced to work. At the mother with two hungry toddlers. "Surely, you just walked the same block I did."

"Come off it, Shannon. Those poor people's misfortunes aren't because we gave our clients some bad advice on a few investments."

I held up the newspaper I'd bought from the child outside. "You know what reports are saying? Unemployment is at thirty-five percent in New York. Forty-three percent in Michigan. They've opened up centers they're calling soup kitchens to help feed the hungry. The mayor of Detroit just launched what he's calling a Potato Patch Plan to allow people to garden in community spaces. People are chopping wood, breaking rock, all in exchange for food."

"We were swindled, Shannon."

"We tricked people, Gregory."

He sat back and adjusted the collar of his shirt, the tightness of it rubbing his bruised neck. "None of this is our fault and the outside world's problems aren't either."

"I don't want it," I said and pushed the envelope further away. "It was you who wanted Stetson as a client."

"Yes, and it was you who funneled every penny into the railroad." He laughed as he pushed the envelope back toward me. "You and your obsession with the railway."

My face flushed because he was right.

Pritchett's enthusiasm for the railway is what first intrigued me about the man's financial investment company. America's railway was the future, and we had an opportunity to guarantee its success.

I was young. I was excited. And I missed my father back home at the depot.

Pritchett hired me to recruit investors in the Midwestern Railway system. With every investor I recruited, Pritchett paid me a commission, which I funneled right back into Pritchett's railway investment. The returns were marvelous. I recruited friends who became clients who then recruited more clients, until I was so far up in Pritchett's scheme that Gregory had both our clientele to manage.

One of them was Mason Stetson, one of St. Louis's most successful businessmen. He was cutthroat, and life always worked in his favor. He made sure of it.

Every month, Pritchett would provide us with a report on our client's return on investments, and we'd contact our caseload and celebrate our successes.

Except it had all been a lie.

The modest yet exciting gains we'd seen led us to believe the Midwest Railway was doing better than it was. The truth was Pritchett had robbed Peter to pay Paul, which ultimately resulted in his own payout and disappearance, just in time for the market to crash. When our clients came looking to pull their money out of Pritchett Investment, they learned that there was no money. We learned along with them.

We were hated by our clients, for certain, and threatened by most. But none took it quite as personally as Mason Stetson.

"I don't need your charity," I said to Gregory.

"You need the help just as much as I do," he said and laughed. "And it's not charity. It's what's left of the office."

"Then use it to pay back the people whose livelihoods we ruined," I said, motioning toward his bruised neck. "Pay back the Stetsons of the world."

Gregory's face stilled as his jaw tightened. He opened his mouth to respond, then closed it.

My temperature cooled as I looked to my friend, his face ashen and afraid. "You've been visited then."

Gregory rubbed his neck, then nodded. "Just a warning. But he told me he'd be back, and that the money should be ready," he said, taking a breath, then gesturing to the envelope. "Look—it's not a lot of money, or else I'd hand it over to him. I sold the office furniture. The books from the study. The big clock in the foyer." He sighed, like he was imagining that grandfather clock in front of us. He loved that clock. "Do what you want with it—but just do it elsewhere."

"Why don't you take it?"

"You're inflating how much money it is. Besides, Anna already bought our tickets to London."

He gave the envelope a final push.

"Well, thank you," I said.

"You sound surprised." He tutted, then smiled, the corners of his eyes crinkling. "We had a good go of it, did we not?"

My fingertips tingled like little needles injecting venom into the tips and shooting up into my wrists. I flexed my hand and it scrunched around the envelope of money. "We did."

Gregory relaxed back in his chair. "I never would have met Anna if not for you."

I placed the envelope in my coat pocket, then shook out my hand as subtly as possible "You never would have made up with her either. After the party at Dramond's?"

Gregory winced. "Don't go bringing that up now. We're talking of happy times."

I held my hands up in mock surrender. The tingle subsided.

Gregory's eyes twinkled with a mist that wasn't because he was leaving me. It was because we loved what we'd done, and we'd loved the lifestyle it had provided. Now, we had to start over. Despite my initial rejection of the money, Gregory had done something I thought impossible: he'd given me the chance to start anew. I knew I had to take his advice and leave.

He pulled a watch from his coat pocket. "I best be going. Shouldn't leave Anna alone too long. She worries."

"I don't blame her."

We stood and for a moment that felt awkward. This goodbye between us. Gregory extended a hand, and I placed mine in his. "You're welcome to come to London with us."

I tried to pry my hand from his. "I couldn't."

Gregory's grip tightened. "I mean it. You are always welcome."

I put on one last smile for my friend. "Better get to packing, then."

Gregory slapped me on my shoulder one last time. "Good boy."

I approached 3rd and Oak with a plan.

I'd start again abroad. In London. Or Paris, perhaps.

I'd throw what few belongings I had into a suitcase. The next steamer departed in three days, and the passenger train from the depot to the port left every morning at eight. I had a night to pack everything and be on my way.

I'd have to write Clara and Henry, but that could wait until I was established. Maybe I'd send them a missive while at the port. Or perhaps it was best—safest—for all involved if they didn't know where I landed.

At least for the first few years.

I'd let the dust settle. Another scandal would erupt in due time, and I'd be a drop in the bucket of society's wrongdoings.

It wouldn't be pretty, and there'd be plenty of low days, but my father always told me that the only way out is through, one step at a time.

The sun was on its way to setting as I reached the entrance of 3rd and Oak Boarding.

The last thought I had before pulling open the door was that the building seemed unnaturally dark. As I twisted the doorknob, I dismissed the worry with a simple explanation—perhaps Mary had shut the place down due to the lice infestation.

But then, why was the front door unlocked?

As the door closed behind me, two hands wrapped around my throat.

Too startled to scream, I gasped as his fingers squeezed.

I knew this man. Although I'd never met him, I knew him.

Stetson's man had found me at last.

We stumbled forward and crashed into the coatrack. The wooden rod bounced off the wall and back into my assailant, distracting him and loosening his grip. My adrenaline surprised me. All this time, when I thought of the hired gun's visit, I expected to feel a debilitating terror and fear. I felt that, but more than anything, I felt a drive. To get away. To be free.

I wriggled and turned to face my enemy.

He regained his balance and refocused his strength into the hands around my throat. His fingers pressed, crushing my windpipe, and causing my mouth to gape and gasp for air, like a fish pulled out of water. Panic mixed with adrenaline. Lodging my forearms between his, I pressed my elbows into the soft part of his arms.

His eyes narrowed, and his grip around my throat tightened.

My temples pounded and my lungs burned as the world in my periphery blurred. My eyelids drooped. I fought the darkness, struggling for air. My hands moved from his forearms to his hands, and I dug my nails in. But his fingers and thumb pressed harder into my throat. My hands moved up his and he swung me back and forth. We stumbled and I landed with my back on the bare wooden steps. He landed on his elbow, hard, and grunted. I took the moment of distraction and slid my middle and forefinger underneath his pinky finger around my throat and pulled hard in the opposite direction. That tactic had always worked on my boarding school roommate.

He yelled and lessened his grip just enough for me to kick him off me and scramble up, pushing to my feet and taking the stairs two at a time, careful to skip the step with the overly polished finish. Close behind me, I heard him stumble on the stairs, giving me a moment of grace.

I reached the third story landing and turned left toward the bathroom, figuring he'd check my bedroom first.

I slammed the door shut and turned the lock.

Frantic, I looked around the small washroom for anything of substance to use for a weapon.

I pulled at the sink base, hoping it was as old and decrepit as the rest of the house and would come off easily. But it stayed in place.

I gave it one last pull as he kicked the door in.

He gripped the back of my neck and slammed my knees onto the hard tiles of the bathroom floor before shoving my head into the dirty toilet bowl's water.

"This is your fault, Alabaster." He pulled my head out of the bowl. I opened my eyes and gulped for air. Behind the toilet was a book—someone's left-behind reading material. A western I'd seen before. My father had loved the series, and I had many memories of his large hands wrapped around the book's burnt-orange cover.

He shoved my head into the water. I floundered, pushing my hands against the porcelain, but each time I tried he just pushed me deeper toward the bottom. "The world is despicable because of people like you."

People like me.

The greediest of mankind who couldn't see outside their own earning potential. Prioritizing a dollar over everything—friends, family, the community's health and wellness. I thought of the young newspaper boy and the hungry twins outside.

People like me.

I had no argument against my attacker because he was right.

The realization of who I'd become—who I'd *wanted* to become—made me feel like I was drowning more than my head being held under water. In shame. In disgust. And a disturbed part of me felt thankful that my father was not here to see the sort of man his son had become.

The only thing that brought me any relief was that I *was* actually drowning.

Perhaps it was time I paid my penance.

I lessened my resistance and he pushed my face further into the water.

People like me.

Me.

I saw myself. Clearer than I had in years. Not in my most expensive suit, or at the office downtown.

I saw myself sitting at the kitchen table of this boarding house, waiting for Mary's scones to come out of the oven.

People like me loved the taste of cardamon.

People like me never won a game of chess against Clara.

People like me raced to their mom when they saw the first robin of spring.

People like me loved to lie awake until midnight listening for the whistle of the train at the station.

People like me read the newspaper with their father every morning.

And no matter how far or deep I'd buried him, I knew that people like me meant my father. Everything good and beautiful, silly and serene, that lived inside me existed because it had once lived inside him.

People like me weren't like this.

The world had to know that.

The world had to.

Something inside me snapped. I pushed as hard as I could, catching him by surprise. He stumbled backward. I gasped, sputtered for air, and reached behind the toilet. With water dripping from my hair, nose, and eyelashes, I grabbed the burnt-orange book and hit him square in the nose. The deafening crack and his cry of surprise told me I'd broken it.

Blood poured from his nose and his eyes widened.

I lunged for the door. The man reached for me, snagging his fingers in my pant leg. I tripped, then shook free. I ran to the staircase in time to see three additional men enter through the front door.

My head swiveled between the men, cursing and screaming, and Stetson's man, stumbling out of the bathroom.

Dodging his hands, I ran toward my quarters and slammed the door tight.

In a matter of moments, the pounding began. Shoulders and feet slammed against the door. It would fly off its hinges at any moment, I was sure of it.

I looked around for something. Anything. The room was bare, except for the bedroll stashed in the corner.

The door rattled. The next kick was it.

There was only one option left.

I opened the window and jumped.

ALL I SAW WAS SKY.

It was almost sunset, and the evening yellow mixed beautifully with the late afternoon blue.

I blinked, the feeling of weightlessness too fresh for me to truly believe I was still alive.

My body didn't ache as I'd expected. My throat was tight from where the man had grabbed me, and my hair was wet from the toilet's water.

But I was alive.

I took inventory of my body. I wiggled my toes, then my fingers, and slowly sat up.

I'd jumped from the apartment's third story window and landed flat on my back. And somehow—an act of God or otherwise—I was seemingly unharmed.

A white bug darted across my black pant leg.

A smirk spread across my face before cracking into a cheeky smile. One I hadn't felt in ages.

I'd landed in Mary's dumpster full of lice-ridden mattresses.

Laughter took over me. The ridiculousness of it caught me off guard. Tears streamed down my face as I tried to catch my breath. But the laughter poured out of me.

My father would love this story, I thought.

I took a breath and wiped the tears from my cheeks, then looked up at the old apartment.

I would not be returning. Of this I was certain.

I scrambled to my feet and fell out of the dumpster just as the boarding house's front door flew open.

"Oy!" Stetson's man yelled.

Wasting no time, I ran.

Down the block, then into the throng of picketers. I dipped and dodged, thankful for the men and their big signs and large bodies.

I could feel the Stetson's man close behind, except he dodged no one. As I bumped shoulders and apologized, I glanced over my shoulder to see a large man gripping Stetson's man by the coat lapels and screaming into his face.

My smile grew. This just might work.

As I turned a corner, I slammed into something smaller than me. The newspaper boy. He stumbled, but I gripped both of his arms to steady us both.

His eyes, big as coffee saucers, stared into mine.

All it took was a moment, and I knew. I reached into my coat pocket and pulled out the envelop. With no hesitation and zero second thoughts, I handed the boy the money. Because I didn't want it. I couldn't. I wasn't who I'd been, and I had to make good on that. I had to be different. And this was the start.

The boy's forehead crinkled in surprise. I smiled at him, then ran.

I made it to the depot right as a train—a no-name freighter—began its slow chug to speed.

I glanced behind me and saw Stetson's man.

I pumped my arms and pushed the balls of my feet off the loose gravel of the train tracks. The open freight car gained speed.

Several men—other train jumpers—leaned out of the car, whooping at me, telling me to run faster, taunting Stetson's man, extending their arms for my salvation. I'd take it, and I'd make something out of it. As my fingers reached for theirs, I made a solemn promise, a sacred prayer: If my fingers reached this man's, I'd spend the rest of my life striving to be different. To be someone familiar to my old self. Someone my father would be proud of.

With one final reach, I took the man's hands. He pulled me forward, wrapped his hands around my arms and pulled me onto the train car.

My knees hit the wooden floor, and I nearly kissed it. I'd always loved trains, but never knew I could feel the love of one in return. I pushed my head outside the open car to see Stetson's man running. But the metal steed was too fast, a silent symphony of iron and steam, picking up speed as he grew smaller and smaller. He pulled out his pistol, raised it, fired it once, then slowed until he was no more than a dot in the distance.

I pulled myself back into the open freight car.

I was alive.

I was whole.

My heart thumped in my chest and my lungs filled with air. I felt like the richest man in St. Louis.

"Where's the train going?" I asked the train hopper who'd helped me.

"West."

I looked out on the sunset, early still, the blues changing to a darkened orange.

"West," I repeated. "Marvelous."

THE ALCHEMIST
SHARON WOODARD

Everyone says it all changed when Dez held up the lottery tickets for me to choose. I know *he'd* say that. But I know it was the moment when I passed that building at 3rd and Oak. Or fell into its spell. Or whatever happened to me then. Because from that point on, me and Dez began unwinding.

Oak Street ends in abandoned wharves, at least the parts that haven't yet tumbled into the river. The whole area stands derelict and spicy with its crumbling walls. We were walking since no way were we leaving the old Buick in that neighborhood and all together, because it was a pilgrimage. Dez, Marco, Grease, Mallory, and me. The boys shambled ahead, loud and excited because one of those old, charred walls now sported a piece by G-dog himself.

Dez, as usual, was boasting, "Our work attracted a true graff messiah. We've hit the big time now." Marco was bragging about his water tower piece. He finished basically a mural 130 feet up and all in with climbing now, he felt leveled up with G-dog's famous death-defying pieces. The ones on bridges and overpasses. Dez had already done that ten story rooftop in Northside so he wouldn't be outdone in swagger that afternoon. The boys argued and shoved each other. That the piece fully trespassed our turf and barely even two stories high didn't enter into any of it.

Mal lugged her kit, paints, stencils, even her stool. She planned to finish what she'd started before we got run off last week. I hung back with her, coming along to see what everyone was so manic about.

When we passed along the building, its ten stories suddenly eclipsed the sun. It made not just shade, but a wholesale and ominous disappearance of all light. It plunged us into a space where cold now ruled. Black steel, not ancient, but old enough, it reigned over the whole block. Walking by, I felt like a helpless duck in the water as a stealth warship glided by, massive, and dangerous. Like it occupied a whole other... scale. It *hummed*. My body buzzed with it, constricting my chest enough to bring on some dizzy.

I snuck a look at Mal to see if she was getting this. But no, her fingers flew over her phone, her face molded in a sultry smirk.

Sexting Duke again.

Ahead, the boys blustered, obnoxious and loud and asinine. Even though the building glided alongside, sinister and ominous, rendering us small and fragile in its shadow.

Crossing 3rd, and back in the sun again, Marco slammed his hands on the hood of a taxi moving on a red light. The boys got involved in the cross smack, even Mal looked up from her screen, her cheeks flushed and eyes sparky.

I glanced back at the building now hunched at the corner. The humming in my chest kept up as we moved on. When we reached the bodega for supplies, I settled a water on the case of Modelos.

Dez scowled. "Come on, Bear. Cider or Claw?" He pointed to the soft alcohol section next to the beer fridge.

I shook my head.

His eyes narrowed. "This is a special night, real celebrity shit."

But a building menacing me, following me, climbing right into my head meant I was due a good dry out. I scanned the crowded checkstand as bored Mr. Vu watched from behind plexiglass. I pointed, "How about two scratchers?"

Dez scoffed, taking in the display. "Come on. That's just throwing money away."

I gestured to the beer. "And you're an investment banker now?"

Marco howled from outside to quit wasting his time.

When did everyone get so self-important?

Dez asked for two scratchers and pulled out his wallet. Mr. Vu was good people so we never boosted from him. Not even jerky sticks. He looked on all curious as Dez shoved his change in his pocket and held out the two tickets. "Which one?"

He'd say that I chose.

He'd say that I carefully and thoughtfully picked one. But that's not how it went.

For me, the floor trembled, threatening to break free, a drum pounded in my ears, each beat, a bomb going off. One ticket glowed and buzzed in an unworldly way, pulling me in like gravity. A flush of sick heat and oppressive dread came with it, like walking by that building. That ticket felt every bit a dark shimmering maw sucking me in.

I lurched, grabbing the other ticket, the quiet one. As soon as I touched it, I was back in the bodega with Dez glaring and impatient and Marco outside harping. That's how that ticket became mine and the other his.

G-DOG'S PIECE TOOK UP THE WHOLE SIDE OF A WAREHOUSE, BIGGER THAN what we usually do. He'd base-coated the whole wall and even left his signature glittered boot print on the ground in front. His colors too, the lime and indigo letters intricately woven through with a splashy river of gold. A mishmash of code and symbols kinetic enough to be loud and dizzying. Real talent for sure, sharp edges added dimension that took real planning and execution, but something made it unsettling. I couldn't tell if I liked it. I swear I'd seen better, in the rail yards across the river and that first time T-square's crew took the water tower. And I may be biased, but anything by Dez. Still, no mistaking, this G-dog, had our attention.

It appeared the night before and, like in London, everyone heard about it word of mouth, not through socials. That's a G-dog thing. No digital trail. "I serve to imprint your retina," the glut of his voice-garbled interviews streaming the internet told us. You could only see it in person, only you, mingling your DNA with the piece, entangling yourself in the art.

His technique was to roll out white, claiming a whole area, like purifying it. He did a four-story warehouse in Newham spanning the whole block. It appeared overnight. Insane right? Then he centered his own piece leaving wide white edges. Nexus, was the word he used. Dog of the people, he called himself. A loyal servant. The opposite of a god.

His colors splashed huge across the middle all framed by white. That edge made a seductive void just begging for graff. But the center, the Nexus, his piece of lime and indigo and gold, was just for him.

And you could be part of it, along the edges.

His invitation.

And you could take pictures, post your art, but with only a flash of his colors. Never his whole piece. Everyone knows his colors, so that frame made yours legit: your bridge to greatness. Not his words, but what others said of the honor of being a part of his work. Goldening you. Not his word either.

Even in this world of outsized egos, his was a bit much.

Of course, Dez loved it. The fanfare and decorum. The rules G-dog set around his work. How rigid it all was. Dez explained, "Anarchy is all about irony." He *loved* irony.

Mal called him out. "Isn't the whole point of anarchy not to have to answer to anyone? No rules? Shouldn't we paint all over his work just to make the point?"

Dez would just laugh at her. "It's an oxymoron, the rules of anarchy. Don't you get it Mal? Irony. It's brilliant."

Mal didn't get it and I kept trying to and now here was the demigod himself.

Dez was excited G-dog showed up. Everyone assumed he was a magician. What he did and where and how fast. He used a kind of quick dry paint he invented or something. So, a chemist, too. A regular Renaissance man.

❧

WHEN WE GOT THERE, NEW TAGS ALREADY SPLATTERED THE EDGES. SOME, I didn't recognize. So yeah, it was a pilgrimage and not just for us locals. I expected Mal to jump in with her tag, maybe do it overly aggressive. But she, like me, gawked at the gilded mess on the whitewashed half-burnt wall saying nothing. Dez, Marco, and Grease pulled on their beers and stood like they were in the Louvre basking in masterpiece shine.

Dez raised a beer. "A great day, my friends." The other two poured some out before raising theirs too. Mal snorted, then rounded the corner where we could hear her working.

I MEAN WHAT MAKES GREATNESS? ART. PASSION. PLANNING. NERVE. HYPE. The *amour-propre*? G-dog had all of it especially planning. In the mathematics of graffiti, balance is key. It takes an eye. A maturation of the craft. And G-dog, for sure, had nerve. Some of his pieces hurt your brain figuring how he got up there. Yet, the morning sun rose on them, quick dry paint and all.

He must be a goddamn spider man.

Dez said every tagger is marinating in *amour-propre*, since our whole goal is to get our name onto as many places as we can. Vanity art. Our need to find worth in the eyes of others, because we'd been tricked to think what's inside wasn't enough. But it was layered too with protest and resilience. Our work screamed: Look, I am here and here and here. Look at me, I will not be erased. Dez called this full circle, humanity checkmating the chaos of inhumanity. A vital link. Like earthworms, turning waste into the building blocks for the resurgence of life.

Dez could really get going.

Especially during his Rousseau period. "Inventing private property," he said, "led to inequality and, inevitably, to deprivation, and an unjust world." So us taking back private property, putting our name on it, became a noble act.

That he could braid destruction, creation, nobility, and righteousness. *That* was the genius of Dez.

THERE WE STOOD, AT THE LATEST ALTAR. BURNING IT INTO OUR RETINAS. Entangling our collective DNA. We'd seen the videos. So many of them, whetting us, prepping us for this coming. And looking at Dez, feeling him, I sure wanted it. I'd never seen a complete real G-dog. Just his colors flashed on the edge of another's tag. Just the glittery boot print. Just the legend.

Dez put his arm around me; something that would normally seal the feeling of gravity and us united in the craft. But the thing with the lottery tickets and the darkness of that building, prowling alongside, eclipsing us, had shifted my world and unmoored me.

While they took up their spray cans, staking their place around the Nexus, I sipped my water. Before they were done, I wandered back up Oak by myself crossing over before I got to 3rd.

AT OUR PLACE THAT NIGHT, I PULLED THE SCRATCHER FROM MY POCKET. Nothing. I tossed it in the trash and took a shower.

When Dez stumbled in, he woke me from a dead sleep.

"Hey." He slurred, hunched over the phone glow on his ticket. "Hey!" He chirped louder. He nuzzled my hip. "Bear, look! I think I won!" He flipped on the light, blinding me, and shoved the scratcher in my face. I rubbed my eyes and it took a bit to focus. But yeah, three bubbles said: $100,000. It looked legit, but I'd been so deeply asleep it felt blurred and dreamy. I pulled him into me and turned off the light.

I awoke to him banging around the kitchen. As soon as he saw me, he pounced. "It's legit. I fully won a hundred grand. Can you believe this shit?" He radiated, warm and electric, making me laugh. "I've been up all night figuring. A third or so for taxes. Pay off those fines." He paced along the counter. I dodged him and poured coffee. "That leaves, like, fifty grand free and clear and I know exactly what I want to do."

I sat down, sipping, letting my head clear.

"Patagonia." His whirlwind stopped.

"What?"

"Patagonia, New Zealand, Thailand, maybe Tibet. Climbing. Just keep going. You know? Like the YouTube guy? Then maybe an ashram in the mountains."

"You're using all the money for a climbing trip?"

He stared at me. "My money."

"Your money." I set down my cup.

His jaw tightened. "I knew you'd do that."

But I hadn't done anything. So, I soldiered on. "For how long?"

His eyes went belligerent. "Long as I want. Long as the money holds. Months. Years if I'm careful. This is the chance of a lifetime."

"You're not inviting me to come?"

"Why? It's not your dream and besides, you couldn't afford it."

That stung. But this was Dez and me. We hadn't defined anything. We were separate-together the whole time. To give myself a minute, I scanned our apartment. The floor buzzed, shifty and unsteady. My eyes landed on the paint.

"What about your work? Your art?"

His eyes followed mine and he snorted. "What do you mean?"

I gestured to the milk crates of spray cans, piles of stencils, our sketch books. "You'll just drop all this?"

He looked at me like I'd lost the thread entirely.

"Bear. " Condescending and lecturing. "The whole point of all that is to scream: I am here. I matter. See me. I don't need that anymore. I have my ticket out." He waved the scratcher at me. "That's all irrelevant now." Sparks of the bodega light shimmered off his hand, falling to the floor. His arms moved through the murky sunlight creeping in our etched windows. "I can launch now."

My knuckles blanched around my mug, and, for a second, I felt it crushed. Black coffee sloshed the table, waterfalling onto the floor. My hand all sliced up. Instead, I softened my breath, my eyes, everything, and surveyed the apartment. "I can't keep this going by myself."

For the first time, he slowed down. "Yeah. Probably not."

"I'll have to move."

His voice sobered. "Yeah."

I fiddled with my cup. Being cool. It is what it is.

"Hey, Bear. It'll take a minute to get it together, I need gear and maybe a visa, I have to figure out the money. And banks. All of it. I'll help you move."

I downed the rest of my bitter coffee because, of course, I hadn't spilled it.

At work that night, Mallory put down her knife to stare at me. "That's it? Just like that? He gets some gift from the universe and leaves us in the dust?"

But really, what did Dez owe us? I wanted to leave it, but she was just getting started.

"What about dedication to the craft? Brotherhood of the crew? Creative destruction? Waging war on capitalism? All that G-dog worship for God's sake? He just grabs and runs?" She seized the sharpening steel and drew the knife back and forth against it. The violence surprised me.

I focused on the bar, rubbing in the lemon oil.

Mal stopped and looked at me, her voice soft. "What about you?"

I wanted to be okay. I thought I was. "I'll look for a new place."

Mal's face was awash in concern. We both knew finding anything affordable would be a nightmare. Since the new bridge went in making it easier to commute across the river, anything cheap was snapped up. Even the warehouse where Mal lived had another rent bump.

She focused on the limes. I finished conditioning the bar and set to wiping down the beer cooler, removing the empty keg. I checked on the mixers. It was the first of our two shifts together. She'd picked up my cocktails and I'd covered Dez's bar shifts since the first thing he did with the money was quit, leaving us short staffed. "I don't get you Bear, I'd be furious. Or at least hurt."

I stood, holding the Bloody Mary mix. Then her arm slipped around me and she whispered. "You deserve better, Mama Bear."

My eyes sparked but I turned away toward her hand on my shoulder.

Mallory's pointer finger was missing most of the tip, so when she makes bunny ears, one ear is broken. It's her tag sign, BrokenBunny around the initials 'YoS,' 'love yo'self.' The little 'o' sheltered between the 'y' and the 's.' All of it protected by the heart-shaped broken bunny. Bunnies are love, even broken bunnies. That's Mal.

I rolled the empty keg to the back before any tears could embarrass me.

$$\sim$$

Later, I found myself in front of 3rd and Oak. I didn't know why. Or maybe I did, because watching Dez buy gear and pack left me feeling undone. This was where the whole unwinding began. By default, that made it my new nexus. The somber building loomed over but remained docked to this corner. Stationary.

Of course.

Jees.

I hadn't smoked since that night, or drank. But this building still had a kinetic power. It was more rundown than I first thought, adding to how sinister it felt. I wandered, circling the block, wasting a good hour. Then, surprised to find the door unlocked, I stole into the lobby.

In places, the floor tiles were worn right down to the cement underneath. A wall of mailboxes lined up opposite two elevators. A smudge of gold on one elevator door winked in the gloom. Past that, a small office squatted with a white-lettered 'Leasing Office' on the door. It was closed and dark. I was peering in it when the elevator dinged and a dumpy middle-aged woman stepped out.

"Oh dear, are you my ten o'clock?"

I glanced up at a clock; it was nearly eleven. She bustled over to unlock the office but her ring of keys was unwieldy and she dropped it before being successful. She opened the door and flipped on the harsh fluorescent light.

"Please." She held out her arm to usher me in.

I scanned the lobby, but besides us, it was empty.

She tugged a folder from the desk. Flakes of sparkly paint sprinkled from it and she brushed them to the floor. "I'm so sorry to make you wait. I'm guessing you're here for the studio?"

Her face was relaxed and expectant. I sat down, careful to tuck my paint-sprayed Docs under the chair. "Uh. Sure, yeah."

Satisfied, she pulled open the folder and shoved papers toward me.

"The application is basic, I need a few references and you can look over the rental agreement. I'll waive the rest of the month since I want it filled quick."

I scanned for the rent and felt my eyes pop. A quarter of what I expected to pay. Barely half of what I paid at Dez's place. I blinked to make sure I'd read it right but she had already opened the door offering a tour.

The studio was at least as big as Dez's place. A full kitchen with room for a sitting area and a place to eat. An archway led into another area big enough for a bed. A fire escape out the window looked down Oak toward the river. The building hummed under my feet, its old mass anchoring. Like it wanted me here.

"3RD AND OAK?" MAL ARCHED HER BROWS. "THAT'S A TERRIBLE neighborhood, Bear. You sure about this? Sure you aren't panicking?"

Of course, I was panicking. Dez had left. I told her the price and that stopped her dead. Mal lived in a warehouse with ten other artists where she bathed with a series of hoses and buckets. Her kitchen was a camping set up. "You can't pass that up."

I agreed as we pulled on aprons. Marco was working bar-back. Even he didn't know the 3rd and Oak building and he was born here. They made plans to help me move. Turns out Dez hadn't made time for me after all, a surprise to no one, except, a little bit, to me.

We didn't even have a sendoff. The closest I got to something real with him was when he told me to stop moping.

I wasn't, but he said "This was your choice after all. You could have picked the other ticket." When I didn't respond, he'd tossed down his new climbing shoes and said, "Look, we both know if you won the money, you would have shared it. You'd see it in your rising-tide-raises-all-boats way." He knelt, ripping off the labels and shoving the shoes in his new pack. "You would have fixed Marco's transmission and bought Mal those French pastels. Paid for art school. Paid to fix Grease's teeth. Made sure we all had good coats. Paid my fines. Whatever. And that would have been right for you."

I pushed back against the wall, away from him and his rational eyes.

"But where would that lead, Bear? Huh?" He zipped the pack and tossed it to the door, squatting, now looking up at me. "Marco would need valves or something, rats would destroy the pastels, there'd be another class, we'd for sure ruin the coats, and rent would be due again. Where would we all be then? Huh?"

I didn't answer. I held my chest rigid letting none of it in, but he shook his head.

"Nowhere. Right back here." His shoulders slouched. His eyes stayed sharp and metal. "It's not a tide, Bear. It's one fucking wave. My wave. I gotta do me. It's one life vest. Not two. Not five. Dividing up a life vest doesn't save anyone."

He wasn't wrong, but I needed to get out of our place before the ghosts unwound me.

When we pulled up to the building, Marco had a hard time finding a parking spot. Me and Mal got out with my plants and he circled the block again. Mal stared skyward, hugging my philodendron. She sucked in her breath. "Woah," was all she said.

I headed to the door, lugging both overgrown spider plants, careful to keep the babies safe.

"Bear, wait!" She stumbled, her eyes were all pupil making her look stoned even though she wasn't. "How have I never seen this building?" She looked skyward. "Is it moving? I feel like it's moving."

Mal was freaking me out, so I didn't answer and headed up to the door. I leaned against it, trying to get my key out. It swung inward and I almost fell. It should have been locked.

Mal followed, tentative under the weight of the philodendron. Marco's truck appeared again and he parked almost in front of the door. He waited there since he couldn't leave the truck with all my stuff in the back.

We rode the elevator up and when Mal saw the apartment, she whistled.

"Oh, Bear." She set down the plant and glided through the big space. More at ease, she leaned on the window with the fire escape. "You can see the river." Her eyes found me and aimed for supportive. Heading into the kitchen, she stepped over the dubious stains on the wooden floor. "It's not bad, Bear. It's got…"

I steeled myself for her critique. "Character?"

She spun in the middle of the kitchen. "Bones. It's got great bones." Flipping on one of the stove's burners flashed out a merry blue circle of flame. She was sunny, trying to make up for earlier. "It's lovely, really. There is so much room." She turned off the burner and peeked into the bathroom. "I'll make curtains. Brilliant yellow ones. And find you rugs. You are gonna be fine." Standing on one of the bigger stains near the archway, bright and dialed up, I almost believed her.

G-DOG'S PIECES SHOWED UP ALL OVER TOWN. ON THE ROOFTOP OF THE old power building, he eclipsed T-square's mural of hell. I didn't know that's what it was until T-square told me, and it wasn't his best, but still. Coming from out of town and covering an existing local piece with a piece of your own broke just about the biggest rule in our world. A tag can cover a tag. That's just spitting. You can also cover a tag with a more complicated throw. That's a move for a local, but if you're a bomber from outside, that can be dicey. It could be dicey even if you're local. But no one ever covers an actual piece. We just don't dis like that. So, to do what G-dog did, come from out of town, cover a full on piece, basically a mural, with his own piece, in a prime spot like the rooftop, was a triple act of war.

But no one grumbled, at least not out loud, since it was G-dog's piece and that was an honor, right? This wasn't New York or Chicago. We weren't violent in this dead-end town. We didn't even have a train yard. Besides, it was living art we practiced, fluid, and transient. The city was the canvas. "Don't get attached," was what Dez would say. But he also would have reclaimed his name; G-dog be dammed.

But he'd been gone for three weeks and more and more of his pieces were covered in the gold and indigo mashup. Sometimes the glittery boot prints showed up before and sometimes after the work was done. G-dog claimed space on his own time, like a power play. When one of Dez's pieces went down, it was like a streetlamp went out and the night grew darker. G-dog's pieces were spectacular feats but they didn't feel like home, like Dez.

Mal clucked and said good riddance. She was firmly Team Bear.

Dez always said ours was a world that went unnoticed. "You only see it if you're in it." It took a long time to understand what he meant because who can miss sudden giant conspicuous throwies of cartoons or sigs or words? Or even the ubiquitous scripts of coded signatures on road signs, mailboxes, and playground equipment?

He meant us, though. Working under cover of darkness, in secret, breeching illegal places. A feral army resisting cancerous urban growth. Creative destruction meeting destructive creation.

A tag—our signature—was personal, the embodiment of our essence. A way to stake claim. Not of the place, but of our place in it.

"Deeds or fortunes made surfing the stock market made you think you owned things but it's all delusion. The whole system is rooted in land stolen from people who had no concept of land ownership." Dez would go off like this all night. Railing that progress was just a veiled orgy of the destruction of the Commons. In his metaphor, we came full circle, now the natives challenging the morality of ownership. "You capitalists think you own this place but every night we show up and defy you. Paint over us and we just come back. Rinse and repeat."

He filled our hearts with purpose and vision.

Like that luxury building in Los Angeles only half-built and abandoned by a Chinese development company. Six years later, it's still empty and a graff Mecca. They sneak in, mark the tenth, thirtieth, the fortieth floor. Hiding not only from street cops, but from helicopters. Our art staking its claim to the skyline.

"Which is the abomination? Who is the criminal?" Dez would argue bringing all of it alive.

But Dez, with all his rants, brilliant or demented, was gone. And his pieces, his words, his essence, were disappearing. I was torn about what to do.

If a tagger died or got injured, we maintained shrines. We honored anniversaries. We poured out beer. We repaired what weather ruined but not what the city painted over. There were expiration dates to grief it turned out.

There weren't rules for when a tagger won the lottery and fucking skipped town though. Seemed like open season. Abandoned family couldn't be expected to maintain your mark. Still, when the piece at the plinth of the harbor bridge went gold, it felt wrong. Some of the Broken-Bunnies were gone, too. Mal wasn't as into tagging anymore since she'd gotten serious with Duke.

~

"I'LL MOVE IN WITH HIM. HIS PLACE UP ON MAHOGANY HAS A REAL bathroom," she quipped, wiping down the high tops, scrubbing the stools.

I listened, refilling cherries and olives and pickled onions. I was more or less permanently bartending now. "You're leaving the co-op? What about your art?"

She laughed, sweeping her hands in the air, gesturing to the bar and the dining room beyond. "Where has art gotten me?" It felt like she was disappearing, like BrokenBunny. "Duke says I should get into real estate. He thinks I'd look good on the posters." She tugged at a curl by her neck.

~

IT TURNED OUT DUKE HAD A WHOLE OTHER LIFE WITHOUT ROOM FOR MAL. He never wanted to move her in. She'd been played the whole time. So, for a bit, we were a crew again, back to cruising the waterfront in Grease's Buick. It was almost like old times, except for Mal's heartbreak, my malaise, and Dez's absence.

A new G-dog showed up at the old crematorium and we all got out to take a look.

The same mishmash, indigo and lime and gold, framed by white space, crowded already with graff. Mal stood back, sucking down a White Claw studying it. Already bored, I watched the river.

"Hey." Mal walked closer to the wall, scrutinizing it. "Hey, Bear. Do you see this?" She waved at the gold. I wandered over and studied it. In a molten crucible, a golden piece liquified. It overflowed, forming a river. Same as ever. So unimaginative. Dez's pieces had stories threaded between the letters. Color and depth, light and shadow, telling a story, our story. Curled at the base of a letter or in a shadow in every piece, Dez would weave in a secret sleeping bear and a bunny. I shrugged turning to the car.

But she grabbed my arm, pointing. "No, Bear. Look. Don't you see it?"

I turned back to where she pointed to G-dog's molten gold. Just a river of it, and yeah kind of cool, all the shades of gold gave it motion when you got up close. But then I saw it. Like those pictures of psychedelic gibberish until you see the jaguar or whatever. Then all you see is the jaguar and it never goes back to gibberish. I saw the sleeping bear, holding her face with one claw out, the others curled in. How Dez always drew me. And then I saw the BrokenBunny. Not whole, but broken, the way Mal saw herself. All in shades of gold, so delicate no wonder you missed it at first.

Marco looked, too. He found the polo mallet, his own joke, barely visible. Grease hunted for a wrench and found it. All of us melted together forming G-dog's river of gold. We saw other things. A horse, a fox, some kind of falling lizard thing. The Liz from Chicago. He fell off a bridge last year. It rocked the whole graff world. Afterward, Dez made us hit the interstate overpass. Not a whole piece, just a quick throwie. Up and down. But all of us.

"You gotta hop back up. Beat your fear."

We hadn't stayed long. Up and down. The fear hadn't won, not all the way.

The longer we looked the more we saw. Mal stepped toward it, mesmerized. I got that sick feeling I had at the bodega with the lottery tickets. The swirling gold was so lifelike, the heat of molten metal wafted off it. Mal reached to it, the gold shine eclipsing her face. Nauseous and dizzy, I leapt, shoving her hand away.

I yelped a fusion of "No!" and "Don't touch it!"

Everyone gaped at me bug-eyed and tinged a sick greenish. We were all stunned looking at each other. Almost as one, we piled into the car then we careened around town, to all the G-dogs.

It was the same wherever we went. A sleeping bear, a broken bunny, Marco-polo, a wrench, the Liz always falling, all of it. Even T-square. Signs we recognized and ones we didn't. The luminous river of ever-flowing gold with us melting in it. But never anything with Dez. Not his 'Z,' not his triangle with the eye, child of God for Desmond, not the purple scarab of reanimation he sometimes did. All of us and a bunch of others, but no Dez. G-dog totally disappeared him. We all felt sick. We scrammed, not sure what we'd seen.

At the bar, we slumped around the hightop full of empties.

"He's good. That's all. Top-rate shading creates movement," Marco decided, gripping his bottle. He wasn't green anymore. He acted like he'd made it back to unshakable Marco. Scale a wall, hang from a rail, outrun a riot battalion, Marco. "Fancy paint tricks. Art student shit. You see what you want, not what's there." He looked around with contempt.

Mal pulled at her napkin and whispered, "Dez said never copy. Only create. What is ours is ours. It's an abomination."

Marco snorted, spinning his glass. "Everyone copies. Everyone steals. Dez was a blowhard. Besides, where is he now?"

Grease picked at the label on his Modelo. "With Dez we could pull off big things like that."

Mal crimped the napkin smaller and smaller. Duke had shrunk her, shattered her sweet BrokenBunny heart.

Dez had shrunk all of us.

I thought about the time across the river at the old theater. Dez on the ladder, me and Marco doing fill, and Grease on look out. Suddenly, red and blue lights flashed everywhere with a hot spotlight up on Dez and a megaphone barking orders. Dez signaled all sly for us to slink into shadow. He'd hammed it up, doing a whole show, pissing off the cops enough to let us tear through alleys to find a place to hide. Dez ended up collared for vandalism and resisting arrest. He took it all and cleaned up trash for nine months. Never gave any of us up. He signed himself rezizAnt for a while before going back to Dez with the lazy 'Z.'

I missed him. The parts I loved, not the part that just up and left. Both parts chewed at my insides. I couldn't help Mal or bring back Dez. So, I turned on Marco, the burn rising up my neck. I pushed away my beer. I couldn't help but growl, "He always had your back."

Marco looked up, surprised. "So? We all did. That's how it works. Doesn't mean I bought all his BS."

But Dez made it make sense. Kept us safe. He gave us purpose. "Why do it at all Marco?"

He sneered, scanning the bar. "Why? For release. Life pents you up. For the hours I'm spraying, I'm peace, connected, totally untouchable. My tension bleeds right onto the wall. I walk away cool, accomplished, light." He spun his glass, thoughtful. "And, in the day, I see it and it's there and I'm there. Maybe I see what could be better. And the whole cycle starts again." He chugged his beer and stood up. "Plus it keeps me from doing worse things. You coming or what?"

I didn't go. I babysat Mal.

∾

Back at 3rd and Oak, it never got not weird. I never saw anyone in the listing office. No other tenants came or went. Weird for such a big building, though between cocktailing and extra bartending shifts, I was hardly home. We rarely painted. G-dog was everywhere. Marco talked about moving to Detroit. Grease already had. We never heard from Dez. It was like he dropped off the planet.

I hardly slept. I lay in bed and saw that river of gold. It flowed through my dreams. I dreamt I'd picked the other ticket, but it burst into flames. I dreamt that Mal melted into the gold and I couldn't pull her out. I dreamt I drowned in that river. I'd awaken soaked in sweat. The building around me hummed and I'd get tangled in my sheets and find myself thrashing to free myself. I was awake and couldn't sleep and asleep and couldn't wake.

One night, glitter paint smudged the foyer. Another night, I was coming home near dawn. The elevator randomly opened on the second floor giving me a glimpse of a tall dude entering an apartment. The doors slid closed, but not before I clocked the glitter on his boots.

"You're Sleepy Bear?"

I spun toward the entrance of the laundry room where the guy from the second floor stood. The one with the splashed work boots. He paused, backlit from the corridor. When he entered, he dropped his bag at a machine.

"Dez's girl, huh?"

"Dez isn't here anymore."

He laughed and started dumping clothes in a machine. "He's not dead."

"I didn't say that."

Digging in his pocket, he pulled out a roll of quarters. He hopped up on the closed washer and sat unrolling a few coins. "But you feel like he is."

I didn't. Well, in a way, I did. In a lot of ways, I did. Things had unwound. My clothes tumbled and clanked with the building throbbing around me.

"You're G-dog." I said, not asking.

He set coins in the slots shooting them home. The washer churned. He shoved the roll back in his pocket and pulled out a crushed pack of Kools. No one smoked Kools. A grandpa maybe.

I backed away when he offered me one. "I know what you're doing."

A cigarette bobbed in his mouth but he didn't light it. "What am I doing?"

"I don't know how, but you're stealing our work. Stealing us."

He nodded, his expression thoughtful.

"That's why you don't allow pictures." I spat the last words. "You're a thief."

I didn't expect the delight on his face. "Thief?"

"You found us because we are good. Then you grow, because of us."

He chuckled. "Damn. I sound like a mastermind."

I didn't like him. Didn't like this. Didn't like how claustrophobic the room felt. All those floors above us, vibrating, moving, threatening to break free of their moorings.

"Why is your tag Sleepy Bear?" He rested his elbows on the back of the machine. His black eyes burned curious under the shaggy, blacker hair.

I thought about Dez naming me. "You sleepwalk through life, not letting anything affect you, numb. Like a lovely, sleepy bear."

Dez was wrong though. I was affected by everything. I just didn't need to advertise it. Besides, nothing meant anything anymore. Creation, destruction, art, vandalism. It was all the same and all nothing. Even Dez left the minute he saw an exit.

The smell of detergent and dryer sheets hung in the air, cloying and chemical. I wanted out. I wanted to grab my damp clothes and run but I didn't. I stayed, frozen. Because, really, that's what I do. That's how I always made it to tomorrow. I froze and didn't say anything. Went back to sleep. A sleepy bear. Just fine.

"Except you're not." He said, as if he'd heard me.

He popped down from the washer and leaned, tall and spare and dark. With paint-splattered jeans and his ridiculous glittered boots. "Not sleepy. Are you?" He cocked his eyebrow."You are a bear though, huh?"

I stepped back. Behind me, the dryer tumbled and clattered.

"Dez's best stuff is yours. Your ideas. Your work. You, right alongside him. On the bridge. The water tower." He examined his fingernails. "No big thing for you. Right?"

I followed Dez. I always followed because he brought things to life. We completed each other. Created together. It was how it was. How I wanted it. The building thrummed above me.

Every one of G-dog's pieces had us in it. That river of us became his gold, drawing others to it. Art, from everywhere he'd been. London to here. Fame. He was the maw pulling it in. But then it became his. The building droned. So loud. I held my ears, my head, but the noise wasn't from the building. It was from him. His black eyes, now on me again, the smirk. I backed against the dryer, hot and tumbling. Zippers clanked out of rhythm.

"This building," I realized, "you got me in here. You arranged it."

He watched me.

"What are you?"

His voice went flat. "You don't have words for what I am. Even you, a creature of the night." He pinched the cigarette in his hands. "I'm also a dark night thing."

I got scared at night, out painting. Even with all of us. Darkness revealed desperation. Darkness prowled sundown to dawn. We hid in it but so did other things. Things I'd rather not know about. My belly roiled, nauseous. Like in the bodega. Like pulling Mal away from the golden river. Like seeing all of us in it.

"That gold, in your pieces, why are we in it? How are we in it?" My voice was shakier than I wanted. "Why does it move?"

His eyebrows arched. "Smart Bear. Much better questions."

"It's alive, isn't it?"

He gestured, a magician showing empty hands.

I thought of what Marco said. 'It's a release. I walk away lighter.

Then the cycle starts again.' What was spilled, that we'd all spilled, in these painting frenzies? G-dog studied me, still as a reptile, and blinked.

"You have a way of collecting what we throw away. Our angst, our pain. You feed on it." My voice edged to panic.

"The life force you spit away. Yes." He brightened, pleased with himself.

No.

With me. Like he saw me seeing him and was grateful. The way Dez looked at me. My heart chilled.

"You sent Dez away."

"How could I do that?" He scoffed, like I'd said something preposterous. But his look was a dare.

"You rigged the tickets. You charmed them somehow. You made sure he got his wish." It caused a sharp pain to think that about Dez. That his ticket out, in his heart of hearts, didn't include me. My chest tightened.

"Bear, you chose." G-dog mocked me. "It could have gone another way, but for you."

I did choose.

But did I? I chose for Dez to go. Not knowing but also knowing, I grabbed the life vest leaving him the shimmering open maw. Backing away, the room tilted, the detergents and perfumes messing in my head.

"Sweet, Loyal Bear. Don't be hard on yourself. He got quite the conciliation prize."

I stared at him. His cold look eclipsed anything warm and human.

But Dez worshipped his work. "The oversized murals appearing overnight. The high bridges, the rooftops, the publicity, how do you do all that?"

"C'mon. Human innovation. It's amazing what you can do hopped up on life force."

"You're evil."

"No." He laughed. "Your religion fails you. There are so many more options than good and evil."

"You're some monster then."

His face darkened, a shadow passing through, chilling the room.

"No, Bear. I gather what's thrown away or given freely. I take something base and transmute it to gold."

"An alchemist."

He waved his finger-guns at me, his smile breaking free, like the sun itself.

The dryer's buzzer shrilled. The silence plunged us into unnerving stillness. "Why tell me all this?"

He hopped back on the washer. "An offer. You can have anything. My offer to you."

"To me?"

"Of course."

"Why me?"

He gestured toward the street. "I love what you've done here. I want it. You are its source. So, I want you."

It confused me. "No. Dez was all of it. It left with him. He's who you want."

G-dog shook his head. "So he led you to believe. But he'll learn. In some jungle, burning with fever, he'll figure out what his source is." He scoffed. "Tragic, but you get what you ask for."

I stared at him, frozen.

His eyes met mine, almost apologetic. "Look, we know who the creators are. Dez had skills, but the real juice—" He fist bumped his heart and cradled his belly. "Comes from women." His whole body shifted to warm and receptive. "Do what you did for Dez, but for me. It doesn't have to be graff. Plenty of places cast away life force. D.C., L.A., Wall Street. Name any game."

His eyes were now rich pools pulling me in. "I'm offering you the world."

I saw the image of gold coalescing into a river. His river. "But what happens to me, in that gold?"

The softness now was raw, hungry…and predatory. "You, immortalized. Legendary."

"By becoming an amalgam of everyone you collect?"

"A path to something bigger. Taken global."

It was wrong. The opposite of what we were, of what I wanted. Shaky, but clear, my whisper escaped, "No."

"No?" His back stiffened.

Just like that, I could move. I stepped away. "You can only take what's freely given, what's tossed away."

"A technicality, but yes." He spread his hands. "In return I offer you everything."

The building wasn't the danger. It never was. It wasn't pressing down but rather holding me. The danger was out there, my worth on a wall or with Dez or G-dog or flowing away from me in someone's river. The buzzing I felt was me. G-dog had no power here. Dez either. Neither could diminish me. Everything I had ever given was still in me. Was me. I straightened.

I repeated it. Still and quiet. For myself. "No."

"Oh, Bear." Annoyance damaged his smile.

I turned, stuffing the warm mound of clothing from the dryer into my basket.

"Bear, you know I'll keep coming back. Food left out attracts rats. It's only nature. My nature." He tried to keep the strain from his voice. The disappointment.

It didn't matter.

He didn't realize he had set me free. My body hummed as I strode to the elevator.

FOR THE FIRST TIME IN WEEKS, I SLEPT THROUGH THE NIGHT. THE MORNING broke to heavy rain. I laid in bed all day listening to it. On my way out, I passed a woman balancing a child and groceries entering their apartment. On the street, I saw T-square's crew-tags on the building.

At work, Marco stopped in for his last drink before moving. "Did you hear about the G-dogs?"

I stopped working and looked up.

"The ones at the wharf and the bridge washed off in the storm last night. I'm guessing the others, too. Must be his crap paint. Just bare walls now."

"Well, they won't be bare for long," Mal laughed, her spark coming back.

"Yeah? You gonna get busy?" Marco raised his glass to her.

She shook her head. "No. I think I'll focus here." She tapped her heart. "What about you, Bear?"

I smiled at her and finished attaching the beer keg.

RECIPE FOR A GOOD KISS
TRISH MACENULTY

Thirteen notifications? Mags clicked on the little heart in the upper right-hand corner of her Instagram feed. She didn't get all that many notifications on Instagram. It was her least favorite social media platform—too small, too cluttered, and she found the constant sales pitches irksome. Of course, she was guilty of stealth sales herself. She wouldn't be on social media if she wasn't obligated to promote her food blog and cookbook.

When she switched the screen to notifications, she saw that twelve of the thirteen were from the same account: MelancholyMan.

Oh, good grief, she thought. *Another cyber-masher.* If she clicked on it, she'd probably find fake pictures of a muscled-up old dude in a military uniform, a widower no doubt. They were always trying to friend her on Facebook. Did anyone fall for these scams?

She did like the Moody Blues song of the same name, and the tune immediately started up in her head. That ear worm would probably wriggle in her brain for a week.

What the heck, she thought, clicking on the account curious to see if MelancholyMan was anyone she actually knew. A picture popped up of a man with whitish hair, a strong face, thick eyebrows, and dark eyes. She took in the name. There was a moment of utter disbelief, followed by, "Holy. Crap. Barry the Abominable Bozeman."

That name hadn't floated across her horizon since the sixth grade. She only remembered it on the rare occasion when a conversation revolved around firsts. Her mind barreled back in time to the school bus stop in front of the apartment building at 3rd and Oak. She saw her younger self, wearing a pleated skirt with a white blouse and saddle oxfords, holding onto her blue three-ring notebook, scrawled with the names of the Beach Boys, and a textbook or two.

My God, why didn't we have book bags back then, she wondered. She inhaled, remembering the smell of crushed acorns in the crisp morning air mixing with the scent of fabric softener on her sweater. Behind her, the low laughter of boys. The screech of brakes as the yellow school bus heaved to a stop in front of her and settled with a moan. The doors opening with a sucking sound.

Every school day she had gotten on the bus and sat in the middle, saving a seat for Katie who boarded at the mouth of a development called Falling Leaves where people lived in houses not apartments. The boys, including Barry, would pass by on their way to the back of the bus where they'd act the way boys did back then—loud, obnoxious, and stupid. Barry sometimes would stop to ask her how she did on a test or a paper. The school was too poor to have a gifted program, so they met once a week in the gifted class. As the top students in the sixth grade, Mags and Barry had an unofficial competition going as to which one was smarter. She did better in science, and he was the whiz in English. The top spots in math and history went back and forth between them.

Mags looked at Barry's picture again. He had aged well. With his wiry frame, long face, and olive-tinted skin, he hadn't been on the cute list back then. She'd never had a crush on him. She'd been too busy mooning for Katie's blond-haired, blue-eyed older brother. Then the fifth and sixth graders in the apartment building at 3rd and Oak started pairing up for their first attempts at making out. Even the fourth graders were playing spin the bottle. The only ones left after the other kids paired up were Mags and Barry.

One early evening, after the other kids had been called in for dinner, Mags and Barry were alone in the playground behind the building. Mags was perched at the top of the jungle gym. Barry looked up at her and said, "Hey, come down." She dropped through the bars and stood in front of him, knowing what was going to happen. He leaned over and planted his lips on hers. It was over quickly, like the strike of a lightning bolt. They stared at each other. Then without a word, she slid between the bars, her red sneakers landing on the dirt, and dashed inside the building to the cramped apartment where her mother had made something dreadful like cubed steak or perhaps canned chop suey and overdone rice. Later they would figure out her mother had Crohn's disease, but in those days, she was just a sickly woman who had no interest in decent food. It wasn't lost on Mags that her desire to be a chef could be traced directly back to this early deprivation.

The next day during recess, Katie whispered to her that Barry had told everyone she was a lousy kisser and that her breath was bad.

"He said you just stood there like you didn't know what to do." Katie seemed to relish telling her the gossip, as if it were someone else they were discussing. Katie was pretty with green cat-like eyes and had a cruel streak that Mags had ignored until then.

From that day on, she thought of him as Barry the Abominable Bozeman. She stopped playing on the jungle gym, didn't compare grades with him, and, in fact, never spoke to him again.

At the end of Mags' sixth-grade year, her mother married a dentist, and they moved out of the dingy, overheated apartment at 3rd and Oak into a three-bedroom ranch house with a swimming pool on the other side of town. Mags' stepfather paid for her to go to private school, and she blithely wiped away all memories of the 3rd and Oak gang, of Barry the Abominable Bozeman, even of Katie, her once-best friend. She never had to look back on that first disastrous kiss with Barry underneath the jungle gym behind the apartments or deal with the fact that he'd told all the other kids she was a lousy kisser. For one thing, she thought, she did not have bad breath. She probably tasted like grape Nehi. And it was her first kiss. How was she supposed to know what to do?

After all these years, now here he was. Following her on Instagram! Of all the nerve.

Since he'd "liked" twelve of her posts—eleven food photos and one video of her making a ginger vinaigrette—she expected he would send a direct message eventually. Something insipid like: "Remember me?" *Oh yeah, I remember you all right, Buster.*

She glanced at his posts. There weren't many. Mainly wildlife photos. Only one of his posts was remotely personal. It was a picture of him and a little boy—a grandson. That meant he'd married at least once and had a kid. Well, good for him.

She'd also gotten married and had a family. First, to a narcissistic pilot in the Air Force who had donated his genetic material in the creation of two beautiful children, only to ignore them completely after he'd left her, married someone else, and had two other children. Sometimes she wondered if she'd been practicing for that betrayal since the sixth grade.

Second, to a kind and selfless manager of a gourmet food market who'd devoted himself to helping her raise her kids. He died of a Tylenol overdose three weeks after his diagnosis of Lou Gehrig's disease. That was five years ago. With the income from his life insurance policy, Mags retired from her job as culinary professor at a community college and started her food blog: the Eclectic Chef. Not a great name in retrospect since apparently many people didn't know what "eclectic" meant and instead called her the Electric Chef.

But Barry the Abominable Bozeman did not send a private message, and she forgot about him and the gang of kids with whom she had played tetherball, capture the flag, and basketball behind the apartment building at 3rd and Oak. She had the launch of her second cookbook to plan and she also had to tape segments for the local morning show on slicing onions—lengthwise, for God's sake—making a gluten-free roux and creating your own vegetable broth from scraps. Not to mention, her daughter had a minor surgery coming up, and Mags had offered to step in and help take care of the grandkids for a couple of days.

Then the email came. From the bookstore in her hometown: "We would love to have you come sign books and do a culinary demonstration here at the store. You're a hometown girl! We consider you one of our local authors!!"

She read the email again. The prospect, even with all the exclamation marks, did not excite her. She rarely went back to her hometown. Her life was in a city two hundred miles away. She closed the email. She'd answer in the morning.

"Of course, you'll go," her publicist said the next day. "You need to sell books, Hon. I mean, cookbooks are not an easy sell these days. First of all, they're expensive to make, expensive to buy, and why buy a cookbook when you can find any recipe you'd ever want on the Internet? People buy them because they feel an affinity for the chef. Go there and make affinity happen."

Mags wrote back to the bookstore. They answered. A date was agreed upon for the next month. She made a reservation at the Marriott and used points for her stay since her publisher was not footing the bill.

THE DRIVE TOOK A LITTLE MORE THAN THREE HOURS. HER HOMETOWN wasn't a bad place. Great airport. Good restaurants. A nice waterfront. It's just that she'd never felt she'd really lived until she went away to college. Before then she'd been a sleepwalker, waiting for life to happen. Once she launched into adulthood, she'd seen no reason to return. Both her parents were dead. She had no siblings. Sure, some of the people she went to high school with followed her on Facebook, but that's because they thought publishing a cookbook made her famous.

As she drove toward the city, the downtown rose in the distance like pyramids in the desert. She passed the familiar exits, then, at the last second, turned off the highway. This was not the way to her hotel. This was the way back through the decades. From the two thousands, the nineties, the eighties, the seventies, smack dab into the late 1960s.

Why am I doing this, she wondered, but the compulsion was too strong to resist. She passed the small library where she'd spent countless hours as a child, passed the park where she used to roll down a grassy hill, drove across the drainage tunnel where she and Katie had smoked Marlboro cigarettes stolen from Katie's dad, and, finally, pulled up beside a down-on-its-heels, concrete apartment building on the corner of 3rd and Oak.

She parked her Prius and gazed up at her former home. The apartment where she and her mother had lived was on the corner of the fourth floor. She found the window to her bedroom, which had been decorated with cut-out pictures of horses taped to the walls. The curtains had been an ugly moss green. One time a bat flew straight through the window and into the bathroom where it scared her mother right out of the shower and into the hallway—naked. Mags had laughed so hard she peed herself.

She couldn't remember what happened to the bat.

Now the whole building looked deserted. The lawn in front was patchy like a dog with mange, and some of the first-floor windows were boarded up with plywood. Mags got out of the car and noticed a big rectangular sign in front. Walking over to it, she read: Future site of Bank of America. She gazed up at the building with a pang. She didn't know why she cared after all these years, but nostalgia could be a heady drug.

Mags wandered to the back of the building. Water oak trees towered above her. The jungle gym was still there—after all these years. As she leaned against the bars, her heart broke a little. The past sat in front of her, a forlorn ghost. She thought of the gang of kids who had played here every day after school, dirty and disheveled, the screams, the taunts, the laughter. Her memories weren't all bad food, loneliness, and betrayal. There had been fun jumbled into the mix of her childhood. Good, old-fashioned, rough-and-tumble fun.

Mags returned to her Prius, pushed the start button, and drove to a Taco Bell. She recognized the irony of discussing eclectic new recipes after eating a bland bean burrito, but she had no time for a real meal. Her demonstration and book signing were scheduled for seven p.m. The demo would be easy—knife skills. The dice, the slice, the mince, the julienne, the chiffonade. Those were always fun. She liked the frisson of fear that skimmed through the crowd when she sliced a carrot on the bias in under five seconds—as if they were watching NASCAR, anticipating a gory crash.

Mags entered the bookstore and looked around. It was a decent crowd, maybe thirty people. The owner got her set up at a table in the back where she put on her apron and let her knife fly. A clerk passed around sliced carrot and celery for the audience.

After the demo, Mags sat at a desk and signed copies of her second big, expensive cookbook: *The Eclectic Chef's Alphabet of Recipes: Beans, Beets, and Bologna*. Basically, any food item that started with 'B.' It had been the publisher's idea: a 26-book series. The first had been *Artichokes, Amaretto, and Apple Pie*.

A book club comprised of women from her high school were there, acting thrilled to buy her book. A few of them pretended they'd been her great friends once upon a time. Except for a couple of nerdy girls who'd moved away as quickly as she had, Mags kept to herself through high school. She was sure none of these women actually remembered her except from her Facebook posts. But she smiled and put on her own pretense. *Oh, yes, that was so funny when that happened. Of course, I remember you, blah blah blah.*

The book-club ladies left, and she signed more books. An elegant-looking woman a few years younger than she, wearing a striped crew-neck top over a pair of white capris and carrying a Kate Spade handbag, placed a book in front of her.

"Who should I sign it to?" Mags asked, digging another pen out of her purse. Of course, the signing pen she'd brought *would* run out of ink.

"Susan Bozeman," the woman said.

Mags looked up. Behind the woman was a tall man in his sixties. He was tanned and fit with bushy eyebrows. Barry the Abominable Bozeman in the flesh.

"Hi, Barry," Mags said.

"Hi, Mags," he answered. "Good to see you."

They stared at each other, sizing up the toll of years. His Instagram photo hadn't lied. He looked great. The scammers could definitely use his image for the studly widowers they used on social media to friend gullible older women. But Mags was no slouch either—Pilates, yoga, and regular swimming had kept all systems go. She might not be as slim and elegant as the woman standing in front of her, but she was the one with the pen in her hand.

She signed the book "To Susan" and handed the book over to the woman.

"Thank you," Susan said.

Barry smiled and nodded at Mags before leaving with Susan. Mags watched their retreating backs. Another book was thrust in front of her. She stared at it for a moment before putting down her pen.

"Will you excuse me for just one minute?" she said to the customer. She pushed the chair back and wound through the remaining people to the exit. She burst through the door. There they were, a few stores down, heading toward a car.

"Barry!" she called. "Wait!"

Barry and Susan stopped and turned around.

She hurried toward them. Barry looked confused. Mags had no idea what Susan's expression was. Her eyes were directed only toward Barry.

"I wanted to tell you something," she said.

As soon as she closed in on him, she reached for his face, clasped it between her hands, pulled him toward her, and planted her lips on his. She released him and stepped back.

"There! Still think I'm a lousy kisser?" she asked.

"I…" he said. "What?"

"I didn't appreciate you telling every kid in the building I had bad breath! And…and that I didn't even know how to kiss. I was just a kid!"

Barry's mouth hung open, and his eyes were wide. A tsunami of embarrassment washed over her. She turned toward his wife, her hand over her mouth. Should she apologize? Try to explain herself. The woman stared at her as if she'd gone mad. Mags wasn't sure what she would have done if a total stranger had come up and kissed her husband back when she had one, but she probably wouldn't have been quite this ladylike.

"Try the recipe on page eighty-three," Mags said. "The Bolognese sauce is divine. Fresh parsley is the secret."

She wheeled around and walked as quickly as she could back to the bookstore. He probably didn't even remember saying she was a lousy kisser, she thought as she took her seat. Who knows? What if Katie had been lying? Perhaps Barry and his wife were driving away, laughing in disbelief about the insane woman who wrote alphabetized cookbooks. She signed six more books, packed up her knives, and drove to her hotel where, after a glass of Kim Crawford, she slept a full eight hours, a minor miracle.

Two days later, after posting pictures on her Facebook page, she checked her Instagram. She had a direct message from Barry Bozeman, aka MelancholyMan. It said: "My sister Susan is enjoying her cookbook very much. She especially likes the recipe for beef tips on rice."

Sister? Mags put down her phone and closed her eyes. From deep in the recesses of her memory emerged a waif-like little girl hovering at the edge of the playground behind the apartment building of the 3rd and Oak gang.

That evening she posted a video of a recipe she had just created using acorn squash, zucchini, and Gruyere, topped with crispy slivers of fried potato curls and sweet peppadew peppers like little smooches. She called it The Good Kiss Casserole—casseroles being a dominant theme of the next book—and noted that it "Pairs best with grape Nehi."

Thirty seconds later a heart flashed in the corner of her screen.

TERRIBLY GORGEOUS
SUE ANN HIGGENS

3rd and Oak.

For Gerald Kelley, it was love at first sight. The house was a time-piece nestled between stately homes on a street lined with big porches and sprawling lawns. His dad always said a three-digit address meant you'd made it. And here it was: 308 Oak Street. *That* address said you were in the mix, not just some phony from a slapped-up housing development with five digits littering the front of the place.

Gerald grew up in a rented saltbox just south of downtown; a four-digit address on a busy street. Rooms too small and too few. Linoleum from the forties and mismatched rugs. On Saturdays, his dad drove him around the grand old neighborhoods downtown, admiring the stately trees, the imposing old houses with long eves and gabled dormers.

"Buy yourself one of these three-digit addresses," his dad said, "and marry a pretty girl. Then you'll have it made."

But Gerald quit school at sixteen when an accident on a backhoe took his dad. He swung a hammer and carried boards to keep a roof over his mom's head. The team he was on was building a dozen matching houses on the south edge of town. The old-timers on the crew complained about the shoddy materials they were using. "Now, take a big gabled beauty like those grand old houses downtown. They used hand saws and planes to shape every window and ornate bit of trim," they said. "Those were built with real craftsmanship and pride."

But construction work was too hot and too inconsistent. Gerald got a job in an auto parts store and got his GED. He didn't have time for friends, but after a couple years he scratched together enough to start college part-time right there at the State University.

He met Hillary, a brainy sophomore, at her job in the campus library. She was cute and helped him find books a few times. He didn't feel at home in a library, but he started going regularly to see if she was working. He asked her out. They both liked movies and R&B. She was three years younger, but only a year behind him in school. She was fun to be with though he didn't have a lot of time for dating. He worked all the shifts he could manage; he was saving for a house someday.

HILLARY WELDON WAS STUDYING HISTORY. SINCE EIGHTH GRADE, SHE'D been fascinated by how caravans of camels and merchants had brought not just spices on their routes, but ideas and beliefs, reshaping cultures. She wasn't sure if she'd be a professor someday. But a history degree would be a good foundation for something, maybe anthropology or archaeology.

"My focus is on the time between the Middle Ages and the Renaissance," she told Gerald on their first date. "See, I think if people don't understand the transformations in art and culture in that period, they can't really understand the present." He nodded, but Hillary wasn't sure he got it. "There was this big shift from agrarian to urban life, and who benefitted? There were some pretty greedy origins to what we call the Age of Discovery."

Hillary liked Gerald's broad shoulders, his hazel eyes, and his silly attachment to his car. He was ambitious, working all hours and studying business. He knew just the kind of house he wanted. He drove her around the old downtown neighborhood on a couple of their dates, pointing out the classic features and big trees. It seemed odd in such a young man. She found it endearing.

When she'd been going out with Gerald for a few months, he met her parents. Hillary knew her mother hoped she'd find someone from an established family. Not rich exactly, but substantial.

"He seems nice enough," Hillary's mom said. "But you don't want to end up with someone who can't support his family. A girl has to think about these things. I don't mean look at his teeth like he's some horse," she'd cautioned, "just have a good look at his parents."

Hillary met Gerald's mother at graduation when he got his business degree with the Class of '74. But his mom didn't have a lot to say and he'd lost his father.

"You'll be graduating next year, dear," Hillary's mother kept reminding her. "Make sure you're dating a man you hope to settle down with and start a family."

She thought Gerald was probably that guy. She wasn't dating anyone else, but she was in no hurry. Gerald was now managing three auto parts franchises. No more grease under his nails. Hillary planned to further her studies and research something exciting. Maybe travel to Europe.

Then, without any notice, Gerald disappeared. He didn't call. He didn't come to the library. She was suddenly sure she was in love with him. What had she done wrong? Why did he drop her?

As luck would have it, one of the guys at work mentioned to Gerald his grandma was selling her old house downtown. "It ain't terribly gorgeous, if you know what I mean," he said. "But it's got good bones and a great big yard."

Gerald always longed to go inside one of the handsome old houses. He asked if he could take a look. "Sure, but I'm telling you, it needs a ton of work."

The white paint was flaking like a bad sunburn. And maybe 308 Oak wasn't as grand as others on the street. But it was from the last century and had a triple lot with big grassy lawn on either side of the house. Oval cameo windows peered from the north side. An old rose clung to a trellis on the chimney. The green bathroom tile held the charm of a prior era and the hardwood floors could be buffed back to a shine. It beckoned him: Have a family here and grow old watching this oak tree shade the house.

He had barely enough saved for the down payment. He bought the century-old house at 3rd and Oak. His very own three-digit address. Gerald jingled the keys to his new house wishing his old man could see him.

He spent every hour he wasn't at work polishing the place up. The paint inside was shabby and the huge yard was overgrown. He worked for months trying to make it more presentable and falling deeper in love with the crown molding and casement windows. He wanted it to be nicer before he showed it to Hillary.

Finally, he called her. He said how much he'd missed her and asked if he could pick her up. "Please, Hills, I have something to show you," he pleaded.

"What do you mean you bought us a house?" He could tell she was miffed. "Where have you been? You haven't returned my calls for months. This is what you've been doing?"

"Can you even believe it? A family home in the heart of the nicest old neighborhood. Pure class; right downtown." He ushered her in the front door.

It was freezing inside. She crossed her arms and shook her head. "How will you ever heat it with these high ceilings and single-pane windows?"

"Wait'll you see it on a sunny day, Hills. This place really shines. Just needs a little elbow grease." He held her close and whispered in her ear, "Let's make history here."

It was sort of romantic that he'd been trying to build them a future. During her final semester, Hillary went to 3rd and Oak on Saturdays to help Gerald on whatever project he was doing. He called these their dates. She couldn't believe he could live there. Often the kitchen plumbing was on the fritz. She held a flashlight and he banged on the old pipes. Sometimes they drank beer and sanded door jambs so the old doors would latch; other times she pulled weeds while he edged a former flower garden.

~

Even Gerald thought the house was too hot in the summer and he nearly froze there in winter. Hillary's appreciation for the place would grow to match his, it would just take some time. They would have the perfect life there. He told his mom he'd decided to propose.

"Well, what do you like about her? She seems a little snooty to me," his mom said.

"Hillary is special in that she's nothing special," he laughed. "Just pretty enough."

"You mean like that old house you bought yourself." His mom gave him a tired look.

"Nice hands; a good smile. Dad would have liked her. And she's a hard worker. She loves the house just like I do—or she will. She wants to go to graduate school. She's the type a man should marry."

"If you think she's the one, go on ahead."

~

Hillary wasn't exactly sure what kind of work she'd get with her history degree. Anthropology was too much theorizing and guesswork; archaeology was more geology than she cared for. Maybe she'd work at a cultural center and then get a grant to do research. Graduation loomed and she didn't want to move back home. Gerald's proposal caught her off guard.

"I can't marry you. You're already married to that house!" But he was persuasive. He'd bought them a house big enough for the family of four they both wanted. Why not Gerald Kelley?

She crossed the stage and her mother framed her diploma. They married that next fall. She cashiered at the pharmacy downtown and picked up shifts at the public library. The too-high ceilings, stuck windows, and dank basement at 308 Oak were now also hers.

Hillary appreciated the special features in the house, she did. Their wedding china looked good in the glass-front hutch in the formal dining room. She learned the difference between balusters and spindles on the staircase. The three bedrooms were small but there was a nice view from theirs when the leaves fell in autumn. It had once been elegant. She wanted to be proud of it like Gerald. But when her parents visited, she saw she was saddled with a drafty old place and neither the money nor the skill to make it beautiful. She spackled and sanded every weekend and dreamed of a job more suited to her interests.

"I joined the Neighborhood Preservation Committee," she informed Gerald. She had explained to the group her interest wasn't modern times, but her degree was all they heard. She was immediately elected the committee's Historian. The committee's sole focus was to get a Historic District designation to prevent any unwelcome development like they saw in other neighborhoods. It was a years-long process and she took over their application and all its demanding detail.

"Get this," she told Gerald after her fourth committee meeting, "Mr. Wilson over on Second and Ash, the one with the Studebaker out back? And all the azaleas? He used to live here. Grew up in this house. His grandfather built it or did the kitchen addition on the back—after their *seventh* kid! Can you imagine? With only three bedrooms? We should have him over. I bet he knows a lot of the house's story."

"Maybe after we get a little further on the remodeling," Gerald said, digging a sliver from his finger.

Gerald hoped for a family right away, but Hillary hadn't gotten pregnant when they planned. Maybe it was for the best. They pecked away at the house's many projects and got the nursery ready.

Finally, their first, Gretchen, came along. They were now a family. He was happy until he realized how foul-tempered a little thing like that could be. Then came feisty Shelburne.

"I really can't live in this project and keep the kids safe, Gerald," Hillary said for the umpteenth time. "Gretchen is running around; Shelburne is crawling. You've got to finish this place or hire someone who will."

Sure, there were tools in some corners. Pry bars, hammers, and levels needed to be in reach when he found a few minutes to work on something. Nothing was painted, but nearly all the woodwork was fully restored. He wanted it to look perfect. After he painted, he'd buff the hardwood floors. He was so close.

Timmy's surprise arrival shocked him; at least he was a placid kid. Somehow, there they were with three kids instead of what Gerald thought was a more respectable number, like two.

"These closets are a joke, Ger. This whole drafty place is too small." Hillary seemed to resent every little thing about the house. "Maybe families in the late 1800s lived on top of one another, but I don't want to. No storage in the kitchen. The draft from the fireplace. And that dark basement. The kids can't play down there. This isn't working. It's time we moved."

"But the triple lot," he argued. "Where would you get big shade trees on a corner lot in suburbia? And that's full dimension timber in those floor joists. Not the crap they use these days. I know it's gone slower than we thought, but look at these leaded windows. We're lucky to have this place."

"Well, it seems like you're more interested in golfing on weekends than doing the list of projects here." Gerald thought she was just weepy after another baby. She would get over it.

WHEN TIMMY TURNED THREE, HILLARY INSISTED THEY FIND ANOTHER PLACE. She circled listings in the newspaper and left them on the kitchen table. "We're both exhausted by this place. You're just too stubborn to admit it."

"Fine. I'll go look at a couple places with you," he grumbled one Friday morning. On Saturday they left the kids with Hillary's parents and drove to a development he'd never heard of.

"This is the best new neighborhood." Her foot tapped in excitement. "See, this one has *four* bedrooms and two baths." She navigated him past several identical houses.

"Good God, Hills, these places have no charm. The lots are small. No front porch. Four- and five-digit addresses. You can't be serious."

"Look, Ger. You picked the wrong house, and now I'm going to pick one that's right for us. The schools out here are more modern. These newer places are actually bigger *and* cheaper."

"But what's that compared to a house with a past?"

"Our kids don't have anyone to play with. Our neighbors are all old."

"What are old people but history? I thought you liked history?"

Hillary rounded up a realtor, a guy named Spence, and brought him to see about selling 3rd and Oak. "It looks like the upkeep has just been too much with a growing family. You'll have to do some sprucing up to sell. Obviously, all new paint. Warm colors are popular. A sunny yellow will brighten up this out-of-date kitchen. Maybe that will make buyers overlook that there's no dishwasher. Shame there's only one bathroom."

Gerald slumped. He'd thought they were as planted as the oak out front.

"I'll take care of everything, Ger. It's going to be great," Hillary made a schedule. The painters started work in the living room.

"God, it looks great," he admitted. "Fresh and bright. We always knew the place needed a coat of paint. Maybe that's all it needs, eh?" Gerald admired the new sheen on the fireplace mantel and windowsills.

"Don't touch that, Ger. Oil paint needs a couple days to dry."

"Well, let's see what we think after they're done painting, Hills. No need to rush into selling it." Hillary shook her head.

That Saturday, to escape the paint fumes, they spent the night at Hillary's parents' house.

The house at 308 Oak caught fire and burned.

To the ground.

Something about rags and mineral spirits used with the oil paint. Freak accident.

"Oh, God, no." Hillary covered her mouth in shock looking at the smoldering wreck. "What if we'd been home?" She and Gerald huddled the children to them.

"Once these old wooden structures catch fire," the Fire Chief told them that morning, "it's hard to stop it." The chimney still stood. And the kitchen at the back of the house. But it was gone. All that was left were some pots and pans. Gerald wiped his eyes as their neighbors, Lynette and Bart, came by. "If there's anything we can do," they said.

The big oak tree was singed but still stood. The painter's insurance covered most of the loss. A new house was no longer a choice.

Spence helped them sell the ruin on the triple lot. Three months later, in spite of neighbors' objections, an apartment building was going up. Part of the city's economic-opportunity zone plans.

"I thought someone would rebuild a lovely family home," Gerald said when Hillary told him the news. The neighbors on the Preservation Committee were furious.

BY THEN THEY WERE SETTLED INTO THEIR BIGGER HOUSE THAT WOULD NEVER catch the eye of a preservationist. There were no trees to speak of, but kids of all sizes rode bikes and bounced balls. The curved streets and cul-de-sacs around the new house made no sense to Gerald. Why were the garages at the front? The new neighbors all seemed a bit self-satisfied. He disliked the new place as much as Hillary and the kids loved it. Could he help it if he retreated to golf and scotch?

"Nothing says you've given up like five digits at the edge of civilization," Gerald moaned on.

Hillary shook her head. "We all made it out alive. The kids are out there playing with their new friends. Let's be happy here."

"If you'd just been satisfied, we wouldn't be in this situation." He swirled the ice in his scotch and stared at her.

"We even had the dog with us, Ger. We're the luckiest people on earth."

Gerald didn't feel the least bit lucky. He started driving by their old corner once a week. The grid of the streets had an elegant geometry, numbers one direction, tree-named streets crossing them. A dark brick structure rose from the ashes of his dream. It was charmless, angular, out of place. The workers were done and people were moving in. If only they'd stayed put.

One evening he couldn't resist seeing the new apartment building up close. It was nearly dark. Walking around it confirmed it was a monster, a scar on an otherwise beautiful street. As he skulked back to his car, he ran into their former neighbors, Lynette and Bart.

"What brings you to this part of town, stranger?" Bart asked.

"Oh, just looking at the progress here."

"Call that progress?" Bart hacked a harsh laugh. "How does an eyesore like that end up in a neighborhood of beautiful Georgian and colonial houses? They put the damned thing up in, what, six months? And to top it off, the City said it had to be brick since your house burned."

Gerald toed a seam in the sidewalk.

"We miss you folks," Lynette said. "Why don't you and Hillary meet us at Angelo's for dinner? Next week? We'd love to catch up."

On the way to their favorite Italian place in the old neighborhood, Gerald drove Hillary by 3rd and Oak. "Just so you know what our legacy looks like."

"It's not what I pictured." Hillary said. "Could it be any less... appealing?" They rode the rest of the way in silence.

"Tell us about your new home," Lynette said after they were seated and their drinks arrived.

"Yes, can't say I know your part of town." Bart lifted his eyebrows at Lynette. "What's it like?"

"It's not terribly gorgeous," Gerald said.

"But we love all the room," Hillary jumped in, "and the schools are just what we needed."

Gerald wondered again if she really couldn't see what they'd lost. "We're saving some money, though, compared to all the maintenance costs back at the old house," he said. "Hillary's got a big trip planned for us."

"It's good for the children to see the world while they're young," Hillary said. "Expands their minds to see history."

"That's ironic," Bart muttered into his napkin.

Gerald shrugged and flagged the waitress for another scotch.

"Well, you're not the most popular folks on Oak Street," Bart said. "That new building is unsightly. None of the neighbors on Oak can park in front of their own house anymore. Twelve apartments, if you can believe it. All strangers."

Gerald swirled his glass. "Sorry about all the—"

"Our *home* was lost," Hillary steamed. "*All* the kids' toys. Our furniture. All the time and sweat we put into the place. All our *photos* and my grandmother's dishes."

Gerald put his hand on her wrist.

"Yes. Yes, of course." Bart stabbed his spaghetti. "Very sad. Don't mean to sound unsympathetic." They all scraped their plates. "Seems like it killed old Wilson," Bart started in again. "He grew up there, you know."

"Yes, we heard he'd passed." Gerald looked at Hillary who was fond of the guy.

"Might sound strange from a history major, but I find it odd how people cling to something historic but shun the present." Gerald wondered if she'd had too much wine. "I mean, trees fall down. New ones are planted. Old homes burn. Dynasties fall. It's just life." He didn't think the neighbors would invite them out again.

Gerald went by the apartment most days on his way home. He'd park near Second and see who came and went from the building. He sipped from a flask he kept in the glove compartment and remembered coming to this neighborhood with his dad.

He was fixated on the corner unit on the ground floor. The guy he glimpsed in the window looked about Gerald's age, late thirties. What would it be like to still live in the heart of town? To play records and wear jeans?

Gerald went to work and got drinks with the guys from the office a couple nights a week. Besides that, and golf some Sundays, his main entertainment was sitting and watching things at 3rd and Oak. When he asked himself what he was doing there, he wasn't sure. Some people took flowers to the cemetery. Maybe he was just paying his respects.

~

Hillary was aware she'd traded her grad school dream for coordinating their children's soccer practices and play dates. She worked half-time at the pharmacy, but with no house projects looming over their heads, she felt unburdened. She volunteered at the library and one night a month she dined with six other ladies at Book Group. Though she preferred biographies, she read the historical novels the group liked. She was making new friends.

They talked about the flute tutor at school and the new soccer coach. Then Sheila asked Beth, a mom who lived a few streets from Hillary, about her family vacation to Ireland.

"I used to complain about how many times on a trip Bob would slink off for a drink. Or go for a smoke and be gone an hour. I felt trapped. Now, when I feel like they're taking me for granted, I ditch my family for a day. A vacation vacation. It's an absolute must for family trips. Usually near the end, when they're fed up with my itineraries," Beth laughed.

"You're kidding!" Hillary was stunned. Beth seemed so devoted and patient. Hillary swigged the rest of her wine. Fat chance she'd ever skip out for a day on family vacation. She couldn't wait for her family's upcoming travels—she'd dreamed of a trip to Europe for years.

She planned a trip to Spain for their winter break. Timmy was in kindergarten; Shelburne was in second grade. Gretchen was nine and resented that she couldn't bring a friend. Hillary insisted this was a family trip.

~

After six days in Spain with three kids under ten, Gerald was about done in. Their hotel was low-ceilinged and dark. Hillary's tour guides dragged them all over. "You didn't want to drive in a foreign country," she snapped when Gerald complained.

"Yeah, but enough Roman ruins and Muslim-era bath houses, eh, Hills? It's too hot. I like to be cold in winter." The sunshine and orange trees were getting under his skin. He couldn't get a decent burger anywhere. And Hillary's tight schedule of sightseeing meant he couldn't sneak away for a round of golf. Three days left of this endless trip. When the kids were bathed and ready for bed, Hillary was going over the next day's agenda of palaces and churches. "I think I'll pop down to the hotel bar and see if scotch tastes like it should in Seville," he said. "I've got my room key."

A gust of air shushed Hillary as the door closed behind him.

THE NEXT MORNING THEY WERE EATING THE HOTEL'S COMPLIMENTARY *desayuno*: a shapeless croissant and too-small coffee. "Can't believe they call this a breakfast," Gerald groused as he had every morning of the trip. "It's not bad enough the shower barely gets hot?"

"Okay, gang." Hillary smiled. She'd tossed and turned all night. She felt sweat on her upper lip from a new excitement. She closed the guidebook and tucked it into her bag. "I'll be back this afternoon. Everyone, remember your sun hat if you decide to go out."

"What's that supposed to mean?" Gerald rubbed his sunburned neck.

"I thought we were going to see a big church or something," Gretchen said.

Hillary stood and gathered her bag. "I realize I've been selfish asking you all to do the things I'm interested in." She tried to sound calm though her stomach was jumpy. "We're all ready for some exploration of our own." She put the map into her bag. "Gerald, you've got your room key? The other guidebooks are up there, if you want them. See you all back here around five."

Gerald's mouth was ajar. She waved and floated out of the lobby.

What a day. Seville was gorgeous. She was studying—not just seeing

—the Giralda Tower. The former minaret, completed in 1195, was converted to a bell tower in the fourteen hundreds. She was not dragging along a hung-over Gerald and her sparring children. Every step held some part of the history she'd devoured in college.

When she rejoined them that night, the children were scowling. "Dad didn't let us go anywhere," Shelburne said.

"We got ice creams," Timmy cuddled next to Hillary.

"It's *helado*, doofus," Gretchen said. "There's a difference."

"Why the hell didn't you get us a hotel with a pool?" Gerald swirled a scotch in his hand.

"My day was fabulous!" Hillary said. "I ate tapas in an absolutely ancient place. For two glasses of wine, I got six little dishes: olives, bread with ham, these darling spears of friend eggplant covered in honey! I couldn't eat it all. I'm just going to have a little nap before we go to dinner. You all decide what you'd like tonight."

She closed the hotel bedroom door behind her.

That evening, they wandered the wide plaza amidst a crowd of locals and other tourists. They looked at Christmas stalls and Hillary talked them into a horse carriage ride. Bells jingled on the reins. A string quartet played between the ornate north and south towers.

"Look where we are, kids." Hillary's gaze swept out over the plaza ignoring Gerald who was in a pout. Families strolled; elegant streetlamps reflected in the grand fountain. The mild evening held the day's last warmth. "What better Christmas gift is there than this view? We're here together. We've seen a new country, *and* we have a nice home to go back to—"

"You mean we *had* a nice house. It burned down, as you may recall." Gerald didn't look at her.

Hillary scowled. "That was really sad. Not just for you, you know. But we were lucky to find a new home that fits us well. The kids are surrounded by new friends. Part of the fun of travel is that we're all going to be excited to get home." Good God, when was he going to let it go?

∼

Back at home, they pulled together their late Christmas. "Our tree always looked so much better at the old house," Gerald said to Hillary.

She shook her head. "Are you blind? The kids made all these snowflakes. And this is where *they* will remember Christmas. Not the old place. Time moves on. Why can't you?"

He threw on his coat and stamped into his boots. "I've got some Christmas shopping to do." He drove downtown where a few shops were advertising after-Christmas sales. He found a board for Shelly's new coin collection. Soccer was Timmy's thing, so he got him some shinguards. Gretchen couldn't stop talking about getting a horse. He bought her a book of stories about real horsewomen, and got a book for Hillary, *Spanish Colonial Impact: Middle Ages to Renaissance.* She would chew on that all year.

He stopped at 3rd and Oak on his way home. The guy's silhouette in the ground-floor window flickered in light from a television. No tree. No Christmas lights.

Gerald pulled out his flask but it was empty. He would go to the liquor store on the way home. He supposed their Christmas tree at home was okay. The kids made their own ornaments at school and loved hanging them. And now that he'd built a putting green in the corner of their rec room he could practice during the winter. The kids liked to challenge him three-on-one with their little golf clubs.

He was freezing and the windshield had frosted over. He scrubbed at it but couldn't see anything. He needed to get home. Their house was always warm. Dinner would be ready. He cranked the key in the ignition, but it didn't turn over. He was shivering. Worry prickled his armpits. "Come on, dammit." He tried several times; it was no good. He was stuck.

"Idiot." He pounded his fist on the steering wheel. Here he was, Mr. Auto Parts exec, sitting with a dead battery on a frozen street pining for a home that had never been warm enough. Even with a fire in the fireplace, 3rd and Oak had been miserably drafty. And they'd lost it in fire. "Dammit all."

He tightened his coat against the cold and walked a few blocks downtown. Nothing was open. No service station. Not a phone booth anywhere. He shambled back to his car. What he wouldn't give to get home and sit by their gas fireplace.

The TV was the only light in that corner apartment. It seemed the guy hadn't moved. Gerald let out a deep breath and went through the front door of the building. There was a bad smell in the hallway, fish cooking or cat box, he wasn't sure. He heard the theme song from *Cheers* as he knocked on the door.

The guy who opened it was tall and his skin looked gray in the TV light. His clothes were baggy. His sofa had seen better days. Milk crates held up a bookshelf. Gerald shuddered.

"Hi, sorry to bug you," he said. "I, um, my car out front won't start. Any chance you could give me a jump?"

"I wish I could, man. But I've only got a bike these days. Can't exactly do landscaping this time of year."

He couldn't call any of their old neighbors. Dread settled on his shoulders. He had to call Hillary. But then she'd know he was in his ice-cold car in the old neighborhood while the family made Christmas at home.

"Could I use your phone then? To call home? My wife can come with jumper cables."

"Sure. C'mon in."

Hillary sounded baffled when he told her where he was parked.

"How do you like the place?" Gerald asked the guy waiting for her to arrive. "Nice tree out front."

"Well, it's hard to get any peace when people are always coming and going. Kids thump around upstairs. Next door the radio blares big band music all day. Not ideal."

All those hours he'd spent wishing he was still here. Then griping about their new house. What if Hillary got fed up with him and he landed in a place like this? The laugh track on *Cheers* jarred. "Nice neighborhood, though," he tried again.

"Neighbors couldn't be less friendly," the guy said. In the kitchen, dishes were piled in the sink, a can of chili stood with the lid open. Gerald thought of the ham dinner Hillary was making for them. The lights on their tree.

Hillary was there in twenty minutes. The kids waited in her car while he jumped his battery. She looked at the apartment building and then at him, clasping her gloved hands.

"I can't really explain it," he said, while they let his car charge. She shook her head and rubbed her arms for warmth.

"I'll see you at *home*." She got in her car and drove away.

He planned to stop at the liquor store, but instead went to the supermarket near the new house. He got champagne to share with his wife. Poinsettias were two for one, so he bought four. Why not?

He wheeled up to their five-digit, split-level house and walked in carrying a bottle of bubbly, his bag of gifts, and a ridiculous armful of tropical plants. Dinner smelled amazing. Hillary and the kids were decorating sugar cookies. He set down the plants and switched on the gas fire.

Timmy ran up to him grinning, holding out a tree cookie, green frosting above his lip. "Daddy, you're home!"

Gerald shrugged off his coat and took the cookie. "Yes, kiddo, I'm home."

JUST DO IT

SUSAN KRAUS

Elke sat at her living room window, sipping chai tea, wondering if this would be the day that she'd find the courage—the will—to "just do it." The window looked out over 3rd Street, but she could see all the way down to Oak. The neighborhood had once been on the road to gentrification, old buildings being torn down and new high-rises built on their footprint. But the virus hit hard, and investments in high-rises had stalled.

Most of the prior tenants had already been railroaded out by steep rent increases, so the building had, instead, been retrofitted into rent-controlled senior housing. Nothing fancy, but the apartments had new windows, and shiny tile and handicap-accessible showers in the bathrooms. The kitchens were modernized with granite countertops and double sinks. The front doors had been replaced and tricked out with a fob entry, and the foyer walls painted bright blue with crisp white trim. Little had been done to improve the exterior, and it remained an unappealing building, resembling the squat block-style that mushroomed after WWII in Soviet-occupied countries.

That very squatness felt familiar to Elke. It was the housing of her childhood in East Germany when housing was to "house" people, like barns are to house animals. The bare minimum was done, no room for aesthetics. So much of her country had been bombed to ashes that people were desperate for a few rooms that they did not have to share with strangers, a few rooms to be a family. But inside, this apartment was much nicer: high ceilings, shiny wooden floors, large windows that opened at night so she could have a cross-breeze. That was—to use the American expression—gravy.

Elke looked down at the street as she waited for the day to begin. It was like a curtain coming up for a play, shrouded darkness lifting so that mundane, daily life could begin. Over and over. And over. And over.

First would come men heading out for early shifts at their jobs. They often carried black bags of trash, depositing them in the large metal trash bins. Then, the shopkeepers would appear, lifting the bars that they'd pulled down at closing to cover display windows, opening their doors, sweeping their front walks. There were fewer shops than a year ago, but a small grocer, a pharmacy, a coffee shop, and hole-in-the-wall restaurants remained. Farther down was a liquor store and what locals called the "China shop." This China shop was stuffed to the ceilings with bits of everything. Walk in and ask for something, and, amazingly, one of the Zhangs—there were three generations—would nod, disappear for two minutes, then present it. Or nimbly climb a ladder and toss it down.

Some shopkeepers lived above their shops, and many other apartments, up long staircases, were tucked into the third and fourth stories. Even above empty shops with "For Lease" signs in their windows, the apartments showed lights and movement.

About eight a.m., the street doors that opened to the staircases leading to upper apartments would all open, as if on cue, and children tumble out in gaggles to walk to school. An elementary school was just four blocks away, a high school seven. A middle school was in another direction, but no more than eight blocks away. This was city life. Cars were a luxury, and few people drove their kids to school. Parents walked them, or older siblings hurried along the younger ones.

This was the first time that Elke had ever lived alone. She'd lived with her parents until she and Juergen had married. Their first apartment had been smaller than the living room of the one she now lived in.

By the time their children had been born, they'd bought a brownstone in Brooklyn, the mortgage paid for over twenty-five years. It had a basement flat with a separate entrance that they'd rented out, often for years at a time, to single professional women or a couple in the early years of marriage.

Their children had been given American names: Robert and Melissa. Their names made it less obvious that their parents were from Germany and spoke with accents that they had not been able to lose no matter how much they practiced, despite hours of listening to the television and repeating dialogue out loud.

Robert and Melissa had been born when Elke was in her late thirties, an age when many of her former peers back in Germany, but also peers here in New Jersey, had teenagers. Elke and Juergen raised them to think for themselves, to be suspicious of power, respectful and deferential with law enforcement, cautious with anyone new. Trust was only to be given after it had been earned.

Robert now lived in London, working for an international corporation, doing something called IT. Melissa lived with another woman whom Elke had thought was a friend and roommate, but who was soon to become Melissa's wife. Melissa worked tirelessly for a non-profit dedicated to teaching children how they could make a difference with climate change.

Elke's children had achieved their parents' goals for them: To be free to make choices, to be educated, to live in a democracy, and to live without fear. They were launched, engaged with their own lives. That was what mattered.

Elke missed Juergen. Missed him with a gut-twisting longing that could take her breath away. She'd used that expression, an American figure of speech, over the years. "Oh, it took my breath away," she'd said about a sunset, or a musical performance, or a magnificent view. But then it was just words, not an accurate description of a physical phenomenon. Now, there were times when she felt a drowning sensation, like there was not enough air to keep breathing; not enough air to live.

The episodes were unpredictable, triggered by a smell, a taste, an accidental touch. The first attack—diagnosed by the ER doctor as a panic attack, not a heart attack—had happened in a grocery store, buying grapes. Juergen had loved grapes, especially black grapes and red grapes, not the green ones. He would eat them one by one, savoring their sweetness, closing his eyes as he crushed them with his tongue.

"What are you thinking, Juergen, when you are eating a grape?" Elke had once asked him.

"I'm not thinking, *mein Liebchen*. I'm eating a grape as I would have eaten a grape as a little boy *if* we'd had grapes," he'd answered. "With gratitude and amazement." Food in post-war East Germany had been limited. Potatoes and…well, whatever could be scrounged to go with potatoes.

That was Juergen. While Elke was pragmatic to the point of pessimism, Juergen lived each day as a gift, a blessing. And, as he sometimes had to remind her, each day was a gift. They'd escaped East Germany at a time when most attempting to escape were shot, killed, or worse.

Elke had grown up in Dresden. She'd met Juergen there when she was twenty-two, working in a hospital as a nursing assistant. He was starting his medical residency. He'd grown up in Görlitz, which had miraculously escaped bombing.

Looking back, and second guessing, which Elke often did, it might have been better to relocate within Europe. But she and Juergen had been fixated on America ever since John F. Kennedy had visited West Berlin and made a speech at the Berlin Wall. June 26, 1963. It had been Elke's thirteenth birthday. *"Ich bin ein Berliner,"* Kennedy had said. *"Ich bin ein Berliner."* Elke had whispered, *"Ich bin ein Americanerin."*

Late one night, when she and Juergen were first surreptitiously dating—achieved despite all the rules, curfews, and surveillance—they shared how they'd each listened to JFK's speech. For each, it had been on a prohibited radio broadcast: Elke in a friend's basement; Juergen in the woods with two friends. Neither had told their parents of the risks they had taken.

Fourteen years after *"Ich bin ein Berliner,"* by then married, Juergen finished with his medical training and a became hospital physician, a surgeon, but Elke—barred from higher education for reasons never known—still working as a nursing assistant, they'd made the momentous decision to escape. Juergen understood that he would not be able to practice medicine in the United States, not unless he could pass the exams in English, not unless the American Medical Association approved his medical education. He knew his education in East Germany was not comparable. Juergen understood all of that. But they had no choice.

Juergen had been informed that he was about to be "recruited" to serve in Verkutlag, a Soviet Gulag one hundred and sixty miles above the Arctic Circle. It was a five-year posting, no spouses or families allowed. Juergen knew he would not survive five years in Vorkutag, even as staff and not as a prisoner. Bad things were done to people, and he would be ordered to be complicit or face consequences. He knew of no one who had returned from such an assignment.

So, they'd left with nothing but their ID papers, educational certificates, and some photos buried deep within two small valises of summer, holiday clothing, a couple on a brief farewell holiday. Juergen had gotten forged papers for them to travel to Burgas, in Bulgaria, on the Black Sea. It was near the Turkish border. A cousin had given him the name of a fisherman who might help them. At every rail checkpoint, as armed guards walked through the train, they'd had their papers ready, trying to look respectful but unconcerned. The fisherman had wanted more money than they had, than they would ever have, but they'd put together a pile of their watches, wedding rings, Elke's grandmother's jewelry. Everything of marketable value was given. But it was their only hope. There was no going back. The journey in the small open fishing boat took twelve hours, in darkness and rough seas. But they made it close to Istanbul, dumped in an unknown location on a beach in a country they'd never been to, with a language they could not speak.

They'd left without telling their parents or friends, without any goodbyes. It was better for families to know nothing, to be able to emphatically disown their disloyal and reckless children to the police, while privately praying for their safety.

IT WAS ALMOST A YEAR BEFORE THEY WERE SPONSORED BY A CHURCH GROUP in New York and approved to enter the United States. A year in limbo, waiting, hoping. Elke and Juergen found an apartment in New Jersey, across the Hudson River from New York City. Rents were cheaper there. Elke got a job at a nursing home.

After a year, once she'd improved her English, she began courses in a local community college working toward an LPN license. Another year later, she segued into a program to be a RN. She worked seven a.m. to three p.m., then took classes three evenings a week. When it came time for her full-time clinical rotations, she waitressed on weekends, only then discovering that she could make more money from tips than full-time as a nurses' aide.

Juergen found work in a hospital, but it became too frustrating to do menial labor when he'd been a physician. Some of his doctor-coworkers wanted to help, offered recommendations, encouraged him to go to school at a community college to be an EMT, or an X-Ray Technician. But every day in the hospital, not being able to do the work he'd been educated to do, trained to do, was too painful. He looked for other jobs, trying to have an open mind. He finally found work translating journal articles, many of them medical, into German. He studied the nuances of editing, of translating. He was able to rise in the company to be an editor, to translate entire books, to supervise other editors.

The Berlin Wall fell on November 9, 1989, and East and West Germany were reunited on October 3, 1990. For Elke and Juergen, 11/9 would always mean more than 9/11.

IMMEDIATELY AFTER THE REUNIFICATION, FLIGHTS TO EAST GERMANY WERE flooded with people desperate to see and hug the families they had not seen for decades, but for Elke and Juergen it was too late. Their parents had died: her parents in a bus crash; his mother when protesting in the

Peaceful Revolution a year before reunification. His father had died from war injuries when Juergen was just fourteen months old.

But that, all of it, so much, was decades ago. It was as if it had happened to other people in other lives.

Elke was now seventy-four. Juergen would have been almost eighty. He'd died of Covid two years ago, in 2022, when the height of the pandemic crisis had passed, when vaccinations were available, when everyone was starting to relax. He'd been ill for a week when the second round of vaccines became available. Juergen could not be vaccinated when ill. He told Elke to go get the vaccine and he would get it in a few weeks. But he didn't make it. Elke could never know if his initial congestion had been early Covid—or if she'd brought Covid home with her after waiting in line to get vaccinated, and then letting her guard down to stroll in the city, enjoying the sunshine and the illusion of safety. She never became symptomatic.

When Juergen got really sick, when his breathing became labored, she pushed him to go to the hospital. But he resisted. He was still a doctor. He knew the odds. He knew he was dying. He did not want to die on a respirator, alone, without Elke beside him. "I'm seventy-eight," he said to her. "We have survived so much. I will survive or I will die, but I want you with me no matter which. Please understand."

Juergen died in the bedroom of their brownstone, after just six days. At the end, Elke had given him every possible pill they had that would help him not suffer: leftover pain pills from when he'd had a hip replacement, anti-anxiety medication that her doctor had prescribed when she had been unable to sleep, OTC sleep and pain meds. She'd ground up the pills and mixed them in a dark, hot coffee that Juergen loved, adding an abundance of sugar and cream. Juergen had sipped it from a delicate teacup in her hand, his head cradled in her other arm, looking into her eyes with gratitude.

Some hours after Juergen died, after holding his hand and touching his face until the warmth had left it, Elke called a neighbor. Initially unsettled at the request, perhaps because Elke shared that Juergen's dead body was in the next room, the friend hastily recommended a funeral home. Within hours, the funeral home came, and respectfully took Juergen's body away to be cremated.

In the past, an autopsy would have been done. But so many people had died at home from Covid, and Juergen was almost eighty. Elke gave them the contact information for his physician who could verify that he'd had Covid although they'd just had a Zoom appointment. The physician had directed him to go to the ER.

For almost a year after Juergen died, Elke stayed in the brownstone. Juergen's ashes were on a bookcase in the living room. She did not consider moving. They did not have many long-term friends, but they had neighbors. They'd never joined a church, which was how many people found community. In many ways, they'd been enough for each other.

FOR A FEW MONTHS, ELKE DID LITTLE, LIFE ON HOLD, AS IF WAITING FOR A sign. But there was no sign. Their children asked about having a small memorial for Juergen but Robert needed to schedule around his work. Melissa's wedding had been postponed, no date set, but Elke did not know why. "I can come anytime, Mom," she'd texted. "Whatever works best for Robert. And we can get it organized."

Neither Robert nor Melissa had been able to say goodbye to their father in person. They wanted a memorial for closure. It was to be a Celebration of Life, so very American. They chose a restaurant, with catered food set on tables along one wall. They had photos of Juergen and the family rotating on a screen, and music playing that they remembered he'd liked. It was all their memories of Juergen when he was *der vater*. He'd been such a good father, this man who'd never had a father. He'd tried to please them, to connect with them, by putting on music they enjoyed, watching movies they enjoyed. He did not impose his preferences on them.

Her children's friends were invited, and many came, but only some that Elke had ever met. Neighbors and his co-workers were invited as well, but his death had been months before. It was as if he was already forgotten. A few came, but more sent regrets. Some never responded.

When Juergen died, she'd received cards from his co-workers and from neighbors. Many said how sorry they were that Joe had died and hoped that Ellie would find comfort knowing Joe was at peace. They offered their prayers and condolences.

It had hit her then that none of them had even known their real names, although that wasn't their fault. Juergen and Elke had adopted American 'short-cut' names when it became clear that their names were too foreign: they'd be spelling them out letter-by-letter and correcting pronunciation for decades if they kept them.

So, Elke had become Ellie. Juergen had become Joe.

AFTER THE MEMORIAL, ELKE FELT UNHINGED. SHE DID NOT HAVE A FAITH TO provide solace. There was nothing to hold on to. The brownstone echoed with memories, and the very emptiness felt loud. One day, reading the local newspaper, she saw an article about senior housing, back across the Hudson, and a building that was being renovated into rent-controlled apartments for seniors. Applications were available online. Elke clicked on the link and completed one.

She and Juergen's retirement plan had been based on two Social Security checks. They'd read articles and talked with helpful people at the Social Security office, so they knew what to expect. When they retired, the brownstone had been paid for. But they'd needed the two checks to cover the taxes, which were inordinate, and repairs and living expenses.

The brownstone was big, three stories high, with long, narrow staircases. It was her home, but without Juergen, it was too much. He'd been the one to handle minor repairs. When they needed an honest plumber or electrician, he'd talked to co-workers.

Elke did not need the space. The fantasies that she and Juergen had occasionally indulged, about grandchildren coming to stay with them for a month in the summers, about holidays with their children—and their spouses and the imaginary grandchildren—had not happened yet. And might not ever. And that was okay. She did not need to be a grandmother without Juergen. She did not even want their dreams without him to share them.

Elke met with an intake manager to get more information on the senior apartments. The rent, calculated on her Social Security—now adjusted to the higher amount that had been Juergen's social security—would be less than she paid in taxes for a year on the brownstone. A lot less. Elke did not understand why the rent was based solely on her income and not her savings. But she was not about to question such a gift.

Abruptly, her decision was made. She would sell the house. The worry of upkeep, and fixing things, even maintaining their small garden, would be gone. She signed a lease for a year, starting in four months when the building's renovations would be complete. She chose a corner apartment from a drawing, with two-bedrooms. She wanted an extra room in case her children did come to visit.

The brownstone sold quickly for six times what they'd paid for it decades earlier. The figure, which the perky real estate agent explained had been reached after a bidding war among three applicants, had, for a moment, 'taken her breath away.'

The tenant in the basement apartment, Beth-Ann, a widow herself, but younger, still working, could remain, at her current rent, for three years. Elke and Beth-Ann had discussed her situation. In three years, she intended to retire and relocate to be near a daughter. Elke had worried that having such a condition might block a sale, but obviously not.

Elke put the proceeds in a trust, although not irrevocable in case her circumstances changed. It would go to her children and any grandchildren. It was far more than she and Juergen ever dreamed they could give. She resolved to not tell her children about the trust, not yet. Inheritances could interfere with developing self-sufficiency.

The next few months passed quickly, every day with one appointment or another. Real estate agents and estate sale decisions, attorneys for making a new will, setting up the trust and learning how to mitigate inheritance taxes for her children. Somewhere in there, Elke decided to give some of the proceeds to a few causes. Immigrant services, mostly, like free classes in English for new immigrants. Writing those checks gave her great satisfaction and she imagined Juergen smiling.

Elke took a month to de-clutter, to carefully choose which of her possessions she wanted to bring to her much smaller apartment. Which, as it turned out, were almost none. She felt little attachment to her old things. She found herself considering leaving it all, starting fresh. Not because she liked newness but because anything new would be…anonymous? No memories attached? Like a hotel room that one finds comfortable, appealing even, yet nothing she would have to think about taking with her.

The more she considered this, the clearer it became. Hiring a moving company was a larger expense than replacing everything. And Elke was nothing if not frugal.

"Frugal to a fault," Juergen had told her, more a lecture, however needed. "You cannot taste money, like you can a splendid meal that makes you moan with pleasure. Money has no texture to feel, like silk or velvet. Money cannot appreciate beauty or delight in new experiences. Money is useless unless it is used, for security and basic needs, of course, but also to purchase joy and adventure. Money can create memories. Alone it is merely paper and metal. Money must be spent to appreciate its value."

It had been a long speech for Juergen. But Elke remembered every word, his sincerity. It had always been hard for her to spend, impossible to spend without worry. But with Juergen gone, she felt regret for her frugality. In the end, all those hours of clipping coupons, of seeking out sales, the chronic anxiety she'd felt at every wasted dollar, meant nothing.

Elke took photos of every room and sent them to Robert and Melissa. She asked them to choose whatever they wanted from the house and that she would put those pieces in a storage unit until they could get them. She did not think they would want much. They had shown little interest in the past and had rather definite tastes of their own.

They'd been more concerned about her than upset when she'd told them she was selling the house. They worried that she was acting impulsively, out of depression, and would regret the move. They asked if she wanted assistance, and if she had someone to provide money management. Elke explained that there were some retirement accounts with Edward Jones, she had an attorney, and that she did not need assistance but would call if she did.

Elke decided she'd take her favorite easy chair, two bookcases, and just enough books to fill them. Some clothing. Juergen's favorite sweater, a cardigan that was now her robe. And some of their art: paintings they had chosen together or given each other; pottery; artifacts collected on family vacations. The rest would be sold at an estate sale to be organized by someone the real estate agent suggested. All of it. Elke would not make any decisions about furnishing the apartment until the building was ready to move into. And then she would sit in her easy chair, thinking and reading, in that empty space. Simply wait and see what happened in her head.

In the end, she'd gone to an IKEA for a day, walking slowly, stopping at every section, testing chairs and mattresses and couches for comfort, sized to fit *her* legs and *her* comfort, not Juergen's much longer and larger body, taking notes on and photos of what she was considering. She'd stopped for lunch, Swedish meatballs as always, to methodically review the list. She'd walked through again, looking for what she might have missed. By four p.m., she'd purchased it all, exactly what was needed for a woman alone. No excess. It was delivered to her apartment, and assembled by two cheerful young men in blue shirts. She'd ordered pizzas and root beer for them from the pizzeria down the street. As soon as the bed was assembled, she'd put on the new sheets and comforter, fluffed the new pillows. She'd unpacked the boxes and put away dishes and cutlery, pots and pans.

The total had been, just as she'd calculated, far less than the cost of a moving company.

The apartment was only seven blocks from where she and Juergen had lived when they first came to America. Walking, she'd found pockets of the familiar, but much had been erased with new construction. Decades had passed since they'd first explored these streets, hand-in-hand, numb from what they'd risked, determined to create a new life. They'd left everything behind. They'd had only themselves.

Elke now sat, every morning, in her chair by the big window. Each morning, she asked herself if this would be the day to "just *do* it." To move on. To take the rest of the hoarded pills in her own cup of sweetened coffee.

After Juergen died, the pull had been strong. But she couldn't burden her children with having to sort through decades of things, to sort out finances, to be pulled from their lives because she had chosen to exit her life. It would be much simpler for them now. She had, to use the American phrase, "settled her affairs."

The pull had lessened. Then she hadn't been able to imagine life without Juergen. Now she didn't try. She awakened, slipped into his sweater, made her tea, and sat. She watched the people go about their lives. She showered and dressed. She walked alone for two hours a day, stopping to buy just enough food for one day. She'd stopped looking at prices, buying for each day as if it were her last. One perfect piece of steak, or one freshly caught fish. One shiny apple. A small chunk of Brie. A loaf of still warm bread. Irish butter. French pastry. Belgian chocolates. British teas. Panamanian coffee.

Yes, her cupboards were mostly empty, her refrigerator almost so. But that was the incentive to go out. Hunger as motivation. One day at a time. Breathe. Walk. Listen. Taste. See.

But the question required an answer. It was a daily decision. She had the pills. She could choose to "just do it" on any random day.

Another question had been popping up in her head: "What do I *want* today?" Her entire life, Elke had debated that question, demanding that the Elke who '*wanted*' have justifiable reasons for whatever she wanted, while the worried, frugal Elke presented reasons why whatever was *wanted* could be delayed or denied. It was a noisy, exhausting process.

But now Elke lacked the energy to debate. It was easier to just go along. To say, "Okay, I'll try it. But don't be surprised if it's a letdown."

Impulsivity intruded into her daily life, her routine. It was disruptive but...fun? To enter a restaurant without reading the right side of the menu? To select a piece of clothing without looking at the price tag? To buy a new book, hardback even, because it looked interesting?

Elke shifted in her chair. The morning play was over. Today would not be the day to "just do it."

But "What do I want today?" remained unanswered.

A strange notion had been brewing, a child-like longing. She remembered a cat that she'd had as a teenager. It had cuddled with her when she'd studied, followed her around their apartment, greeted her when she'd returned from school, slept at her feet. She remembered talking to the cat, gently rubbing behind its ears or under its chin as it purred at her touch.

"Why not?" she asked herself, simultaneously listing multiple sensible reasons why taking on a cat was not a good idea. It was a commitment. A responsibility. But Juergen's voice prevailed, the voice that told her she was loved, that she deserved to be loved. That she was his *liebling* and she could have *das katzchen* if she wanted. It would bring her *sonnenschein.*

There was an animal shelter about a mile away. Elke had never been in it, but she'd heard dogs barking. She would walk there. She would ask about adoption protocols. Maybe, perhaps, today was the day she would bring home a cat.

A HEAVY POUCH

K. FUFKIN VOLLMAYER

Murder Gully Ravine, Placerville El Dorado

April 1850

Hangtown earned its name from three different men accused of stealing claims and nuggets. Their fate was decided by the long swing of hemp rope. Stealing a man's gold, his water, his cards, any of these brings a quick death. If I cocked my pistol to run the claim jumpers off, Murder Gully would be an even bigger cemetery. This was the choice on this bright Sunday morning, breathing in air so cold it nipped my lungs: do we let them run us off? Or do we run them off?

When they came in last night, they spoke in a foreign tongue. Holland talk? No, French. A few hours later, in the pitch black before dawn, I said to myself, Jean Baptiste, you are losing your ear, for they are rattling on in German. And if there was any lost soul in these foothills who knows German, it was me. Long ago, my top lip had a bit of fur from my first whiskers, I heard *yah* and *nein* all day when I was a prisoner inside a silk cage, locked up in the Duke's castle in Germany.

But last night, I failed. I was charged to stand sentry to protect our Long Tom against thieves, Mexicans on mules, Boston bandits, and wealthy Europes all seized with gold mania, who might have sold their wives for a ship passage to the foothills of California. In other words, I was to guard against the very squatters who'd arrived last night.

Any hope of placer mining rested on the workings of the sluice box. All day long, we shoveled rock and mud into the Long Tom. Built about waist high on wooden stilts, one end let snow melt gush through the wood trough, washing gold flakes and even a few pebbles to separate from rocks. On a good day, the American River washed a fistful of gold dust into a little bitty trap beneath the trough. The Long Tom rock shoved rock against rock and sounded like a landslide of boulders inside the sluice. My poor noggin. Jimmie and I slowly grew rich and deaf. The hooves clattering inside my ears may be how I missed the sound of the claim jumpers last night. One of them, a man with a screech of orange hair, big ears, and a scorched face as red and raw-looking as one of them boiled crabs so popular at the tent restaurants in San Francisco, led the way for his mates. He put his finger to his lips to hush the *yah-yah-yah*-speaking men. Mind you, I am no stranger to men armed to the teeth with a necklace of hemp slung around their shoulders in case they itched to hogtie some red man they'd caught beneath their boot. But this gang had mules and packets.

Jimmie had the ague and snored beside me. Bingham moaned about a sore tooth all week and limped off to Auburn to plead with a surgeon. Romeo, the fourth man in our company, said he would escort Bingham. As he was wont to give Bingham a blow on his head as easily as a smile, I suspect he wanted to land more of the former than the latter. This left me and snoring Jimmie.

I was a dwarf compared to Jimmie. But my small stature was perhaps what saved me a few years ago, on that death march across the southwest. The Mormon march was men on horses and mules, moving from Missouri down to New Mexico and Arizona; a journey to distract Mexico as it fended off the U.S. Army. So, I suppose the Mormon trail across the desert that I had signed up for, and where I scouted for water for the horses and mules, finding them a bit of green willows to eat and some shade in that hellscape of the desert, made me a claim jumper. Not for gold, but for trying to cheat Mexico out of its lands in Alta California for the Mormons.

Our forty feet of riverfront was filled with boulders, rocks, river clay, and if we were very, very lucky, a bit of gold. Even a strike. Which was why, on this nose-numbing April morning, here was Crab Man with his funny talk, a singsong heidy-ho up-and-down lilt to his speech, calling to his mates.

These men were jowly, too well fed to have been here long. Pained hunger, cold, and mud up to your knees—that is what mining was. Shoveling top dirt into the trough all day every day, sifting through the mud in the riffle, waking up to rain or ice falling, have turned my feet into swollen, rotting cabbages.

Anyone not foolish enough to abandon all reason to be a miner asked: How were they able to put up their three canvas tents on our river-front and move into our claim? Simple. Our shanty was set back from the river on account of snowmelt flooding us when our tent was beside it; seeping in at night and giving us the very ailments we complained of now. We had all manner of fevers, Chagres, cough, weak-limbed nerves.

Do not forget that Jimmie—James P. Beckwourth—was a mountain man whose exploits rightly proceeded him. He was an Indian fighter who married the daughter of a Crow chief. He trapped, scouted, marched, ran dry goods, and could put his ear to the ground and hear ants moving. When he was not hired as a guide, he gambled. He never lost at Monte or poker. Jimmie, all six hulking feet of him, who would not bat an eye at any regiment of white men with muskets and pistols staring down at him, was a bit feverish this morning.

"A dozen men tiptoed in last night, and a Europe man with a face like a cooked crab," I said to him by way of good morning and how do you do. "Crab Man on two spindle legs he is, with a cigar jammed in his mouth and a pistol shoved in his britches."

Jimmie yawned. Scratched like he had a tickle. "We'll get us some dogs that is hungry enough to bite. Not one. Two. Three even. No. Better yet. We get us some mad dogs with fangs foaming as white as the currents of the American here. That is how we get us our claim back."

I was still lightheaded and loose-lipped enough from my whiskey tippling last night to ask, "So, I am to walk to Sacramento City for a big dog and her litter and trot them back? I wager there are no big dogs for sale. Or rabid ones to catch." I laughed.

Jimmie took his musket and put the barrel to my chest. "I got the gun and you got to run. Not to Sacramento. Fetch the rabid ones from Hutchins' settlement. All that skittle-scattle you did with the god's army down south? You is short and fast as a mountain goat, Charbo."

"But Jimmie, they are dearly departed." I winked at him.

He cocked his head. "Where did you hear that?"

"Hutchins shot and burned those dogs. McMurtry's Irish gang told me when I went to trade for vinegar."

He stared, swatting the air like the stench of a rotting rat had drifted over. He had the mountain fever, but his eyes were still a polished brown. His cheekbones were dark curved wings sloping down to his chin, the kind my mother had.

"So we have visitors who are sleeping on our claim, and we have no rabid dogs to silence them?" Jimmie asked.

"Worse, they have guns, whiskey, and accents that sound like the talk from my time when I was a guest of a prince over in Europe."

"Guest of a prince? What in the devil is you speechifying on about?" Jimmie jabbed me. To say that he dwarfed me in his size and might did not do him justice. He was a Negro Daniel Boone in his buckskin and hatchet, and my chin reached his arm pit.

"Some history. Back when you lived among the Crow, I was captive of Prince Paul Wilhelm in Germany. Even if I wanted to escape, where would I go? For months, I did not speak a lick of their German tongue and did not have a penny to my name for the passage back across the Atlantic. He promised me an education, but I was his servant, bowing so low my nose bled."

"That where you learned to write and talk fancy, Charbo?" Jimmie belched.

"Indeed. For all its hardships, I would take your life with the Crows eating scrub and acorns. The castle was a jail of velvet and beer."

I held up the muddy rag of canvas flapping beneath our calico and pine bough tent. Out we went into the clear cold of April in the mountains, with snow and ice still on the ground, and air too thin to breathe.

Jimmie stopped, held out his hand. "My hat, Charbonneau." He winked at me. "Hide the curly and you hide the Negro. If there's one false claim we do not need, it is that there's a free man mining. They will accuse any Negro of stealing. Never mind that we wish to steal our own claim back." He scooped up his hair in his slouch hat with a flourish.

"Right you are, James P. Though we are half-starved, your musket is oiled and ready. She will talk for both of us."

"Not today. My heavy pouch will." Jimmie patted the lump of canvas he wore at his breast. It was an ordinary dirt-smudged bag, only this one squirmed.

My eyes watered. I wondered if it was scurvy and not a mountain fever that tormented him and me and every other man who forsook all reason to live in water and mud and cold, and eat water, mud and cold for his dinner.

Jimmie bent over his musket like it was a cane, pounding his chest, while the whooping and hollering German bandits continued to fire shots into the sky.

He took his pointing finger to the deep plow lines at his eyes. "Remember. These ain't wrinkles, Charbo. These are maps." He poked his own eye. "One for my time as a guest of the Crow, another fighting the Seminole in Florida, and this one for my journey over the Sierras. My face is my map."

"Here you be." I handed him the brown jug. "Spirits to raise your spirit there, James."

"The dregs? I see, Charbo. Well, no matter. I am revived. Now, them claim rats who sneaked in last night—" Just then, like a church bell ringing the faithful to mass, a hurrah and more shouting *yah yah yah* with muskets. It being Sunday, they celebrated not in church with hymns, but with bullets.

"Over yonder," I said.

Jimmie slapped his thigh. "Off with you. Grab some charcoal and let's gussy up our faces, wrists, and feet."

We darkened our joints up with the charcoal.

"You are the loveliest picture of scurvy if ever I did see one, Charbo. Now lean into me while I limp along with my musket."

Crab Man and his assembled party had several brown jugs, pick axes, shovels, and buckets. They were not even panning or shoveling top dirt but hammering away at rocks. Fools pounding after fool's gold.

"Aye, we salute you and is so grateful that you have come here to share our humble abode for it is the scurvy and the Chagres fever that wear us down. Why, Charbo, we could use an extra pair of hands on the Long Tom, ain't that so?" Jimmie grinned, saluted, and fell upon one of them. He dragged me with him and I heaved my stomach out onto Crab Man as I clutched my throat as if a snake had bitten me.

Beneath me, I felt Jimmie clutch his belly as he loosened his pouch, coughing into my head, "Garters," as he let the yellow-striped snakes escape. Fat as two fingers together, they slithered toward Crab Man.

A white man with a wet face and neck, and eyes the color of yellow slugs, stepped forward. Whatever ailment he had, I did not want. "I am Mister Cuthbert. We have journeyed from New York and we left behind so many poor souls from the cholera. And here you are heaving, poor souls. Ach. I would encourage you to find a new claim. We, too, have been infected and do not wish to sicken you." He spoke like that surgeon in the Mormon regiment, all hushed, gentle words, who would then reach for his blade to saw some soldier's gangrened leg off.

Behind him, the Germans stood frightfully tall and yellow-haired. They stepped back, dragging their pickaxes, staring at the shore. Cuthbert called to them in their tongue, but they rolled up their bedrolls and backed off, tripping over the river rocks. The serpent never did much for Eve, but right then as the garter snakes from Jimmie's pouch wriggled up toward the men, they saved our claim. Even Crab Man stumbled and fell in fright.

They were gone by supper.

Weeks later, Jimmie and Romeo pounded rock in the holes they dug while Bingham and I worked the Long Tom on the river. Bingham shoveled in top dirt, I worked the riddle, adjusting it to catch every bit of mud and rock as the river water drained through the sieve. Bingham, a man of few words and many moans, had a milky eye. Every shovel of dirt he lifted, half went in the trough, half went on me. My feet were as blistered and water-logged as ever, worse from Bingham's second helping of mud.

A tang of pine scented the air and grasshoppers jumped about. Skunk cabbages sprouted up like green buckets. Still, as mild as spring was in Placerville, Bingham and I were somehow boiled up, the color of rooster jowl.

"Hold your shovel and I'll sift through the riddle. I got to halt and take a bit of shade," I said.

Jimmie always gave the orders, but the sounds of men calling out and echoes from clanging axes on slate and granite up and down the river hurt my ears. My eyes fooled me, for when I pulled my hands out from the slurry of mud, rock chips, and ice-melt river, there lay five little piggies. Dirt lumps with yellow edges. But it was gold. Then I moaned.

TROUBLE HAD COME WITH MUDSLIDES THAT KEPT THE MULE TRAINS AWAY from the south fork of the American. No potatoes, no sugar, no beans. Beef and eggs were dreams from long ago. To say we were starving sounded like we were hungry. We had loose teeth and bowels from water boiled with pine sap, waiting for supplies to make it to the south fork of the American.

But now, as we sat inside the shanty tent, Romeo hollered and Jimmie grabbed him by the neck. "Close your mouth. All these grabbers and grubbers around us? We will lose it by sunup. So you bite your tongue, boy."

Somehow, word spread fast. For the next seven days, we worked the river and sentry. Five lumps became ten and Jimmie's pouch grew fat. We four men finally had a strike.

On a Saturday night, when most of the companies and claim-stakers had left our stretch of the river for a Sunday in town, the German squawkers came back. I slept until my ribs cracked from Bingham's kick. Cuthbert and Crab Man stood outside with muskets, ordering a dozen Negros and red men, Kanaka by the look of them, to circle our poor canvas shanty.

Crab Man told the Negros to light torches from the sentry fires. But spying the hemp rope was when I knew we were licked. Fire, bullets, hanging.

There he was, Cuthbert, talking slowly like we were deaf and dumb, "Good evening, gentlemen. Now. Please, kindly, hand it over."

In minutes, the tent was in flames, a musket was at my chest, another one pointed at Jimmie. Bingham and Romeo were tied up. Without fuss or fight, Jimmie gave Cuthbert our heavy little pouch of gold dust.

Cuthbert took out his kerchief, waved it against the smoke, blew his nose, mopped his eyes as if he was weeping for his theft. "Thank you for your generosity. For that is what it is. A gift for the loan that we made you to fund your, your, your addition to the Long Tom. We filed it with the justice in Auburn."

The swindle of filing with the Auburn sheriff was to hide his claim jumping. Even with his slug eyes, he was still a white man, which neither Jimmie nor I would ever be, so what justice or lawman would listen to us? In the end, that spring Jimmie had grown too sickly to fight. Me being on the small side, Cuthbert and Crab Man won the battle of Murder Gully.

In the end, it was Jimmie who earned his money back. "I will open another dry goods at the pass on the Sierras and mine the miners, take them for every penny, selling them mules and salt and canvas at forty or fifty cents a pound," he said.

"A mercantile?"

"You watch, Charbo."

He did just that. Opened one high up in the Sierras and earned as much in selling dry goods as any miner hitting a strike. But the promise of another strike in Colorado lured him away; a mermaid in the mountains singing.

For years now, I have slept in a bed with a roof over my head. No more tent on the river fighting off scurvy. My hands are soft, not swollen red from working in snow melt and feeding rocks into the sluice. At night, I lay my head on a bunk in Mary's room and board in Auburn. All I have to show for my mining with Jimmie are hands that ache in the cold and a ringing in my ears from feeding the forever hungry Long Tom cannon.

That winter after Cuthbert and Crab Man plundered our claim, I kept my lips from turning blue with whiskey in a tavern here. Well, it was little more than a tent that sagged from the snow. When the grippe tore through the foothills, felling men like lady death herself, O'Connell the Irishman who served spirits in the tent laughed. "You, my mate, are not laying down, so let your stool grow cold. Off with you. My mate over at the hotel needs a clerk."

The delirium that captured so many men to chase the gold fever was truly a madness. For me, it has mercifully said its prayers and hushed. I count myself lucky. I have passed my years as a desk clerk at the Auburn Hotel, never during the day, only at night as my hair was a little too black, my skin a little too Negro Mexican for the daytime according to O'Connell. Somehow in a slumber of nights and cold and the silver moon shining down, I have worked ten years.

Like all the night clerks, my main job has been to make sure that none of the drunken prospectors burn the place down when they stumble in. I have kept them steady when they return from a visit to Lil's. That establishment is filled with Chinese and Native ladies, a beehive of females. I spied a girl, a Mojave, for she had blue lines on her chin, so they are girls at Lil's, kept under lock and key. No one ever sees them, for they never go out.

One night, a rooster crowed far away, his calling out that dawn was here and my long night at the desk was done. He must have been atop a steep hill, for his hollering neared me, then moved farther off. Wherever he was, the rooster always announced the day clerk, and that I could finally sleep. Here came Jack, the day clerk. He marched in, whistling, proper, tall, and spoke in a sing-song way.

"Good day to you, Jack my boy. The gentlemen Corbett has not returned," I called out.

"Aye, a pleasant Sunday to you, Charbo. Are you to church then?"

"Yes, I shall leave directly," I lied. I gathered up my newspaper and jug and turned to face a man in a gentlemen's jacket grunting as he slumped into the door.

"Good day to you, Mister Corbett," Jack said in his curly talk brogue.

I froze. Mister Corbett was the miner who plundered our claim.

Bloodshot eyes, his belly straining against his vest, swaying back and forth as he tried to steady himself, it was him. The claim jumper.

"You. It is you." Cuthbert drooled, raising his fat finger at me. He was drunk, but he recognized me.

"Mister Corbett. Welcome back, sir." Jack held out his arm. "You must be tired. Allow me to unlock your door."

Cuthbert who called himself Corbett raised his right fist and took a wide, wobbly swing for me. He succeeded only in knocking himself down

"You river rat, you," he mumbled. He took his paw to cover one eye, fixed the other on me and hissed, "Well, well. Here you are, you cockroach." He succeeded only in falling down again, and his neck wagged like a dog's tail.

Just then, a crash of plates, followed by a long silence. A female voice that could only be Esther the cook screeched, "Tarnation and Jesus-Mary-and-Joseph."

Jack turned to me, "Take the gentleman to his room. I shall see what ails Esther."

The crash roused Cuthbert. He muttered, "Charbo, what kind of name is Charbo, anyhow, when it is a common fact that it ain't European but some other name for a half—"

He fell back onto the floor, his head banging the planking.

The toe of my boot met his chest, silencing the rest of his slander.

But he did not stir. He had fallen to the floor like a sack of sand, heavy and quiet.

Cuthbert looked like one more belch would upend his belly. I did him the courtesy afforded an honored guest of the Auburn and dragged him by his boots down to his room and tried to hoist him up to his bed. I cursed him and the long evening he enjoyed at Lil's, for he reeked of whiskey seasoned with a dash of musk perfume. He was a tangled jumble of hair and stink and thus earned another kick. My foot tangled up, only it wasn't in his hair.

My boot was in a web of woven thread that had wormed its way out of his britches and was attached to a bit of calico. Lo and behold, tucked beneath the cliff of Cuthbert's belly was a long heavy canvas pouch.

Heavy enough that it could only be gold dust. Miners fastened their gold to their persons. But what was Cuthbert doing with this much gold?

He snored. I stared. A fat but tender bundle. All the monks at the Catholic school I went to taught Thou Shalt not Steal, yet plundering was all I saw in the foothills.

The rooster crowed again, a warning. I pondered. If I helped myself to half the pouch, Cuthbert could accuse me: half-stolen by the half-breed, his word against mine. Like how he had robbed us of our claim years before. He filed his paper in court. Jimmie and Romeo being Negroes and a red man, none of us had any rights. Cuthbert could bring his men to my room at Mary's boarding house to seize whatever he took a fancy to.

Then again, if Jimmie were here, he'd wink and send me off for snakes and rabid dogs. He always had a plan. With a quick snip, I relieved Cuthbert of his canvas pouch. I know the comings and the goings of who has gold and who, like Cuthbert, has a cow's udder of gold dust so fleshy and swollen, it could only be an ill-gotten pouch. A month before, a white man mining his strike on the Feather River was found doing the dead man's float. Common enough here in the Sierras. His body was found, but not his bag of gold.

Whether it is salt or iron or a bridle or a bushel of corn, it costs a quarter of an ounce of gold to move anything up into the foothills. Costs even more to move an ounce of gold out. Cuthbert was an agent of Gregory's Express. All these years later, after he introduced himself on

Murder Gully, he now oversaw wagons. He loaded the coaches with gold bound first to Sacramento City then on to San Francisco, where it came to rest in banks and vaults. That was how Cuthbert had grown fat and rich, just keeping his eye on teams of horses and wagon wheels and roads.

And stealing a dead man's purse.

Chilblains and a limp and a blurry eye, that is what prospecting left me with. So my prospecting, after ten years up here in foothills, is on 3rd and Oak at the Auburn Hotel and laying claim to Cuthbert's stolen pouch.

I left Cuthbert sleeping. The morning was bright and hard, a spring sun trying to shove the cold and chill of April away.

I put on a collar and a yellowed but clean shirt. I needed to find a church. I grabbed some quick bread, shoved the pouch in my pocket, and left the planking and canvas hotel on Oak Street. All these foothill miscreants might rob each other blind, stab a man in his sleep, or set fire to his camp, but none of them would steal from a church. Most of them had never even set foot in a church. Every last American and European believed Catholics were cultish and blind, obeying a big fat pope in Rome. As the priests had taught me, every Catholic church has a secret passage, a fake door, a priest hole to hide the faithful when they are hunted for being false believers.

So, I left Auburn for Placerville, the only town with enough Catholics to invite a priest for a baptism or a funeral when the road was passable. I would find the church and hide the pouch in the priest hole. Who would think of searching a church? Besides, the gold that Cuthbert stole from me and Jimmie was in this pouch. After all these years, it was like bullion in a bank. I had every right to claim my deposit.

THE PILOT'S STORY
ELYSE GARRETT

June 1983

With a cigarette hanging from his mouth, the cab driver slammed on the brakes. "This is it, lady. 3rd and Oak." Andrea Nolan peered out the cab's window. Something was wrong. Evelyn Lyon Gates would never live in an old Soviet-style apartment building, made with cement blocks and begging for paint, at the very least. The driver opened the cab door. "Are ya sure you've got the right address? That place looks like a rundown prison."

She smoothed the skirt of her uniform and wheeled her flight bag along the cracked concrete walkway behind the cab driver, who carried her suitcases. Placing them next to the tinted glass door, he squinted at the address on the wall. "I'll wait in the cab until you get inside."

"Thank you." She searched for a doorknob or a handle, but only spotted a security camera. Should she get back into the cab and wait? Why did Evelyn Lyon Gates invite her to stay here for six months? She claimed all her ideas and inspiration to write her ten novels were found in this building. How is that possible?

After publishing Andrea's first novel, the publisher mandated that she write a second book with a December 31st deadline. Twelve months, but she spent the first six months trying to create an idea for a story. Andrea's brain, like the building, was solid cement. No premise, conflict, plot, or setting.

Someone opened the door from the inside.

A man with wide shoulders, wearing a black suit and tie, extended his hand. "Good afternoon. May I see your driver's license?"

"Well, sure." Andrea reached into her purse and pulled out her license.

He squinted. "You're far from home. What brings you here?"

"I'm a guest of Evelyn Lyon Gates. You know, the author?"

"Yes." He handed back the license. "Ms. Nolan, I'm James, Ms. Evelyn's official greeter, known by others as the doorman." His handshake consumed Andrea's hand. No one would dare hassle him. He reached for the second door and a gun on his belt caught her attention. "Ms. Evelyn flew to Paris a few weeks ago to research her recent novel."

Judging from what she had seen, she expected a dark hallway with peeling wallpaper, faded carpet, apartment doors on each side, and a clunky elevator. Had she sublet her own apartment for this? She might leave soon, and for good.

Andrea stepped through the second door, hesitated, her jaw dropping as she tried to take it all in. Instead of six apartments, the entire first floor appeared as if she had stepped into a Potemkin Village. A façade that appeared to be authentic, like a Disney creation of a European village. A mural encompassed the walls and ceiling depicting a setting with green grass, trees, rolling hills, and a blue sky overhead. Ceiling lights mimicked the brightness of mid-afternoon. She stood dumbfounded.

James chuckled. "Everyone reacts like that. I'll carry your suitcases to the fifth floor. Follow me please."

As Tchaikovsky's Violin Concerto played through overhead speakers, Andrea followed James through the village shops. "Sounds like you've worked with Evelyn Lyon Gates for a while," Andrea said. "I suppose you've read her novels, too?" They stepped into the elevator.

"We don't use her pen name in the building and the residents refer to each other by their original names, not the American names that Ms. Evelyn helped them legally acquire. And they never ask personal questions while on the first floor. The privacy clause is in the contract. And like you, Ms. Evelyn personally invited all the residents to live in this building. Judging from your uniform, I can only assume you're a stewardess. Which airline?"

"Well, just so you know, the airline industry replaced the term stewardess with the more gender-neutral term flight attendant. Since seventy-five, to be exact. And no, I'm not a flight attendant. I'm a pilot, First Officer, for TWA."

"And a writer, too?"

Andrea nodded. "That's right." Evelyn must have shared her dilemma with him.

"So, they allow women to fly commercial planes? With passengers? Since when?"

"Seventy-three."

James shook his head. "Well...I need to get out more. Anyway, your host, Ms. Evelyn, and her husband designed and constructed this apartment building during the war, nineteen forty. He was the mayor of our great city at the time, then became our governor. Years later, after he passed, Ms. Evelyn moved here and wrote her famous novels. But you and everyone else already know that."

"I didn't know her late husband was a politician."

"And an excellent politician, too. Anyway, Ms. Evelyn's apartment, where you will reside, occupies a third of the square footage on the fifth floor and the rest is used for," he made air quotes, "other special guests. She hasn't invited anyone to the fifth floor for quite some time."

The elevator stopped and opened in front of double doors. James unlocked the left door. "Welcome to your home for the next six months." He handed her the key and carried the suitcases into the apartment. Not like any apartment she could recall. Not even in those home and garden magazines found on the airplane.

With sunlight flooding from the skylights, Andrea gazed around the spacious living room that resembled a hotel lobby. James pointed toward Evelyn's office. "You can see two phones on her desk. The black is for your personal calls. The red is to reach me. Twenty-four-seven. I live in this building, too."

The office where Evelyn Lyon Gates created her stories drew Andrea in. A Victorian desk sat in the center facing the window. An old L.C. Smith typewriter sat on a polished side table. She pictured Evelyn Lyon Gates sitting at her desk, tapping the keys, and creating another compelling story. Maybe some of her magic would rub off on Andrea.

"May I show you the kitchen?" James asked.

Walking behind him, through the dining room, passing an Amish dining table with sixteen chairs. A bouquet of dahlias and roses wrapped with green florist paper lay on the edge of the table as if waiting for someone to rescue it.

With a sweeping motion across the kitchen, James indicated the pantry. "Everything in here is available for you." He opened the pantry door, the size of a large walk-in closet and yanked a chain attached to a light. "You're welcome to everything in here, too."

Baking goods, cereals, loaves of bread, jars filled with jam, coffee, tea bags, a row of crystal vases, and a full wine rack filled the shelves.

James pulled the light off. "I must go." He turned toward the dining room and proceeded to the door, then halted and faced Andrea. "Why aren't you flying now?"

"The fuel crisis resulting from the conflict with Iran led to layoffs, and since I didn't have enough seniority, I was furloughed for at least twelve months. Perfect timing for me."

James rubbed his chin. "Interesting. Well, be sure to visit and enjoy all the facilities downstairs. I hope the time here allows you to be productive and successful with your novel."

"Thank you, James."

Running her fingers over the smooth polished wood of the Amish table. It seemed odd to see a bouquet lying on the table instead of soaking up water in a vase. She carried it into the kitchen and unwrapped the paper. An attached note dropped onto the counter.

Hello Andrea,

I'm glad you accepted my invitation. I guarantee you will have plenty of ideas for your story. Please put the flowers in a vase with water. Fresh flowers will arrive every week. Enjoy! — Evelyn

She went to get a vase from the pantry, but it seemed to be stuck to the shelf. She wiggled it a few times until it pulled away, along with the back wall of the pantry. It opened like a door. "What the…?" She gasped and slammed the pantry door. A crystal water pitcher in the China cabinet caught her eye. Perfect. She put the flowers in the pitcher, added water from the kitchen sink, and set it on the table.

Exhausted from a long day, she plopped onto an overstuffed chair with a footstool, sinking into the soft velvet fabric that persuaded her to relax her tense body. The place felt cozy, but odd. Assigned names? Invitation required to live here? A wall that moves in the pantry and opens into…? Why was Evelyn Lyon Gates so sure Andrea could write a story just by living here? She glanced into the office, to the typewriter on her desk.

She had decided against bringing her own typewriter, too big for her suitcases, and planned to buy a new electric one, as if buying an upgraded model would magically pop ideas into her head to write about.

The first six months she had searched for a story idea, but her mind had refused to cooperate. Out of desperation, she'd attended a writing conference and during the lunch break, she'd grabbed the opportunity to sit next to Evelyn Lyon Gates, the author of several *New York Times* bestsellers.

During an engaging conversation, they discovered a shared relative. Andrea's aunt had been married to Evelyn Lyon Gates' brother-in-law. What had seemed trivial had opened the door to being invited to stay in Evelyn Lyon Gates' apartment for six months to write her novel while Evelyn toured Paris. *Open the door.* The pantry door?

A knock on the front door. She peered out the peep hole then opened the door to James holding a tray. "I've brought your dinner. I didn't know what you would prefer, so I guessed." He smiled. "Baked salmon, stuffed peppers, steamed mixed vegetables, fresh bread rolls, and, of course, an American dessert. A slice of chocolate cake with vanilla ice cream." He pointed to the kitchen. "The menus are in the kitchen. Fill out your choices and slip them under your door every morning. And be sure to include the time for delivery and the day and time for the housekeeper to arrive. We don't want to disturb you. I hope you're settling in and writing. Questions?"

Speechless, Andrea shook her head.

After he closed the door behind him, Andrea turned to investigate the back of the pantry, just to ease her mind. She crept up to its door, as if expecting it to open by itself and put her ear to the door. No sounds. What might harm her? Just a pantry with a wall that moves? She swung the door open and stared at the crystal vase innocently sitting there. She wiggled it, like before and the back wall rotated open, and she stepped in to get a better look. What's in there? The space was dark until tiny lights, like those along the aisle of an airplane, illuminated the floor and followed a downward stairway. She waited until her eyes adjusted before grabbing the railing on the wall to guide her down each step until the narrow stairway leveled on a landing. Judging from the number of steps, she should be on the fourth floor.

Along the wall, at eye level, a glowing circle of glass beckoned her. A folded kitchen step stool leaned against the wall. She found a toggle switch on the wall and flipped it. The sound of a ticking clock came from the other side of the wall. She peered into the round glass the size of a hand mirror and gasped. A man in a worn t-shirt and underwear stood on the other side scratching his head and standing in front of an open refrigerator.

"Natasha, where's the milk?" he shouted in Russian.

A woman answered. "Bottom shelf, Boris. Where do you think it would be? In the bathroom? Use your damn eyes."

Andrea's Russian lessons from high school and college classes let her understand the gist of their brief conversation.

The man seemed unaware of Andrea's face inches from the inside of their kitchen. She stepped back with both hands over her mouth. How in the hell did that happen? Were they not aware of the portals on their side? How was it camouflaged?

A few feet down the passage, was another portal, with a view of their dining room where a dim ceiling light illuminated a long dining table, a China cabinet with glass doors, and an oak buffet with framed photos and house plants. Judging from Boris' voice coming from his kitchen, this was a view into his dining room.

A third portal drew her attention. She flipped the switch, and the volume of Boris' TV startled her. It echoed in the passage until she found a volume control on the switch. She had a full view of Boris' living room with a sofa and two upholstered chairs set around a glass coffee table. A baby grand piano with sheet music scattered on the floor consumed an entire corner of the room. Violin cases on shelves alongside books whose titles she couldn't read. Above the sofa, a wood-carved frame held a painted white flower with multiple petals. Not a daisy or sunflower, but similar. Vaguely familiar, but from where?

Around the corner, more glowing portals streamed dim light into the dark passage. Most with folding stools under or nearby. Someone could sit and relax while spying on these innocent unsuspecting people. How could anyone stoop so low as to spy on people in their homes?

Continuing down the narrow passage, bumping her shoulders against the walls, she turned a corner to what must be apartment 4C. Each apartment had three portals: one in the kitchen, the dining room, and the living room. The kitchen portal had a view of the hallway leading to the bedrooms and bathrooms. God forbid should there be portals inside the bedrooms or bathrooms.

As curiosity opposed and defeated her sense of integrity, she continued to locate the portals, without spying on the residents, on the third and second floor, all with the same pattern in passages. Surprisingly, there were several on the first floor. Next to the pool, the tables in front of the café, the exercise equipment, inside the hair salon, the barber shop, and facing the chairs set up in front of the movie screen.

Surely, this couldn't be legal or certainly not moral.

She followed the floor lights toward the stairs leading back to the fifth floor. But she couldn't resist the urge to see that white flower in

Boris' apartment again. Where had she seen that specific flower before? Ah, it's an edelweiss, like in the movie *The Sound of Music* where the Von Trapp family sang the song *Edelweiss* as they fled Austria.

Overwhelmed by what she saw, Andrea raced up the stairs and back through Evelyn's pantry. She assumed Evelyn and her husband had incorporated the passage and portals during the construction of the building. Such an elaborate system to spy and hear every word of the residents' conversations in their apartments, near the pool, in the bakery, playing checkers, or having lunch with friends in the café. Why?

In the kitchen, she glanced around the walls. Were there portals in here, too? With her back to the window, it seemed she had been a little higher than eye level while watching Boris. She focused on two wall lamps mounted on each side of the window. The back of a portal must have been on the right side of the window, inside the wall lamp. Sitting on the counter, she practically dissected the lamp and found nothing. She studied every wall and ceiling fixture and any object at the same height from the floor that might disguise the portal. Of course, she found nothing. Why would Evelyn and her husband spy on themselves?

Searching the labels on the wine rack, she found a California wine, Robert Mondavi, and poured half a glass. Enough to help her make sense of what she'd found to be so disturbing in the passage. She'd never experienced something constructed to watch and listen to people inside their home and community areas. Why would Evelyn Lyon Gates invite them and then spy on them?

What kind of person was she?

After carrying the wine glass into the living room, she settled into the recliner chair and admired the city lights on the skyscrapers and the arched bridge over the river. Then she straightened. The windows. The passage must be under all the windows. That made sense because the passage dipped down a few steps and back up at about the same intervals as the windows in each apartment. Clever.

Either Boris or Natasha played the piano and the violin. Oh, look at herself using their names as if she knew them. If she ever ran into them on the first floor, she could introduce herself, "Hello, I'm the voyeur on the fifth floor." She shook her head. "Despicable."

THE NEXT MORNING, ANDREA SIPPED HOT COFFEE AND FACED ONE OF THE built-in bookcases in Evelyn Lyon Gates' library. On the eye-level shelf, *Valley of the Dolls, The Hiding Place, The Bluest Eyes, Sophie's Choice, Scruples, Looking for Mr. Goodbar, The Thorn Birds, Roots,* and *Shogun.* She set her coffee on the end table and pulled out books, one by one, and read the autographs and notes written to Evelyn.

Framed photos between the books showed Evelyn smiling, while sitting or standing next to world-renowned individuals. Henry Kissinger, Betty Friedan, Golda Meir, Billy Jean King, Martina Navratilova, Olga Korbut, and Mikhail Baryshnikov. What did they have in common?

Who the hell was Evelyn Lyon Gates?

"MORNING, JAMES. MAY I ASK YOU SOME QUESTIONS?"

He set the breakfast tray on the table. "Of course."

"I discovered the passage yesterday. Why was it built?"

"Ms. Evelyn's husband was very popular, but there were others who would have liked to end his career or even his life. He got the idea from the American saying and kept his friends close—but his enemies closer."

"Does Evelyn still use the passage?"

He shrugged and smiled on his way out the door.

Were the residents Evelyn's enemies?

IN FRONT OF THE FIREPLACE MANTEL, ANDREA STARED AT ALL THE BOOKS Evelyn Lyon Gates had written and received awards and recognition for. She ran her index finger across the spines and pulled a book out where she saw the white flower on the cover. That's it. She'd read that novel, and learned the flower, edelweiss, was not only the national flower of

Austria and Switzerland, but it became the symbol of the German resistance against Nazism.

Were Boris and Natasha the main characters in a novel that Evelyn Lyon Gates wrote? The thought stunned her as she pulled another book from the mantel where the main characters were a married couple and musicians in an orchestra. He played the violin, and the wife played the piano. They'd escaped from the Nazis and risked their lives to rescue the Jewish musicians and their families.

After taking the rest of Evelyn Lyon Gates' novels from the mantel, she carried them all to the table. The back covers refreshed her memory of each story. Her heart pounded. Did Evelyn write other residents' stories?

One back cover described two gay men who had led the patrons and employees of an underground bar through a tunnel to escape the raids. And the man who swam laps in the pool downstairs must be that character in one of her earlier novels who had been a Soviet Olympic swimmer. He carried Jewish orphans on his back as he swam across the river to safety. Despite making several dangerous trips, he managed to save at least fifty orphans.

"Oh my God! They're all heroes!"

～

James set the lunch tray on the table amongst Evelyn's books. "Oh, I see you have discovered the source of inspiration for Ms. Evelyn. What do you think?"

"I'm not sure. I'm absolutely shocked and yet emotionally moved. If Evelyn finds out I've made the connection, will she be angry?"

"Of course not. Why do you think she invited you here?"

"But I can't spy on someone and steal their personal story for my own benefit."

"I understand. But these stories have been hidden from the world and need to be written and shared, especially for naïve Americans who during the war didn't personally experience the Holocaust except through news reels in theaters. Don't you agree?"

"I need time to think about it."

"Just in case, there's a woman we call The Pilot, who lives on the third floor, 3B. She has a compelling story that will inspire you. Her name is Zoya Petrova. But only use that name for research. Do not write or repeat it to anyone. Promise?"

"Yes. I understand."

The thought of a pilot writing a story about another pilot grabbed Andrea's interest. After tossing the idea around all evening, Andrea concluded that if Evelyn Lyon Gates could do it, so could she. Besides, she was desperate, and time was running out.

JAMES BROUGHT BREAKFAST, SLOWING IN FRONT OF EVELYN'S NOVELS AND framed photos spread across the table. He scanned the situation and smiled. "Where should I set your tray? On the veranda?"

"Yes, that would be fine. Thank you, James."

"This morning, around ten, may I suggest you take a notebook and pen into the pantry and to apartment 3B." He smiled. "To research your story."

"How do you know someone will be there?"

"I have my ways."

Andrea raised her eyebrows.

"No cameras." He held his hands up. "I promise."

ANDREA FOLLOWED THE TINY LIGHTS ALONG THE PASSAGE THAT DIPPED under the windows to the third floor where she checked all three portals, but didn't see anyone in the kitchen, dining room, or the living room. James had made a mistake.

She unfolded the step stool and pulled it close to the third portal. Someone had mounted a cup holder on the wall and a plastic pocket to hold her notebook, pen, and pencil. Two cushions made the cold metal seat comfortable. Evelyn had thought of everything.

While waiting, she maintained her focus on the front door in 3B. After thirty minutes, with no sign of anyone entering, she reconsidered her plan. A sign that she shouldn't get her information through the portals. What the hell was she doing, anyway? She scooted off the step stool and grabbed her empty cup, her notebook, and pen when the front door squeaked as it opened.

Andrea spun around and saw a young man and woman, in their early thirties, wearing t-shirts and shorts. They slipped off their sandals and set them in a small shoe rack and seemed familiar with their surroundings. With her hands on her hips, the woman stood and glanced around the living room. "I'll put my clothes and stuff in the guest room."

"Mom's going to appreciate having you here to help her…until she can walk." He opened the closet door. "I've always been curious about this guest closet. Why didn't Mama allow us to play inside or even open the door?"

"She didn't want it messed up. What did you think about Mama's prognosis? Do you believe she'll be able to walk within a few weeks?"

"I hope so," he said. "Mama's a strong woman. I know she'll get herself up on her feet sooner than expected. Don't you?"

"Of course, she's strong physically, mentally, and emotionally," she said. "Anyone who can survive in the Soviet Union, and get themselves to the States, and make a good life, is strong."

"Let's get busy. We only have today to dust, vacuum, and make sure it's as clean as she usually keeps it. We'll get groceries from downstairs before Mama comes home."

Ben reached for the top of the closet door and peeled something back. Tape? He swung the door open and stepped aside. Kristina walked into the hallway leading to the bedrooms.

Andrea hoped the portal could hear both of them, like it did for Boris and Natasha in separate rooms.

Inside the guest closet, Ben's voice could still be heard. "Kristina, what do you think these sheets of plywood are doing in here? Looks like some nails are gone, like someone tried to pull them out." He tossed a nail out onto the floor. "It looks like a second wall behind it, or something."

Could the guest closet lead into the passage? Andrea cringed.

"Come and look at these old suitcases behind the plywood. They're really old."

Kristina joined Ben in the living room and studied the suitcases. "I've never seen them before. Are they Mama's?"

"Must be," Ben said. "Mama got rid of Papa's things after he died."

With the suitcases on the floor between them, Kristina and Ben sat and nodded in agreement. "Here's a black-and-white photo of an airplane parked on a landing field that looks like it could have been built before the war," Kristina said. "And look, isn't that Mama standing next to the wing?"

Ben squinted. "Yes, it certainly is. She looks so young." Ben turned it over. "There's a date on the back. Nineteen forty. She would've been about twenty years old and still in Byelorussia."

"Here's a license issued in nineteen thirty-nine," Kristina said. "I can read some of the Russian words, but Mama's name and the word *pilot* are the only words I can make out."

"So, Mama was a pilot?" Ben asked. "She never told us."

"She hates to fly," Kristina said. "Remember when we practically had to force her to fly to California with us?"

"Here's some maps of the forested areas in Byelorussia, along the border of Lithuania."

"And more government documents, all with official stamps and seals. And a hat. What kind of hat is this? Her surname is written inside. Petrova."

"It's a pilot's hat. Wow, she really did fly planes."

Kristina opened the third suitcase and held up a notebook with a soft cover and lined pages. "Journals. There's a stack of Mama's journals in here."

Inside the passage, Andrea shook her cramped hand and took a deep breath.

Kristina read the journal. "Mama trained in the Red Army."

Ben sat closer to Kristina. "Only nineteen years old."

"In this notebook she wrote: *I flew over the tops of the trees, then turned the engines off and glided into small clearings, hoping to come to a stop before crashing into trees or running over someone anxious to escape. Parents sent their children into the fields alone, in hopes of getting on the plane, to safety. We reached over and lifted them by their arms, legs, hair, whatever we could grab and tossed them into the plane.*"

Ben shook his head. "She never told us."

"Here's something else Mama wrote. *Someone had spotted my co-pilot and me. Flashlights raced between the trees toward our airplane that sat in the center of the field. We didn't have enough clearing to take off without turning around, and there was no time. We fired at the enemy until the flashlights were on the ground and not moving, before they could shoot the Jewish families running toward the plane. I didn't expect to write in my journal tonight. God be with us.*"

Kristina held the journal to her chest. "I wonder if she'll ever tell us about her life in the Soviet Union."

"I don't think so. She must have horrible memories. Let's put these back and not tell her we found them."

"Okay, I'm ready to start vacuuming." Ben set the suitcases and plywood in the closet, closed the door and smoothed the tape down to its original place.

What a strange thing to do. Andrea sat with shallow breaths as shame washed through her. I cannot sit here and watch them engage in a private conversation any longer. I should have left sooner. Or not been here at all.

IN EVELYN'S APARTMENT, ANDREA POURED HERSELF A GLASS OF WINE AND sat in her favorite chair, the one with a view of the city again. Her head reeled from all the ideas for a story. *The Pilot's Story.* With her notebook in hand, she began writing a summary of what she had witnessed in 3B. She'd need to consult with someone who knew Soviet culture and history. Even though the pilot's children spoke English to each other, they read the notes in Russian. Andrea's basic and rusty use of Russian didn't help her much.

James set the dinner tray on the table and set a second tray across from her. "Mind if I join you?" he asked.

Andrea nodded and motioned to the chair across from her. "The pilot's story is incredible. Evelyn was right." She sipped from a glass of water. "But I can't believe I sat there and watched her children in their home. The pressure of a deadline persuaded me to watch even though it was wrong. When Ben opened the closet door, I was hooked. As if reading a good book."

"I'm sure you'll write another compelling story." He smiled. "I've read your first novel."

"Why was tape on the guest closet door?"

"It's a common idea." He shrugged. "To see if anyone had opened the door while they were gone. Sometimes a piece of paper is wedged between the door and the frame."

"And why were there sheets of plywood in the guest closet?"

"As an afterthought, Ms. Evelyn and her husband built hiding places for the residents and their personal belongings, but the materials had to be easy to remove, without loud construction."

"Incredible." Andrea stared at her notebook and wiped the dust. "Am I doing the right thing, James?"

"Yes. I know there's much to consider, but please keep in mind that we must tell these stories to remember the heroes of the Holocaust. When you write the pilot's story, and I hope you do, you will remind the world that we must never allow that kind of evil to take control again."

"I don't recall being taught these stories in history classes. I remember reading *The Diary of Anne Frank* and Corrie Ten Boom's book, *The Hiding Place*, but at that time I didn't grasp the horrific reality, like many Americans, I suppose because the Holocaust happened on another continent, and decades ago. But the contents of the suitcases have impacted me. Made it real. It would be an honor to write the pilot's story, but I can't imagine revealing to her how I spied on her children and used the contents of her hidden suitcases to write it."

"You don't need to tell her or anyone. I'll always honor that secret. So will Ms. Evelyn. After dinner, go to the first floor and swim in the pool. Relax. Let it all soak in. Not the water, but what you witnessed today. Think it over and let it settle so you can organize your notes tomorrow."

James accompanied Andrea down to the first floor where it seemed every resident had congregated. Loud conversations, boisterous laughter, and lively music met her as she stepped out of the elevator. Andrea had pictured a serene environment to soothe her nerves after absorbing such a heartfelt story.

"Enjoy your time here," James said.

After setting her towel on a chair, she eased into the warm water and floated on her back, being supported by the buoyant water. Across the pool, the main character in Evelyn's novel swam laps again. She pictured little children clinging to him as he swam them to safety on the other side of the river. Soft lights in the bakery where a woman arranged a display of bread rolls. She must be the woman who had hidden Jews in her bakery's basement in Poland. Two men playing chess in the corner were possibly the men who had stowed Jews in the underbelly of a truck and crossed the border. The reality of having the privilege of joining these heroes overwhelmed Andrea. The pilot deserves to have her own heroic story written to remind the world of the atrocities of the Holocaust.

THE ELEVATOR DOORS OPENED ON THE FIFTH FLOOR. SHE UNLOCKED THE door to Evelyn's apartment and stepped inside. After she changed her clothes and grabbed her notebook, she thought a cup of tea would help her to focus while she read through her notes and wrote her ideas.

As she passed the dining table, she tripped on something that had not been there before. The pilot's suitcases stood next to the table leg. Waiting for her. A note on the table.

Andrea,
You'll need these.
Call and I will translate for you.
James

ANDREA AND JAMES SPENT THE EVENING SORTING THE SUITCASES' CONTENTS into stacks of photos, journal notes, letters, official documents, newspaper clippings, and maps. James's knowledge and experience of living in the Soviet Union was crucial for making sense of everything. He translated the notes on the back of photos, the documents, newspaper articles, and letters. They continued until two in the morning.

After James left, Andrea relaxed on the recliner with a view of the city and a treasury of ideas keeping her awake. Thinking of how Evelyn Lyon Gates wrote her novels by braiding in the facts with fiction so meticulously and grabbed her readers, Andrea would structure her novel in the same manner. She would fictionalize the story in order to incorporate and weave the information from the suitcases.

DAYS LATER, AND AS JAMES SUGGESTED, ANDREA WAITED AT A TABLE IN front of the café with her notebook and pen in hand. She checked her watch for the fourth or fifth time. Maybe they weren't coming. Ben and Kristina must have jobs or children to care for, but James said their mother was supposed to come home this morning, around ten.

The glass door opened. Ben pushed a wheelchair into the European village, and Kristina walked alongside her mother, carrying a modern purple suitcase. Andrea set her cup down and leaned forward to get a better look. Her heart rate increased. There she was. The pilot. A woman who saved the lives of children. Andrea sucked in her breath and hoped James had returned the empty suitcases to the hiding place in the pilot's closet. Would the pilot want to see her suitcases? Check the contents? Maybe not with Ben and Kristina present. But later?

Next to Kristina, Ben maneuvered the wheelchair into the elevator. Andrea raced to the fifth-floor elevator, ran through the apartment, and scrambled into the passage. Equipped with her notebook and pen, she sat on the stool, awaiting their entry into apartment 3B.

The pilot glanced around her living room and squinted at the top corner of the guest closet. The corners of her mouth turned up.

After they discussed their mother's prognosis and the bulky wheelchair, and how she refused to go to the hospital again, even though the nurses were so kind to her, Kristina made tea and was reminded to add two spoonfuls of strawberry jam, not just one.

Ben rolled the wheelchair to the table where Kristina poured tea into the cups.

"Mama," Kristina said. "Tell us about your life in the Soviet Union."

Their mother scowled. "Nothing to tell." She waved her hand as if chasing the memories away. "Not important."

Andrea climbed the steps back into Evelyn's apartment with a knot in the back of her throat. She couldn't sit on that stool another minute, not because she was physically uncomfortable, but morally uncomfortable. How could Evelyn have done this for at least ten of her novels?

The only potential benefit from watching the pilot and her children was learning how they spoke to each other, their mannerisms, expressions, and how that could be described in her novel. She considered the beginning. Should she write chronologically, starting when the pilot was a child in the Soviet Union? Or start in the present with a backstory, as if the pilot were telling the story to her adult children. Andrea wanted to interview the pilot, but surely she would refuse.

For the next three months, Andrea made a habit to write early in the morning while the birds chirped outside. If she finished before dinner, she rewarded herself with a swim in the pool and time in the hot tub. But her brain never turned off writing. While on the first floor, she observed and listened to the Soviet residents greet, interact, and converse, to develop the characters in her story.

Three afternoons a week, Andrea took a bus to the city library to research the details and facts related to the story. She uncovered more photos and descriptions of the plane the pilot had flown from Byelorussia to Spain, the hidden landing strips, detailed maps of the areas, and historical events.

Sometimes, the most crucial information showed itself in places Andrea never imagined. The librarian noticed the book titles, newsprints, interviews, and photos Andrea had gathered and showed her a tattered book with crumbling pages. Andrea read personal accounts describing how people who hid in the forest survived and where they had originated before the Holocaust.

She hadn't heard from Evelyn, other than updates from James. She pictured Evelyn in the Café de Flore in Paris interviewing a character in her novel or researching in the Bibliotheque Nationale de France. Did she ever regret writing someone's personal story without permission? Andrea couldn't berate Evelyn, because she had graciously invited her to stay in her apartment and practically tossed the pilot's story in Andrea's lap. Andrea hoped she would believe she had done the right thing, once the novel had gone to the publisher and she no longer had control of it.

In mid-November, Andrea finished the second draft of the manuscript. She wrapped it with butcher paper, put it inside a small travel bag, and carried it toward the post office. She fought the urge to skip like a child full of confidence and pride for finishing such a compelling story before the publisher's deadline.

Up ahead, Andrea spotted Kristina and her mother walking toward her. She tightened her grip on the bag that suddenly seemed heavy. "Breathe, smile, look calm," Andrea whispered to herself.

"Hello, Andrea." Kristina smiled.

The pilot extended her hand. "Hello, Andrea. I'm honored to meet you. I am Zoya."

"Oh," Andrea said. "I'd heard physical therapy had helped you walk again. Good for you."

"Yes," Zoya said. "Very hard work, but now I walk." Her smile faded. "Have you written your book?"

A small choke escaped Andrea. "It's going well. It's taken longer than I had expected." She glanced at the sky. "Isn't it nice to walk after a storm?" She took a deep breath and relaxed her shoulders, but her stomach churned.

"Are you walking into the city?" Kristina asked.

"No. Just to the post office." As soon as the words left her mouth, Andrea realized she had left the door open to be asked what she was mailing.

Kristina rested her hand on Andrea's arm and looked straight into her eyes. "You found a story to write. Correct?" She didn't wait for an answer, smiled, took her mother's hand, and they continued toward 3rd and Oak.

What did she mean? Andrea glanced toward the post office, but something had changed. Zoya had such a kind expression, smiling eyes, and for the first time seemed like a real person. Not just viewed through a portal, but a woman who had risked her life for others. Andrea's justifications for spying to meet a personal deadline slipped away.

She considered dropping the manuscript in the trash but feared someone might discover it and possibly harm the pilot and her family. Or someone could claim the story and make themselves the hero, abusing Zoya's personal journals, photos, and documents. The thought of that made Andrea cringe, but her own behavior had been absolutely disgraceful.

THE PHONE RANG IN EVELYN LYON GATES' LIBRARY. WHO WOULD CALL THIS late?

"Hello?"

"Well, hello, Andrea," Evelyn said. "I heard you finished your manuscript early. Congratulations."

"Yes, I did. Thank you so much." Andrea sat at Evelyn's desk. "I appreciate the gracious invitation to stay here in your lovely apartment. You said I would find ideas for the perfect story, and you were absolutely right. Now, I understand how you've come up with so many compelling stories, in such a short time."

"Oh? And how's that?"

"I found your secret passage and was alerted to the pilot's heroism through the portals."

"You did what?" Her shrill voice pierced Andrea's ears. "Oh my God! That's not how I got my stories! How did you get into the passage? I sealed it after my husband died."

Andrea's stomach dropped. "I pulled the crystal vase in the pantry, and it opened."

"What made you think I spied on my friends and stole their personal stories?"

"Well, I've read most of your novels and recognized the residents as the characters."

"Does Zoya know?"

"No. She doesn't."

"You didn't get her permission?"

"No. I couldn't imagine her agreeing to work with me. And I had a deadline, so I forced myself to sit in front of the 3B portal. Did you ever feel that way, too? Did you justify it as a means to show the world—"

"No! I didn't spy on them. Never. I asked each of them for permission to write their stories, and we signed contracts. I spent months sitting with them in my office, while they shared their experiences. They read and approved each chapter and then the entire manuscript after I completed it and before I sent it to the publisher. Have you sent the story to the publisher yet?"

"I almost sent it today, but when I saw Zoya with her daughter, I knew I had made a horrible mistake. I couldn't send it."

"What have you done with it?"

"It's here. In my suitcase."

"You must tell Zoya what you did and apologize. At the very least.

Ask her if she wants the manuscript. If not, burn it." Evelyn cleared her throat. "You thought I did this, too?"

"Yes. It was hard to believe at first, but after I connected the residents to the characters, I assumed you had invited me to do the same."

"But Andrea, look at my books! The dedications are to the survivors and in the acknowledgements, I described how we worked together and what an incredible experience it was to hear their stories unfold in their own words."

Andrea gasped. How could she have been so stupid?

After the enlightening conversation with Evelyn, and Andrea's implicit promise to meet and confess to Zoya, she set the phone into the cradle and collapsed into the recliner chair.

THE NEXT MORNING, ANDREA FOLDED HER CLOTHES AND PUT THEM INTO HER suitcase while she struggled to find the best words to convey her apology to Zoya and her children. There were no words. Andrea couldn't explain how she acquired the information. She refused to expose the passage, or how Ben and Kristina found the suitcases, or that James stole them from the pilot's apartment and made the contents available to her.

A knock on the door. Couldn't be James. Someone else had delivered breakfast. Hopefully, Evelyn hadn't fired him. Andrea had made that dreadful decision to spy and use private information to make a deadline. Not James.

She opened the door.

James stood with his hands clasped. No tray. "May I share my thoughts with you?"

"Of course. Come in and grab a cup of coffee."

James sighed. "I apologize for misleading you and encouraging you to use the passage." He tapped his fingers on the table. "I'm ashamed to say that I also believed Evelyn used the passages for her stories, but now I'm sure she didn't."

"And why is that?"

"The passage gets dusty from the heater and air vents. Evelyn is allergic to dust."

"Who oversees the cleaning crew?"

"Evelyn. Since her husband died. The maintenance and cleaning crew are trusted family members. But as far as I know, she has only allowed them to clean the passage a few times."

"When was the last time the passage was cleaned?"

"The day before you arrived."

Andrea leaned back in the chair and sipped her coffee. Something about his answer bothered her. Cleaned it for me? "I spoke to Evelyn on the phone. She plans to convert the passage into additional storage space inside each apartment."

The doorbell chimed. Who? A friend of Evelyn's? Andrea peeked out the peephole and saw Ben and Kristina standing on each side of their mother. Andrea had expected to meet with Zoya and had prepared to accept her justified fury, but not so soon.

Andrea's hand trembled as she opened the door.

Kristina smiled. "May we come in?"

Momentarily speechless, Andrea stepped back from the door. "Yes, please come in."

With the familiar suitcases in hand, Kristina and Ben accompanied their mother into the apartment. Andrea motioned to the dining room. "Please join James and me at the table," she stammered. "Would you like coffee or tea?"

"No. Thank you," the pilot said.

Ben helped his mother onto a chair. "No tea for me, thanks."

"Nor for me," Kristina said. "We must speak with you."

"I'm so ashamed of myself." Andrea felt nauseous as the words tumbled out.

Zoya smiled. "No need." She nodded at James. "Would you explain what happened? My English...not so good."

James seemed surprised. "Of course." He straightened. "A couple of months ago, Zoya requested that I ask Evelyn to write her story. But Evelyn had already started another novel and planned to live in Paris while writing and researching ."

Zoya placed her hand on her chest. "I was…how you say…disappointed. Continue, James."

"When Evelyn told me Andrea would stay here for six months and needed to find an idea for a story before the end of December, of course, I thought of Zoya."

Everyone smiled at Andrea.

"But a week before your arrival, Andrea, plans changed. Zoya was hit by a car and sent to the hospital. I had to find a way to convince you to write her story. And fast. So, I told Kristina and Ben to go into the apartment and look for anything from her life in the Soviet Union and how she became a pilot. They found the suitcases, and after a discussion with their mama, they gave the suitcases and the contents to me, to give to you."

"I finally told my children the truth." Zoya shook her head. "I never told them. Too dangerous. They would be angry with me, but if they read my story, they would understand. A book can tell my story." She smiled. "They visited me in the hospital and told me they found my suitcases and I must tell my story." She held both hands over her heart. "Now, I stop fearing my country, and punishment for what I have done. I have carried this fear for forty years."

Kristina's eyes filled with tears. "We're so proud of you, Mama."

"Andrea," Zoya said. "Did you write my story?"

Andrea broke out in a sweat. "Yes. I did. But I should have asked for your permission." She leaned across the table and took Zoya's hand. "I'm so sorry. I took your story to save myself. I was desperate to meet a deadline, and I made an extremely selfish decision."

"May I read it?" Zoya asked.

"Of course," Andrea said. "It belongs to you." Andrea handed the bag with the manuscript to her.

"You have a deadline. Yes?"

Andrea nodded. "End of December."

"If you have time, I will tell you my story. Do you agree?"

"I'd be honored to write the novel with you."

"When do we start?" Zoya asked.

"Now?"

"Yes. Of course." Zoya handed the box on her lap to Andrea. "Letters from the children in my airplane."

EIGHTEEN MONTHS LATER, ANDREA WAITED WITH THE CREW AT THE GATE IN the JFK terminal for an agent to unlock the door to the jetway. Above the counter, the sign read Flight 827 Honolulu. Home for Andrea. Passengers filled the gate area. Some stared at the desk waiting for a boarding announcement, others read newspapers, or paperback books. The woman closest to Andrea seemed enthralled with the book she was reading. Andrea recognized the cover.

Across the top, *The Pilot's Story*.

At the bottom, *Andrea Nolan and Zoya Petrova*

Across the back, *Lest we forget*.

DEALING WITH DEMONS AT 3RD & OAK

ANNIE TUPEK

The city bus slowed as it approached the corner of 3rd and Oak. Selma Fairbright wrapped the half-finished sock around her knitting needles and flexed her fingers. Her special arnica-mint lotion kept arthritis from worsening in her seventy-year-old joints, but she had been knitting since boarding the bus, and her fingers were locked in place from the repetitive movement. Knitting was the tried-and-true method to get her into the meditative state necessary for facing a demon.

The apprentice witch—a woman in her early twenties—whose name Selma couldn't quite recall, sat next to her on the barely-cushioned seat and took the cessation of kitting as a signal to ask, "What are you making?"

Her name was something like Kelsey or Chelsea. She blended in with the other young witches Selma had scared away from the Demon Investigative Services. Selma had long-since stopped learning their names. This one had come prepared, likely having heard stories from the other apprentices previously assigned to Selma.

Half a dozen bracelets circled the apprentice's wrists protectively. Another chain around her neck bore an amethyst pendant as a talisman. She wore jeans and a dark flannel over an even darker t-shirt. Her brown hair was pulled back into a sensible braid.

The bus ride had been spent in blissful silence until that point.

"Socks. For my grandson." Selma said. She secured the knitting project in her ample market bag.

The apprentice carried a small purse, a boxy thing like the plastic lunchboxes Selma's children had carried in the eighties. It wouldn't hold much more than a sandwich and thermos of soup. The girl would learn.

"It's cheating," the apprentice said. "Imbuing magic into his socks."

"I am reinforcing the socks to last longer," Selma explained. "The boy goes through socks like a fish through water."

"You're casting speed into each stitch," the apprentice accused.

The girl was sharp. Why did the coven leaders always stick her with the lawful ones?

"He gets bullied," Selma said. "He won't fight back, so he runs."

The apprentice had the decency to look away. Selma would see how the girl did when faced with a demon of the netherworld. Most ran away. But this apprentice wore sensible pink and black sneakers. Good for running.

Selma didn't mind. She preferred to work alone. She hadn't had a real partner since Old Madge had died. Old Madge, the witch who had taught Selma everything she knew, wouldn't have stood for this generation's entitlement and lack of respect. Or cowardice in the face of danger.

A pothole jostled the city bus. Then the brakes screeched the bus to a halt. Selma and her apprentice rose. Everyone else was listless, eyes down, shoulders slumped. Even the apprentice had lost some of her pep. Selma's calculations were correct. A dark force had taken up residence at 3rd and Oak. If not for her own amethyst pendant, she would have felt the depression the demon had cast over the neighborhood.

"Thank you," Selma said to the driver and received the barest smile. The man had been jovial when they'd boarded. The demon's influence on the neighborhood extended to those passing through. It gave her hope that none would recall overhearing the apprentice's accusation. Modern as the world was, city people still did not look kindly on witches.

Selma went to the shade of the bus shelter to get her bearings. Across the street stood a Brutalist movement apartment, its concrete crumbling into the sidewalk. It was as old as she was and, like her body, the building had seen better days. Its façade was a dull, weather-worn gray. The cracks across its ancient face contrasted against the sparkling new developments that surrounded it. A perpetual cloud, invisible to normal sight, cast the building into shadow.

This was the place.

"We need to confirm it's there," Selma said. It was obvious to her, but she needed to set a proper example for the apprentice. Madge had taught her that every moment was a teaching moment, even though the odds were against the apprentice returning for the next mission.

Selma grounded herself on the crumbling sidewalk and pressed her palms against the bus shelter's clammy metal wall, sticky with years of splashed sodas and city grime. Her kinesthetic senses reached through the foundations and plumbing. Her empathy reflected the psyches of the humans inhabiting the area.

Her shoulders slumped and she wilted from despair. Dark energy seeped into her. Geriatric residents waited to die. The landlord filled vacant rooms with halfway-house transients at the top of their eventual downward cycle. A man on the third floor had a handgun in a shoebox under the bed. A woman on the second floor toyed with a bottle of pills. The demon fed, and it fed well.

The coven's leaders seemed to know when she had located a new demon and took the opportunity to stick her with an apprentice. They'd been doing it on and off since Madge had passed ten years ago. Seventy wasn't that old for a witch, but the coven's leaders kept pressuring her to settle into a desk job and pass on the demon hunting role to someone else.

This was supposed to be a reconnaissance mission, but the neighborhood was a nexus of despair. The demon needed to be neutralized immediately. Only then could they begin the area's spiritual restoration.

Selma took her palms from the bus shelter's walls, and balled her hands into fists. She rubbed the carnelian in the ring on her left index finger. Madge had given it to her; a ring of protection. Selma liked to think her mentor's memory increased its strength. The demon was rooted in this place. They were going to need all the crystals they had brought.

"Ground zero," the apprentice said. Selma was surprised to see Christy—or Chrissy?—had delved the neighborhood alongside her. The apprentice asked, "What do we do now?"

Selma gathered her shawl around her. The cloaking and protection spells she had knit into it were still potent. "What do you think we should do?" Selma asked.

It was important to instill standard procedures in young witches. Madge always said self-discipline turned young witches into old witches. The undisciplined youth rarely made it to maturity. But part of that maturity was knowing when to risk deviating from the regulations. Like when lives were at stake.

The apprentice looked at Selma as though expecting a test. Chelsea-Kelsey said, "It's in there. I can feel it." She pointed. "Second floor."

Selma nodded. Part of her assignment was assessing the apprentice's decision-making skills. "It's there. What should we do?"

"The coven will take too long to decide. Anything by committee takes ten times longer. And they're just going to send us back here to take care of things."

Selma eyed the apprentice. It seemed she was figuring out the right time to deviate from the rules. "Take care of things how?"

"We're going to trap the demon. That's why you've got the salt, bottle, and black candle."

"Could be." Christie?—Chrissy?—was showing off her book-learning. Selma tried to recall her name.

"Distract and capture," Christie-Chrissy-Chelsea-Kelsey said. "I know how you operate."

The corner of Selma's mouth rose in a smirk. This one was quicker than the others, and had something of a backbone, too. Selma was aware of what her reputation was among the apprentices. She saw some of herself in this one, but she also saw a cockiness that needed tempering. Today's mission was likely to do just that.

"You're close," Selma said. She was certain the coven had sent the apprentice along to keep her from doing exactly what she was about to do. Take care of the problem. Selma pulled from her market satchel the wine bottle, sealed with a cork, the canister of salt, full, and the black candle, unlit. She pressed the lot into the apprentice's arms. "I distract while you capture."

The apprentice juggled the items until they settled in her arms. "I'm wearing my protective charms. I thought I'd be the one doing the distracting."

"You'll need them," Selma said. "Even without the demon's focused attention, the close proximity will drain your reserves." She wondered if her own protective charms and talismans would be enough. She adjusted her rings so their stones faced inwards, the easier for her thumbs to rub against and awaken their energies.

"You know how to capture a demon?"

"Salt circle," the apprentice said and shook the salt canister. "Then uncork the bottle and offer it a home."

She knew the basics. Selma handed her one of the narrow three-strand braided loops. She had one just like it tied around her left wrist. "Hold onto this. When it breaks, come into the apartment and draw the circle. Got it?" Selma asked, then left the bus shelter and crossed the uneven street. The apartment building's walkway and entrance cut imposing lines and sharp angles. Selma led the way inside.

Whole banks of lights had dimmed or gone out. The fans in the ventilation system clacked and the air they stirred smelled of vinegar and sulfur. The apprentice blanched and started mouth breathing.

"You'll get used to it," Selma said. The stench revolted her, too. It had taken years of training, but she had mastered the ability to ignore rank odors. Demons loved to make a stink. This one tested her limits. For focus, she rubbed her right thumb along the hematite ring on her right index finger. They climbed the stairs, the railing slick. Generations of hands having rubbed the finish away to bare metal. There was a time when she hadn't needed assistance climbing stairs.

The door to the second floor half-hung off its hinges and was propped open against the wall with a cinderblock. "Definitely this floor," the apprentice said.

The apprentice's instincts were good. She had a natural talent for demon locating. Perhaps the Demon Investigative Services might have a new recruit. If she survived this demon. And if Selma could remember her name. Casey?

"Silence from now on." Selma started down the hallway.

At the door to apartment 2B, the apprentice pulled one of her bracelets off her wrist and hung it over the doorknob, its clear quartz appeared dull in the uneven light.

Selma gave her the stare; the one that stopped countless apprentices in their tracks.

"For protection," the apprentice whispered. She visibly shivered. "I could hear the pills rattling."

The apprentice had the right attitude, but needed to follow directions. Selma held her finger to her lips. "Silence."

The fresh, cheerful welcome mat in front of apartment 2D felt out of place on the mottled brown and threadbare carpeting. Selma motioned for the apprentice to stop and stay out of sight of the door.

The apprentice did as she'd been told. Selma took a centering breath, and did her best to filter out the sulfurous stench. Then she took a deliberate step onto the welcome mat, lifted her hand, and knocked three times.

Around her, the building went still. The whirring fans silenced, the groaning floorboards muted, and the building held its breath. The apprentice's eyes were wide, probably as wide as Selma's own, and just as fearful.

Selma gestured for the apprentice to stay where she was, and remain out of sight. Selma returned her attention to the door and drew up her power. Posing as a supernatural archetype to confuse the demon would take all her concentration. "Water and power," she said. "Here for an inspection."

"Water and power?" a voice hissed on the other side. It sounded amused.

The door opened to reveal a scruffy young man. His dishwater-blonde hair was mussed and hung in his eyes, hiding his gaze. His scraggly beard and mustache parted in a grin that revealed clean, sharp teeth. His long-sleeved t-shirt and jeans conformed to his lean limbs. That the demon showed this human form meant it wasn't sure who, or what, Selma was. Her cloaking shawl was still effective.

"Are you here to inspect my power?" The demon's smile lengthened into a leer.

"I can see from here it's large enough. May I come in?" Selma took half a step forward so the toes of her left foot stopped at the threshold.

The demon tossed its head back to get the hair out of its eyes. Black eyes bore into Selma, inspecting. It would find none of the tools of capture: the salt for containment, the bottle for storage, the candle wax for sealing it in. The apprentice held those. Selma smiled at him and projected confidence. When dealing with demons, it was all about confidence. She did not look at the apprentice on her right.

"You do not look like one of my neighbors," the demon said. "Who are you?"

"They call me Old Woman," Selma answered. "And I know better than to give my name to the likes of you. May I come in?"

The demon tilted its head, an expression of curiosity on its face. "You may." The demon stepped aside, its blond hair fell forward to veil its eyes once more.

Selma scuffed her shoe across the threshold leaving a line of rubber and creating a small gap in the ward the apprentice could sneak through. She hoped the girl was smart enough to see it. One of Selma's amethyst bracelets failed as she crossed the threshold. Despair tugged at her with greater force.

A narrow wall divided a small kitchen from the rest of the apartment. Mismatched chairs filled the open space. Lopsided draperies hid the room's windows. Pictures in broken frames on the walls depicted unspeakable acts of torture. Those would be burned. That was one thing the Brutalist-movement building was good for: all those concrete floors, walls, and ceilings made for exceptional fire control. There would be nothing left by the time Selma and the apprentice were done with the demon. The units to each side wouldn't be harmed.

"Who are you really with?" the demon asked.

She was pleased she had it wary. That was the way to defeat them, through confusion. Humans usually acted one of two ways around demons: scared or fawning. She had done neither, knowing her indifference would intrigue the demon. She needed to retain her hold on its attention long enough for the apprentice to draw the salt circle trap around it.

"Manners," Selma scolded. She knew when to take advantage of her crone aspect. She focused on the revered matriarch, an archetype long established in the esoteric traditions, and said, "I'd expected to be offered a seat. Back in my day, we showed reverence to our elders."

Back in her day. This demon was infinitely more ancient than her seventy years.

"Please, sit." The demon gestured with nicotine-stained fingers to the mismatched furniture.

"Thank you," Selma said, her smile one of magnanimous approval for the demon's improved manners. She selected the tattered armchair that would force the demon to sit with its back partially to the door and give the apprentice a better chance to sneak in.

Selma leaned into the armchair, sweat seeping into her shirt. The demon seemed to fill the apartment's single room. A loft they called it, though there was nothing lofty about it. The shadowed corners encroached on the rest of the room, drawing the sparsely sunlit spaces into darkness. She rubbed her carnelian ring on her finger for courage.

"They say hospitality is dead," she said, continuing to manifest her crone aspect, "but I disagree. What is your opinion?"

"Hospitality?" The demon then muttered to itself. It appeared utterly confused.

Selma cocked her head, displaying composure that she did not feel. "Tea."

The demon took it for a demand and put itself under her power. That boded well. The demon went to the kitchen's hot plate. Selma tugged the three-hair braid from her wrist and snapped it, signaling to the apprentice it was time for her entrance.

The demon filled the kettle at the sink, its back to her. As the apprentice slinked into the apartment, staying in the shadows, the demon shut off the water and put the kettle on the hotplate.

"It will be two minutes," the demon said as it came and sat in the chair across from her.

Selma very carefully didn't look at the corner where the apprentice stood, stock still and nearly in the peripheral vision of the demon. She held its full gaze and reinforced her will.

"Most kind," Selma said. Two minutes was all the time she needed. "Why use these human contrivances?" she asked. "We both know there are other ways to make fire." She snapped her fingers and blue flames danced above her hand and disappeared.

The apprentice used the distraction to cut behind the demon's chair, pouring a thin line of salt as she went.

The fire had been a magician's trick. Not magical. The friction of the snap had ignited the chemical compounds painted on her skin.

The demon stared at her. Selma was suddenly intimidated by the intelligence in its eyes. The demon wrinkled its nose.

Selma struggled to maintain her composure. She hadn't thought the demon would smell the chemicals over the brimstone and soot that choked the air, but demons had their special affinity to fire of all kinds.

Selma stood, drawing the demon's eyes away from where the apprentice crouched. She walked to the small counter where the electric kettle was bubbling. "Water is almost boiling," she said. She deftly stepped over the line of salt the apprentice had laid.

"Human," the demon growled and rose to its feet.

Selma ducked behind a narrow counter. Her knees twinged when they bumped the floor. Her body not as resilient as it used to be. She braced her shawl in front of her. Its magic shielded her from the curse the demon threw at her.

"I know you," the demon said. "You're Selma Fairbright. My siblings will rejoice with me as their savior when I pull you down to the nether-world with me."

Selma shivered at the mention of her name. "Better demons than you have tried." Selma crouched in the small kitchen. She shielded another curse with her shawl. The spell that had been spun into the yarn and knitted into the shawl unraveled a little more. She could take one more hit. Maybe two.

"I've got a lot of your siblings at home in bottles. Snuggled into sawdust-filled crates. Safe and sound," Selma said. "And I've got a space for you." She peered around the wall to see what was taking the apprentice so long.

The demon cackled and came closer to the kitchen. "But you left your bottles at home and came here unarmed."

The apartment's windows were too smudged to show any reflections. The whole place was dark and growing darker. Selma couldn't tell which shifting shadows were the apprentice, but she needed to trust that the girl was doing her job.

The demon's hot breath filled the apartment. Selma's defenses were taking a beating from its dark energy. She had only so much light in reserve, and it would take time to regenerate it. She was getting old.

She clutched a red jasper charm for luck. The salt canister rolled across the floor, in front of the demon's feet. A trail of salt leaked out of it.

The demon looked down, its eyes following the canister's trail. It rolled short, not quite closing off the circle. The demon's lips parted and it turned to look over its shoulder, to where the canister had come from. The apprentice.

Selma dove as the demon moved toward the apprentice. Her muscles ached as she stretched and dragged the canister through the pile of salt and closed the circle.

The apartment building shuddered. The demon was trapped. It hollered and scratched its nails along the barrier, taking care to avoid the grains of salt.

"Not so tough, now?" the apprentice said.

"Hush," Selma barked, breathing heavily from the brief exertion. "Don't taunt it. It can't help itself. It is in its nature." She turned her attention to the demon. "What is your name?"

"I won't talk to you," the demon said.

"You have to answer," the apprentice said. "We've got you."

Selma kept her smile to herself. Working with the apprentice was a little like working with Madge. They had the same bravado in the face of evil.

"Yes, you do," the demon said. "But for how long?"

"Eternity, as far as you're concerned," Selma said. "What is your name?"

"Not telling."

Selma rolled her eyes in exasperation. "For the third and final time. What is your name?"

Compelled, the demon answered, "Riaza Firestrike."

"Very well, Riaza Firestrike," Selma said, feeling the power in its name. "No demons are coming to rescue you. They've left you all alone up here. I'm giving you a choice. Banishment to the netherworld where your siblings will torture you for being caught by me. You won't be allowed to visit the human world for a million years." She leaned forward conspiratorially and added, "Between you and me, I don't think we're going to last that long."

"Or?" the demon asked. "What's the offer?"

"Bottle-bound and in the employ of the Demon Investigative Services."

The demon scoffed.

"Banishment it is." The apprentice pulled out the black candle. "See you at Armageddon." She snapped her fingers and fire danced on her fingertips. It was the right time to bully. The apprentice's battlefield timing could use improvement. She had taken way too long to draw the circle, but her psychological game was strong.

"Bottle-bound, bottle-bound," Riaza said quickly.

"Excellent," the apprentice said. She pulled the bottle out of her bag. "Get in."

Riaza complied, transfiguring into smoke and shifting to the bottle. The ward shimmered with the demon's passing and the apprentice closed the bottle with the cork. She poured melted black wax around the mouth, sealing it tight.

Selma swept her foot through the salt circle, breaking it. The apprentice offered the bottle and Selma took it and tucked it into her market bag. At the apartment door, Selma nodded to the apprentice. "You do the honors."

The apprentice snapped her fingers again and flicked flames to the old mail and flyers on the counter, the ragged armchair Selma had sat on, and the clothes piled on the floor. Fire crackled as the flames took hold. Sudden heat built within the room and acrid smoke filled the air. Within moments, everything would be ash. They hurried to the hall and closed the door behind them, sealing the fire inside.

The smoke alarms went off as they reached the first floor. The residents were slow to exit and the fire trucks slower to arrive. Smoke poured out of the second-floor apartment the demon had resided in, but hadn't spread to the other units.

Selma and the apprentice stood under the bus shelter waiting for the next bus.

"What are we going to tell the coven?" the apprentice asked.

"There is no demon at 3rd and Oak," Selma said.

The apprentice nodded. "Adding the bottle to your personal collection?"

The apprentice had proven herself resourceful and calm. She had the spark of defiance that would come in handy when dealing with the coven's leaders. Selma put her hands on her hips and leaned back. Her neck popped. She was getting old. It was time to spend more time on her research and let the younger folks take to the field. This apprentice would make Old Madge proud.

She remembered the apprentice's name.

"Your personal collection, Demon Investigator Chelsea." Selma handed Chelsea the bottle. She pushed her suddenly-cold hands into her pockets. The carnelian ring caught and Selma heard Madge's cackle in her head. It was time.

Selma pulled the ring from her finger and gave it to Chelsea. "Take this, too. Wear it for protection. You'll need it."

She rubbed at the impression the ring had left around her finger. The bus arrived. Selma used the railing for help up the steps. She looked over her shoulder at Chelsea. The young witch seemed perplexed by her new possessions.

"Are you coming?" Selma asked.

Chelsea slipped the carnelian ring—Madge's ring—onto her finger and clutched the demon bottle. They found seats together near the front.

"Next stop: Elm Street," the voice on the PA announced as the doors closed.

"We have a lot of work ahead of us," Selma said and pulled out her knitting. The bus lurched into motion, away from 3rd and Oak.

CARLY KIT WATERS

MARYKA BIAGGIO

I was in love. Up to my eyeballs. And down to the tips of my toes. But I'm sure she didn't know, even though my cheeks burned like a bonfire on homecoming night every time I saw her. She was a sophomore and lived in an apartment off campus—a three-story cinder-block building on 3rd and Oak. Sure, it was just a blocky gray building, but in my eyes, it was a shining castle. Her name was Carly, but she went by Kit. She'd written her name on her notebook: Carly "Kit" Waters. Could there be a cooler name than Carly "Kit" Waters?

But me? I'm Wendy Ragnow. Talk about a dumb name. It sounded like some pig-tailed girl in overalls who collected rags.

From the moment Kit walked into our Shakespeare class with a swagger that would've made John Wayne envious, I was a goner. Kit was an English Lit major, just like me. She hailed from downstate, had a mother and stepfather there, and was an only child.

I'd learned all this over the first four weeks of class because I had leap-frogged my way closer and closer to her desk. She claimed the front seat farthest from the door. I had worked my way up to the row next to hers and one seat back, and from that not-so-lofty perch I could eavesdrop on her and her roommate Jennie's conversations. I knew they weren't an item because I'd seen Jennie hanging like a coat on a rack all over a lanky, straggly-haired guy. And I knew Kit was a lesbian because

I'd heard Jennie teasing her about which girlfriend she was taking out that night, to which Kit responded, "Like I could ever find a girlfriend in this godforsaken town."

I was a wet-behind-the-ears freshman, second semester, and a townie, although my parents had moved out of town right after I started college—dragging my younger sister and two brothers along with them. So, I was a townie without a house in town. And also a kid without any family nearby to have me over for Sunday dinner after Mass or to take me down a notch when they thought I was being an uppity college student. That made me kind of an only child, just like Kit.

All freshmen had to live in the dorm on High Street, and I'm telling you: that street lived up to its name. I kept my pot and Zig-Zag papers hidden with the spare tire in my '69 Barracuda. Everyone called it the fishmobile, which bugged me to no end. Really, it was a pretty classy car, even if it was eight years old and had more creaks and groans than revs and purrs.

Getting caught smoking or stashing pot in my dorm room would have been a disaster. I couldn't afford tuition, so losing my scholarship would mean I'd have to quit college. And then I couldn't see Kit unless I hung out like a forlorn Romeo below her window on 3rd and Oak. I'd already made a fool of myself once by following her after class to see where she lived. I wasn't positive she'd seen me, but she'd swung around before she entered the building and I had to act all casual, as if I was just out for a late Wednesday morning stroll. Like anybody with a brain couldn't see through that! I was such an idiot sometimes.

After that, I went back to driving my Barracuda to spy on Kit or to hang out with my friends. Whenever we cruised around smoking pot, I was the driver of choice. My friend Lucy said I was the real deal behind the wheel. It got so that every time I slid into the driver's seat, I had the urge to light up a joint—like Pavlov's dog, minus the drool.

Being in love with a girl was complicated. Ever since seventh grade, when my girlfriends were making eyes at boys and I was crushing on my teacher, Miss Stecker, I'd worried there was something off about me. But now that I was past the age of schoolgirl crushes and consumed by grown-up love and obsession, I couldn't avoid the truth: I had what the priest in the confessional called impure thoughts. That was just for confessing I'd tingled when a boy kissed me. He'd grilled me about every piece of my impure deed with that pimply-faced boy. That taught me to never again confess that kind of sin! I knew kissing a boy was small potatoes compared to kissing a girl, which left me all confused and in an epic tug-of-war between my feelings and my cursed Catholic conscience.

Damnation, I thought, if I'm going to consult priests about my every thought and deed, I might as well get me to a nunnery. Being an excellent student, I decided to do some research on my affliction. I figured bookish types or psychologists or psychiatrists would be more up-to-date than the Catholic Church, which was as old as God. I took myself off to the library one afternoon and plunked down in the stacks of psychology books. I pulled one book after another off the shelf, flipped to the index, and read everything I could find about homosexuality. It wasn't a pretty picture. By the time I finished my research, I'd learned that, according to all the experts, I was a deviant of the highest order and might be destined for the loony bin and, after that, hell.

I didn't care. That's how much in love I was. Still, I thought I should play it safe and visit the Counseling Center to see if there was an easy cure for my supposed derangement. I got paired up with a lady counselor who was so frumpy I almost turned tail and ran. She told me everything I said would be confidential—unless I planned to kill myself or somebody else, and I assured her I'd crossed those things off my to-do list. Imagine my surprise when I told her I had feelings for a girl—which was like calling Niagara Falls a trickle—and she didn't bat an eye. We had a good heart-to-heart talk and she told me there was a movement afoot in the fields of psychology and psychiatry to destigmatize homosexuality—which sounded like some kind of Catholic ritual to me. She said being gay was nothing to be ashamed of, but that I might want to be circumspect (she loved spouting big-ass words) about who I came out to. Nevertheless, she said, it might be judicious to seek support and affirmation from my social support network.

I had already told my two best friends from high school, Lucy and Marcia, who were psych majors, that I thought I was gay and they'd been pretty ho-hum about it. So, I decided I could tell them I had a crush on someone. I didn't dare tell them I was madly in love. Who knows what kind of stunts they'd pressure me into if they knew *that*.

So, one night when we were at the Big Boy chowing down on burgers, fries, and malts, I let the cat out of the bag. Of course, they wanted to know who my crush was, and I finally gave in to the pressure and told them her name was Kit, and that she was in my Shakespeare class.

"Ooh," Marcia said, flouncing her chestnut locks off her shoulder like she was Farrah Fawcett. "It's about time you busted out of the closet, you little chickenshit. Have you asked her out yet?"

"No," I moaned. "You think it's easy being a rookie gay girl? All *you* have to do is make eyes at some guy and next thing you know he's following you around like a puppy."

"Well," Lucy chimed in, "why don't you take a lesson from Marcia? She knows how to get the guys."

"Yup," Marcia said. "You ought to take social psychology and pick up a few tricks about attraction and intimacy."

"I'm taking my time, sizing up the situation," I said. "Why should I jump into something before I'm sure she's worth the effort?"

"Oh, come on," Marcia clucked. "You're hoping she'll ask you first, aren't you?"

"That'd sure solve a lot of problems. Like figuring out who's supposed to ask who out. And to what? Some movie with a guy and girl making out? It's not like I have a roadmap here."

Lucy giggled. She had the most delightful laugh, and I was grateful she wasn't turning up the heat on me like Marcia was.

Marcia tapped a finger to her lips and then mine. "Well, just let me know if you want me to make her jealous."

I swiped the back of my hand over my mouth. "Jeez, Marcia, you're such a flirt."

"Well, you're like the only virgin left standing in our class. It's about time you got laid."

"Oh, brother," I said. "Stop already."

Lucy said, "Let us know if you want us to hang out at Tony's Pizzeria while you wait for her to walk in."

"Yeah, but that's a townie hang-out. I doubt she spends time there."

"Didn't you say she lives on 3rd and Oak? That's just a block away from Tony's."

"Yeah, so what?"

I really didn't know how to play this. Especially with Kit being a sophomore and more worldly than I was. Heck, I'd never even been downstate, and Kit had a family and tons of friends there. She'd probably even had a slew of lesbian lovers, and the only gay girls I knew were maybe the two old ladies who lived on Rock Street next door to my family—before they all ran off and turned me into an orphan and free spirit in one fell swoop. Everybody on the block had gossiped about them: "Those poor things, they don't have a man to shovel their snow in the winter" and "How in the world do they decide which one of them takes out the trash and which one cooks?"

So, I was completely on my own when it came to wheedling my way into Kit's world. I figured I'd ease my way bit by bit into her conversations with Jennie, and I was forever plotting ways to do that. By the time I'd thought of a clever comeback to whatever they were talking about, they'd moved on to a new topic. It was driving me crazy. I was as slow on the uptake as a turtle sunning on a rock.

Then I came up with an idea. For our Shakespeare class, we were supposed to write a term paper on one of his plays. I'd decided on *Romeo and Juliet* and the subject of forbidden love, which I was quickly becoming the world's expert on. Next time Kit and Jennie started talking about our class, I'd ask, off-handed like, "Do you know what you're going to write your term paper on?" After they told me what they were writing about, I'd nod thoughtfully and ask a few brainy questions. Once they inquired what my topic was, I'd say, "The Forbidden Love of the Montagues and Capulets" and look straight into Kit's eyes without flinching one bit. But that all assumed I could keep my tongue from twisting into a pretzel when I talked to her.

I waited and waited for the chance to ask them about their term papers. One week went by, then two and three, and I still hadn't found an opening. Either they talked about stuff that had nothing to do with class or, if they talked about class, they never brought up their term papers. I just couldn't summon the gumption to up and ask about their papers.

Marcia was right. I was chickenhearted and fated, like some spineless jellyfish, to forever and ever stay in the dreary closet. Or should I say the aquarium? Marcia and Lucy were always watching and prodding me like I was some stubborn donkey, so sometimes I felt like I was on display in a fishbowl. Oh, jeez, I'm getting my metaphors all mixed up.

Each passing day left me feeling more and more like a desperado, and by the time the end of the semester was four weeks away, I decided my plan was as doomed as Hamlet's.

Then one Friday night I was hanging out with Marcia and Lucy at Tony's Pizzeria, and in walks Kit with Jennie and Jennie's boyfriend. They snagged a booth across from ours. My heart thumped and jumped like a rabbit in a gunny sack, and I couldn't keep myself from looking at them every thirty seconds while we gobbled up our large pepperoni pizza.

Marcia, who sat across from me, asked, "Do you know those three?"

"Uh, yeah, um, that's Kit and her friends."

"Well," she says, "looks like you're in luck. Time to make your big move."

Lucy took her time sizing them up. "That's your crush? The blond? She's cute."

"I know," I said like some dumbstruck idolizer. I was still high from the joint we'd smoked on the way to Tony's, and I could feel my ears burning and my mouth turning as dry as the Sahara.

"You know what," I asked. "Why don't we order another pitcher of beer? And maybe some breadsticks, too."

Marcia shook her head. "You're just stalling. The munchies are no excuse for passing up your shot at everlasting love." She winked at me. "Or a good old roll in the hay. You wouldn't even have to worry about birth control, you lucky duck."

"I don't know. Maybe she doesn't even remember me from class."

Lucy, who sat beside me, side-eyed me with her big brown eyes. "You've been sitting kitty-corner from her in class like forever. You're just making up excuses."

Marcia leaned over the table. "Lucy, this is going to take drastic measures. Bump her off the seat."

"No, wait. I'll go. Just give me a minute to think of what to say."

Marcia jerked her chin at Lucy. "Do it."

Lucy scootched me over until I had only one cheek on the seat and was about to topple off. "Go on," she said. "Go say hi."

Before she could push me completely off the seat and make a buffoon of me, I grabbed my beer and stood up. I guess my legs walked me over to their booth because the next thing I knew I was standing there. "Hi, Kit, hi Jennie. I'm Wendy from Shakespeare. Um, I mean, Shakespeare class."

Jennie said, "Yeah, hi, Wendy. This is Bob."

I stood there shrinking like a violet, but I knew I had to muster some social grace. "Nice to meet you, Bob."

The skinny rail of a guy gave me a quick once-over. "Likewise."

Kit scooted over. "You want to join us? These two lovebirds won't mind since all they can do is play kissy-face."

I sat down next to Kit and plopped my glass of beer in front of me. "So, I've never seen you here before. Their pizza's the best, especially the pepperoni."

"Yeah, we just ordered a large with sausage."

Jeez, I thought, is this what passes for dialogue between lit majors? I might as well take up business or math or some other boring subject.

I decided to resurrect my term-paper strategy. Glancing from Kit to Jennie, I asked, "So, what are you writing your term papers on?"

Jennie smirked like I'd made some kind of joke. "*As You Like It.*"

Bob planted a smooch on her cheek. "Yeah, babe, I know how you like it."

"God, you two," Kit said. "You're embarrassing yourselves."

They were embarrassing me, too. I clapped my sweaty palms together on my lap and looked at Kit, hoping she'd salvage my lame attempt at conversation. I'd never seen her so close up, and I was drinking in every little detail. She had the cutest, teensiest beauty mark right next to her eyebrow—like a period at the end of a short, sweet sentence.

She swiveled around and locked her eyes on me. Those sky-blue eyes, Kewpie-doll lips, and shiny blond hair sent me to Pluto and back.

She smiled and said, "I'm writing mine on *Romeo and Juliet*."

After I landed back on earth, I said, "Really? So am I."

We were off to the races, talking about our papers: mine about forbidden love, hers about the tragedy wrought by hatred. We completely tuned out Jennie and Bob. Even when the pizza arrived, the two of them just sat there scarfing it up and ogling us like we were creatures from another planet.

Once we finished telling each other about our papers, I asked her, "What's your favorite Shakespeare line?"

She angled her head like she was thinking hard, and I almost swooned from wanting to reach out and stroke her cheek. She looked me in the eye and said, "The course of true love never did run smooth."

"I really like that one, too," I said as casually as I could, but the way she looked at me was melting me like butter in a frying pan.

I'd been slowly nursing my beer, and now it was all gone. I didn't know what to do. If I rejoined Marcia and Lucy—who were sneaking peeks at us and giggling like grade schoolers—I knew they'd ridicule me for not making a move on Kit. Inviting Kit to my dorm room was sure as hell no way to impress a girl who had an apartment with a bedroom all to herself. Should I wait to see if the three of them invited me to do something with them?

While I was furiously debating with myself, beanpole Bob piped up and said, "Jennie and I are going over to my place."

"Sure, okay," Kit said. "See you later."

As Jennie and Bob slid out of the booth, Jennie said, "Later, alligator."

I was sitting next to Kit in the booth. I felt like I should either move to the other side of the booth or disappear into the abyss. Otherwise, people would wonder why we were sitting next to each other instead of across the booth. They'd think we were queer.

But I was stuck like glue to my seat. She put her hand on the seat between us, nuzzled it up against my thigh, and stroked me with her pinkie finger. She was trying to seduce me!

Kit turned to face me and tilted her head back like she was sizing me up. "So, tell me, do you have a special someone in your life?"

Now she was flirting with me. What was I supposed to say to that? Words banged around my mind like cars at a demolition derby. I wanted to flirt right back, but the best I could come up with was, "Forsooth, not unless that someone is keeping a secret from me."

She cracked up. "You're funny, Wendy."

Which made me go all woozy. I was finally getting the hang of this flirting business. I asked her, "What about you? Do you have someone to write sonnets to?"

Her pinkie was still strumming my thigh, lighting up my nerve endings like Fourth of July sparklers. I wondered if I should give her the pinkie treatment, too. But my hand felt as sluggish as molasses.

"Nope," she said. "It's not easy meeting the kind of people I'd like to date."

I gulped down the lump clogging up my throat. "Yeah, I know what you mean."

Kit nodded and sighed like we were travelers at the end of a long, dusty road. She slugged down the last of her beer and latched her eyes on me. "Would you like to come over to my place?"

Oh God, oh God. She was inviting me to have *lesbian sex*. I didn't know the first thing about lesbian sex. What should I say? I was terrified. I was excited. It was almost curfew time at the dorm. If I didn't spend the night with her, I'd have to stay overnight at Marcia's—if she'd even open the door to me in the middle of the night. What a tangled-up can of worms this was. My heart raced a mile a minute, and my legs twitched like I was at the starting line of a big race. "Uh, I, uh, have to be back at the dorm by midnight, so I'd better not."

Just like that I'd blown my chance.

I kicked myself for the last four weeks of the semester. Sure, I'd broken the ice with Kit, but I'd probably also severed the invisible bond of forbidden passion pulsing between us.

Come finals week, I knew it was now or never. Kit and I might not have any classes together in the upcoming term, and I decided if I didn't make my move, that'd be the end of my grand almost love affair. So, after I took my last final on Thursday, I rolled a joint and drove over to 3rd and Oak.

It was a sunny spring day, and I was wearing a blouse I'd bought for the occasion—a silky, light blue number with a V-neck that, when I leaned forward, afforded a glimpse of what little cleavage I could manufacture by clamping on my tightest bra. And, of course, my favorite bell bottoms, which showed off my girlish waist and slim hips. I traipsed into that apartment building like I owned it, rehearsing my line: "Hi Kit, now that the semester's over, how about we go hang out in the cemetery and smoke a joint? The cops never patrol there."

I checked the list of apartment numbers inside the building's entrance, and there was her name next to Unit 314. I bounded up the stairs, knocked on the door, and held my head high. I could do this.

The door swung open. My knees went wobbly.

Jennie stood there looking at me.

"Uh, hi, Jenny. Is Kit in?"

"Nope, sorry. She left for downstate this morning."

"You mean for good?"

"Practically. Until fall semester."

"Oh, well, if you talk to her, tell her Wendy says hi."

And that's how my crummy freshman year ended—with chickenshit Wendy Ragnow ruining her chance for eternal love with Carly "Kit" Waters. All I could do was give myself a serious talking-to: when Kit comes back to town, you better chuck your wimpy ways, dust off your big-girl boots, and boldly go into gay girldom.

ACKNOWLEDGMENTS

This anthology could not have been finished without the generous time given by Novelitics Writers Collective members. Thank you for stepping up to help with the various moving parts that make up a book and send it into the world. You are all an inspiration.

CONTRIBUTORS

Maryka Biaggio is a psychology professor turned novelist who specializes in historical fiction based on real people. She loves unearthing the stories of people overlooked by history and bringing them back to life—portraying their challenges and foibles and rekindling their emotional world. Doubleday published her debut novel, *Parlor Games,* in 2013. Her second novel, *Eden Waits*, was published by Milford House Press in 2019. In 2021, Milford House Press released *The Point of Vanishing* and in 2022 *The Model Spy*. Her fiction has won several accolades, including Willamette Writers Award, Oregon Writers Colony Award, Historical Novel Society Review Editors' Choice, La Belle Lettre Award, an Upper Peninsula of Michigan Notable Books Award, and a Regional Arts & Council grant. She has served on the Board of the Historical Novel Society North America Conference since 2015. You can learn more at her website: www.marykabiaggio.com.

Kim Taylor Blakemore (editor) is an award-winning author, book coach, and developmental editor. She teaches editing and craft workshops to organizations like Women Writing the West, Willamette Writers, History Quill, Women's Fiction Writers Association, Sisters in Crime and more. Her novels include *The Deception, After Alice Fell* (Killer Nashville Silver Falchion Award), *The Companion* (Tucson Festival of Book Literary Award), *Bowery Girl* (NYPL Best Reads for Teens), and *Cissy Funk* (WILLA Award for Best Young Adult Fiction). Novels written as K.T. Blakemore include *The Good Time Girls* and *The Good Time Girls Get Famous*. She is the editor of *Echoes: An Anthology of Short Fiction* and *3rd & Oak: Stories*. Learn more at www.kimtaylorblakemore.com.

Kerry Cathers (editor) runs the website, A Curiosity of Crime, a research resources for writers of historical detective fiction. She published her first reference book, *A Writer's Guide to Nineteenth-Century Murder by Arsenic*, in 2022. Its follow-up on poisons is coming early 2025. She has given seminars on forensics, poisons, and weaponry for the History Novel Society North America's conference, various Sisters in Crime chapters, Mystery Writers of America, and Kiss of Death's COFFIN series. For more information on forensic science, crime and policing in their social context visit her Substack "Bandits Roost" and follow her on Instagram @acuriosityofcrime.

Elyse Garrett lives in the Pacific Northwest and considers Oahu her second home. When she's not writing, she tends to her flower garden and collects sea glass on the beach with her four rescue dogs. Inspiration for her story came from her experiences working for a major airline during the 1980s, when she had the opportunity to explore the world. Learn more at www.elysegarrett.com

Sue Ann Higgens has been a pastry chef, a high school teacher and principal, a sweatshop sewist, a track coach, and a birth doula. Her writing looks at 20th century women, cultural friction, and entangled families. Her work has appeared in *Echoes: An Anthology of Short Fiction*, and *Our Hidden Conversations: What Americans Really Think About Race and Identity*. She lives and writes in Portland, Oregon, and works to make peace. And very thin lefse.

Susan Kraus lives in Lawrence, Kansas, and worked for decades as a therapist, custody mediator, and award-winning travel writer. Then she segued into novels: *Fall From Grace, All God's Children, Insufficient Evidence*, and *When We Lost Touch*. Her novels have been called "socially conscious" fiction, with characters that compel connection, page-turning plot lines, and themes that make readers think about their own beliefs. You can check out her work at www.susankraus.com.

Sally K Lehman is the author of the novels *The Last Last Fight, In The Fat,* and *The Unit–Room 154*. Her serialized short novella *Small Minutes* was included in the Best Of edition of Bewildering Stories. She is the editor of the anthologies *Bear the Pall, War Stories 2016,* and *War Stories 2017*. Her work can be found in multiple literary magazines including The Coachella Review, Another Chicago Magazine, Lunch Ticket, and 34th Parallel. Sally has an M.F.A. in Creative Writing from Wilkes University where she worked as Managing Editor for River & South Review. She lives near Portland, Oregon. Learn more at www.sallyklehman.com.

Trish MacEnulty is the author of a historical novel series, crime novels, memoirs, a story collection, scripts, and the award-winning, historical coming-of-age novel, *Cinnamon Girl*. She has a Ph.D. in English from the Florida State University and taught writing and film as a university-level professor for two decades. She currently writes book reviews and features for the *Historical Novel Review* and teaches magazine writing at Florida A&M University. She lives in Tallahassee with her husband and publishing partner, Joe Straub. More info at her website: www.trishma-cenultybooks.com.

Tonya Mitchell is the author of *The Arsenic Eater's Wife,* an historical true crime Gothic mystery set in 1889 Liverpool. Her debut historical novel, *A Feigned Madness,* won the Reader Views Reviewers Choice Award and the Kops-Fetherling International Book Award for Best New Voice in Historical Fiction. She is a member of the Women Fiction Writers Association, the Historical Novel Society, and the Author's Guild. She lives in the US with her husband, three boys, and an over-weight golden doodle. Visit her at: www.tonyamitchellauthor.com

Katie Nelson Stone lives and writes in Portland, Oregon. A Public Involvement Specialist by day and a historical fiction author by night (or early mornings, or lunch breaks, etc.), Katie's love for historical stories runs deep. She received her Master's in History from Portland State University and is a historical research consultant with her company River City Historical. Her clientele includes journalists, historical fiction authors, and documentary filmmakers. When she's not working or writing, Katie enjoys camping with her husband and dogs, bike rides, themed parties, good food, captivating books, and bad reality TV. You can learn more at www.katienelsonstone.com.

Micah Thorp is a physician and writer in Portland, Oregon. His first novel, *Uncle Joe's Muse*, and its sequel *Uncle Joe's Senpai* were published in January 2022 and March 2023, respectively. *Uncle Joe's Muse* won a Next Gen Indie Award for Humor and a Foreword Indie Gold Award for Humor. Some of his other literary works have been published in Cleaver Magazine, Fictional Cafe, and Blind Corner. In addition to his literary writing, Dr Thorp's clinical research has been published in numerous medical journals. His book, *Handbook of Common Problems in Clinical Nephrology* (Nova Science, 2010) helps clinicians with medical decision-making and helps others mitigate insomnia. He currently lives in Portland, Oregon.

Originally from the Midwest, Annie Tupek went on a road trip to Alaska and never returned home. After spending over a decade in the frozen tundra, she moved south and now resides in Oregon. She is a licensed private pilot and when not making up stories, she can be found exploring the Pacific Northwest by land and air.

Journalism took K. Fufkin Vollmayer from Alaska to Washington, D.C. When one of her kids parroted the same frontier myth learned in school —of brave, white pioneers in covered wagons—she remembered the captivity and slave narratives she read with her professor, Michael P. Rogin. Combing through the Lewis and Clark journals, she focused on writing about York, the Métis, and the other enslaved member of the expedition, Sacagawea, in her novel *I've Known Rivers: York's Account of the Lewis and Clark Expedition*. In every Latin American country she's visited, she's learned about maroon communities and the Black African diaspora. Learn more at www.fufkin.co.

Sharon Woodard is fascinated by stories. The way they hold us, feed us, seed our dreams, and collectively knit us into existence. And what do those stories sit on? A peek behind the curtain reveals its stories all the way down. But what fascinates this writer are the edges and liminal spaces where stories are inconsistent or split apart to allow the birth of something new. The places where new understandings and ways of experiencing the world can emerge and shift the whole Jenga tower of collective beliefs and thus subtly, change the world. Sharon is a licensed Naturopathic Physician practicing in the Pacific Northwest and mom of two fascinating and radically independent people. When she isn't lurking around gathering fiction fodder, you can find her paddling, hiking, or biking the verdant byways of her home in the Pacific Northwest.

ABOUT NOVELITICS WRITERS COLLECTIVE

Our community is a gathering place for dedicated novelists who are passionate about storytelling, mastering their craft, and navigating the world of publishing. We believe that connecting with like-minded writers is essential in creating a supportive and inspiring environment where everyone can thrive.

Here, you will find a diverse group of novelists at various stages in their writing journeys, from aspiring authors to published professionals. Whether you are starting out or have several novels under your belt, joining our community will provide you with the opportunity to connect with fellow writers who share your enthusiasm.

We prioritize the exchange of ideas and feedback. We encourage members to share their work and seek constructive criticism, enabling everyone to grow as writers. Additionally, we create an annual anthology of short fiction, host regular discussions on various writing-related topics including techniques, plot development, character building, and offer workshops on the craft of fiction and the ever-changing landscape of the publishing industry.

Novelitics has virtual meetings, write-ins, and workshops, and local Portland, Oregon area retreats and meet ups.

By being a part of our community, you will not only have access to invaluable resources, but you will also find motivation and encouragement to keep pushing forward. Our supportive network fosters an environment where writers can celebrate their successes, seek guidance during setbacks, and find inspiration in the accomplishments of their peers.

If you are serious about your writing journey and are looking for a community of dedicated novelists who share your aspirations, our community is the perfect place for you. Join us today. We're happy to meet and write with you. Learn more at www.novelitics.com.

Happy writing,
Kim Taylor Blakemore, Founder

9 798999 125910